The Brothers

The
BROTHERS

ALLEN D. ANDERSON

Langdon Street Press

Langdon Street Press
212 3rd Avenue North, Suite 290
Minneapolis, MN 55401
612.455.2293
www.langdonstreetpress.com

ISBN-13: 978-1-936782-91-8
LCCN: 2012936339

Distributed by Itasca Books

Cover Design and Typeset by Nate Meyers

Printed in the United States of America

Chapter 1

At 2:00 PM on Friday, May 14, 1948, Peter and I were called to the counseling office at Northeast Junior High School.

A man with a serious face, seated behind his desk, said, "I'm Ralph Hayes, school counselor." He nodded toward Peter, "You must be Peter?" Peter didn't respond. Mr. Hayes then turned to me and asked, "And you must be Andrew?"

"That's right," I answered.

Mr. Hayes gave Peter a quick questioning glance, and then said, "We received a call from Hennepin County Hospital. They want you boys to go down there."

"Why?" Peter asked.

Mr. Hayes's brow furrowed. "Your mother was rushed to emergency this morning."

"Bet our old man hit her," Peter said, raising his fist in a threatening gesture.

"Dad drinks once in a while and gets a little carried away," I explained.

"He's a god-damned drunk," Peter added.

Mr. Hayes pressed back in his chair. "You want me to take you there?"

"We can make it okay," I responded, preferring to be alone with Peter so we could talk.

As soon as we were out of the school, Peter said, "Bet anything Dad beat Mom up again."

"We better wait and see," I responded.

Peter started jogging. I ran to keep up. Upon reaching the hospital, we rushed to the reception desk. "We're here to see our mother," I explained.

"What's her name?"

"Simona Amonovitch."

The receptionist forced a smile and made a quick call. "Someone will be down to show you to your mother," she said.

Within seconds a nurse approached us. She was tense as she extended a welcoming hand. "Before you go in to see your mother, I need to talk with you." She directed us into a small room. "Don't be shocked when you see her," she said. "She's heavily bandaged." Her voice mellowed as she added, "Your mother sure loves you boys."

"What happened?" Peter asked.

The nurse paused. "We're not quite sure. She suffered a severe blow to the head. She was found at the bottom of the basement stairs by a neighbor. There were multiple bruises, but a blow to her head was most serious."

"What's Mom say happened?" I asked.

"She's confused. She hasn't said much."

Peter stood. "Take us to Mom! She'll tell me and Andrew what happened."

"Before going in there, you need to know that she's in critical condition."

"Will she be okay?" I asked, worried by the despair in the nurse's voice.

"It's not looking good now. The next four or five hours will tell the story."

"Show us where she is!" Peter insisted.

The nurse hesitated, her eyes studying Peter. "One more thing, be careful not to upset your mother. The doctor was against you boys visiting, but your mother insisted."

When the door to Mom's room opened, there was a nauseous antiseptic smell that irritated my nose and throat. Mom's bed was tilted at an angle, and her head bulged with a gauze wrapping that covered all but her eyes. I swallowed to hold back the gastric upsurge.

There was no sign that she recognized us. Her motionless eyes focused far away. The nurse took Mom's hand, checked her pulse. "Your two sons are here to see you, Simona." The nurse gently squeezed Mom's hand and said, "I'll leave them here with you."

After the nurse departed, we stood dumbfounded, looking at each other, unsure how to proceed in this unfamiliar circumstance. Simultaneously, we moved to the bed, Peter on one side, me on the other.

"What happened, Mom?" Peter asked. There was no response.

I reached out and took Mom's right hand. Peter took her left hand. "Do you recognize us, Mom?" I asked. No answer. Tears swelled in my eyes. I glanced at Peter. He turned away as he wiped the wetness from his cheeks.

Seeing the hurt in Peter, I started to sob, helpless in my effort to hold back. Peter dried his face with his shirt sleeve, his teeth clenched and his body shaking with anger. "That drunken son of a bitch," he muttered.

"Peter," Mom said, not loud, but firm.

Peter glared at Mom. "What happened?" he demanded.

"Peter!" Mom said in a pleading voice, squeezing both our hands. "You can't let your anger destroy you. Do you understand, Peter?" Her voice was shaky.

"Dad pushed you down the stairs, didn't he, Mom?" Peter persisted.

The strength of her grip faltered. I gazed with fear toward Peter. "I better go for the nurse," I said.

Mom squeezed my hand. "No! No!" she whispered, laboring to catch her breath, her eyes closed. My heart pounded. I braced to run for the nurse.

"I ... I must see each of you boys—alone," Mom pleaded.

We both started toward the door, each offering the other to be first to talk with her. "You talk first," Peter said. "I need time to calm down." Peter departed.

"Come close," Mom said, extending her hands to me. "I ... I worry about Peter," she said in a halting desperation. "I worry about the destructive anger inside him." Mom squeezed my hand, amazing me with the power she mustered in those thin, taunt forearms. "You must help protect him from his anger!" she begged. "Peter respects you." She glared into my eyes with a fervor I'd never seen before. Then her head dipped forward as her mind drifted. Her grip weakened and her fingers fell away from my hands.

I readied to rush for help. Mom sensed my intent and chanted, "Andrew, Andrew." She attempted to lean forward to give me a hug, but the strength wasn't there. I pulled her close. "Andrew," she whispered.

"Yes, Mom?"

"Promise me you'll watch after Peter. The war-damaged mind of your father has transplanted his demons onto your brother. Without your gentle influence, this evil force will be his downfall." She clutched at me, her feeble grip frantic to convey the magnitude of her plea.

"I promise, Mom."

This brought a prolonged grateful hug. "Can I see Peter now?" she asked.

"I'll send him in."

Peter was pacing outside Mom's door. The instant he saw me, he snatched my arm. "Is Mom okay?"

"She wants to see you."

Peter dashed into her room, leaving the door open. Just like Peter. I closed it. I walked back and forth, much slower than had Peter. I tried to make sense out of what had transpired, but my mind wouldn't focus.

Mom's door opened. Peter burst out, his face twisted in a fearful grimace. "We need a doctor, quick!"

Peter raced to the nurse's station. "Mom needs help!" he demanded. A nurse hurried to Mom's room. Within seconds several small lights flashed on the switchboard. Two men in white jackets rushed down the hall and disappeared into Mom's room.

We stood with our eyes fixed on the door. I felt numb. Peter's face reddened. The veins on his muscular arms and neck protruded, his fists squeezed tight.

Soon the nurse and two men emerged from Mom's room. "This is Dr. Abrams," said the nurse.

Dr. Abrams shook our hands. He spoke softly. "I'm sorry, fellows. We weren't able to revive your mother. As we feared, the blow to her head proved fatal."

My body sagged, my mind in a fog as we left the hospital. Peter walked with large steps, an angry glare in his eyes. I wanted to share my pain with him, but didn't think it wise to do so now.

It would only intensify his anger at Dad. Any suggestion that Mom's fall may have been an accident would further agitate him. Too many times he'd seen the intensity of Dad's irrational anger, and felt he owed Mom a lot for how she protected him when he was young.

Many times she stepped in to protect him. She paid the price, but Peter was spared the brunt of Dad's violence. As Peter grew older, bigger, and stronger, he felt obligated to repay Mom for her protection through the years. He came to consider it his responsibility to protect her.

I felt desperate to ease the guilt and anger Mom's death brought to Peter. "You can't be blaming yourself," I blurted out.

Peter yelled back, "Everyone knows who killed Mom and that fucker's going to pay for it."

I decided to keep my mouth shut. As we got close to home, Peter's pace quickened and the look in his eyes more intense. A fast walk for Peter was a run for me, but I had to remain at his side. Mom's dying words weighed heavily on me.

As we approached the house, Peter burst ahead. I couldn't keep up. He charged through the front door and searched the ground level by the time I got there. He dashed upstairs, slamming doors in disgust after failing to find Dad. Then, he bolted to the basement. I followed, watching him squeeze behind the furnace to peek behind the coal bin.

After finishing his search, Peter came toward me with clenched fists and fiery eyes, eyes that mellowed as we made eye contact.

At that instant we saw the blood stains on the concrete. My mind drifted into a trance as I gazed at the floor. I turned to Peter and in the glow of the overhead light bulb I saw tears in his eyes. I wiped my own face.

My vision blurred. Had it not been for Peter's deep throaty sobs, I'd have never known the intensity of his pain.

Somehow, Peter's misery hurt more than my own. I reached out and stumbled forward.

We came together in a convulsive hugging that confirmed the closeness that had always existed between us. If there was anyone with whom I wanted to share my hurt, it was Peter. I knew he felt the same.

Between us was a love Mom had ignited and nurtured, a love intensified by the evil force that plagued the mind of our father. The more ominous that devastating threat, the stronger was our need to stand together. Never had we felt the need to support one another as we did now.

Our sobbing and pain became as one. This closeness strengthened the urgency of my commitment to uphold the promise to Mom. No one knew more than Mom about the destructiveness and suffering that anger could bestow.

Mom recognized in her final words that death was not far away. She knew what had killed her. Yet, a dimension of her mind remembered the husband she knew before the war and she had patiently waited for that beauty to return. She watched for that same beauty in Peter, just as I did.

As Peter backed off and glanced at the blood stain on the floor, instant anger flashed in his eyes. My body stiffened as I gazed upon my brother.

Chapter 2

The emotional drain brought on by Mom's death sapped my energy. I wanted to rest, but had to keep an eye on Peter, who was adamant about waiting up for Dad's return home. I tried to make my presence as casual as possible. Any confrontation on my part would only fuel Peter's anger.

Peter gave me a sympathetic glare. "Thanks for keeping me company," he said.

We sat quietly. My eyes drooped, my head sagged. Suddenly, my head popped up. I had dozed off. Thank God something had awakened me. I took a worried glance at Peter, who was as wide awake and intense as ever. His endurance amazed me. I'd always been curious about how long he could go without sleep. Never had I been able to stay awake long enough to find out. I had witnessed his stamina as an athlete, but never thought much about it, since it was always overshadowed by his athletic ability, that already at his young age was legendary in Northeast Minneapolis.

"Maybe we should go to bed," I finally suggested.

"I'm staying up," he responded.

"Tomorrow will be another big day."

"Could be."

I sat up in my chair and resolved to wait it out. Soon, I slumped again, mumbling, "I doubt Dad's coming home tonight."

This brought a hard glare from Peter, who responded, "So where the hell is he?"

His threatening voice bothered me. "It just seems a waste of time to wait up when we don't even know if he'll be here."

Peter glanced at the clock. "Maybe you're right," he said.

"I think a good night's sleep would do us both good," I proclaimed with finality.

Peter popped to his feet. "I'm going out lookin' for Dad," he said.

I felt like the wind was knocked out of me. "What chance you got to find him tonight?" I asked.

"We know his hangouts."

Peter was right. There were many nights when Mom had sent Peter and me out to look for Dad. We almost always found him.

Peter opened the door. "Hold it! I'm going with you," I said. As soon as I got to my feet, I felt dizzy.

"You okay?" Peter asked.

I rubbed my eyes. "Guess I got groggy sitting so long."

"You're not lookin' too swift, little brother." Peter smiled. "Maybe you better stay home and get some sleepy-poo."

Peter knew how to spark my anger and jack me up. That's exactly what happened. It made me face the tough reality of Mom's dying words. To fulfill my commitment to her, I'd have to forget my frailties and do what had to be done. Keeping up with Peter wouldn't be easy.

We started our search on Central Avenue near Columbia Golf Course. The bartenders in every hangout along the avenue recognized us. By 11:00 PM we reached the bridge at St. Anthony Falls. Beyond was a proliferation of downtown bars that would complicate our search.

We had only hunted for Dad beyond the bridge a few times. The fact that his plight had brought him this far was a sure sign that he was determined to escape the pain of his troubled world.

"Where to now?" I asked.

"Last time Dad came this far we found him in lower Hennepin, down by the hooch joints," Peter said impatiently.

"It's tough finding anybody down there."

"Let's get going," Peter responded. He took off. I followed. We went to Augie's, the most popular strip joint. There was a doorman blocking our entrance.

"We're lookin' for our old man," Peter said. "He's a big guy with curly hair. Name's Theodore Amonovitch."

"Nobody tells names in dis place," said the doorman, a burly punch-drunk boxer type. He sized us up. "Bout haf an hour ago der was dis sloppy drunk, an old fart. Came outta da Saddle cross da street. He was wid a young whore. Dey cut out cross da avenue, goin' dat a way." He pointed north on Washington Avenue.

Before the man finished, Peter was on the move. We ran to the corner and headed north on Washington. This area was a sharp contrast to the brightly lit hustle and bustle of downtown.

On the east side of Washington was an endless line of warehouses; on the west side were grand old dirty brick office buildings.

The bars on north Washington were few and far between, just like the street lights. At the end of each long block was a single light. Like everything else on the avenue, the lights were covered with a dark film of soot from the locomotives that continuously chugged back and forth in the switchyard parallel to the street. Beneath the low-lying heavy cloud cover, the oppressive humidity and smoke smudged the air and cushioned the crash of coupling railroad cars.

It weighed me down, making it tough keeping up with Peter. He looked back and slowed.

I pressed hard to catch up. It was too much for me. Peter decided to move on ahead. He knew I could take care of myself. His foremost desire was to find Dad.

I had intense pain in my side, sweat oozed from every pore of my body and my clothes stuck to my skin, resisting my movement. I had to rest.

Without me, Peter moved faster. His physical endurance was no surprise to me and caused me no shame. It was a simple fact of life: Peter was physically gifted. Often times he'd performed beyond the limits of the ordinary.

Peter disappeared from view. The pain in my side had diminished, but had not gone away.

I couldn't afford to wait any longer. I proceeded at a slow trot, increasing speed as I felt more comfortable. Several blocks ahead I spotted a dim light. After advancing another block I was able to read the sign: BURLINGTON HOTEL.

It was located on a corner, a three-story building with a bar on the ground level, with guest rooms above. I opened the squeaky door and was hit by the nauseating musty smell of booze and vomit. One step inside told me the place was deserted. I was about to leave when I heard a throaty contralto voice, "Whatcha want, handsome?"

A female figure came into view. All I could distinguish was the glow of red as the light at the end of the bar reflected off her pompadour heap of hair. Standing such that her body didn't catch the direct ray of light, the lady presented a seductive profile. It caused a stir inside me and raised my already hot body temperature. "I … I was checking to see if my brother stopped in here. He's a big husky guy."

She moved behind the bar. "The big man. He was here looking for his father," she said, her voice shaky.

"That's him."

"He was here and moved on," came a loud voice from upstairs.

Then, echoing down the stairway came angry shouting, "MOVE ASIDE!"

My muscles tightened. That was Peter's voice. I headed toward the stairway.

The lady maneuvered in front of me. "Get the hell out of here! Understand?" she said, trying to sound tough. From close up I was amazed at her grotesque appearance and momentarily forgot what was happening beyond the stairway. She was an old woman, hiding behind a bulging red wig; mascara plastered eyes and wore elevated high heels, which gave a precarious lilt to her walk.

"Pardon me," I said, as I jockeyed to get around her. She grabbed my arm and held tight, showing surprising strength. I jerked to free myself. She fell back. I darted toward the stairs.

She recovered and came at me swinging. Hesitant about hurting an old woman, I restrained her arms. She kicked at me in frustration, her knee catching me in the groin. It wasn't a direct blow, but enough to briefly disable me and kindle my anger.

I intensified my grip on her arm. She became a wild banshee, twisted free, flung off her heels and charged at me, going for my groin. I let loose with an angry blow that knocked her back like a rag doll. She slammed against the bar and slumped to the floor.

I scurried up the stairs and raced through the hall in the direction of the wild noises. I found nothing on the second floor. I dashed up to the third floor, puffing hard and sweating. There, I heard a thud, followed by a sharp crunching smack of a fist.

I arrived just in time to see an obese black man crumple to the carpet. As he collapsed, Peter scrambled for an object on the floor. He picked it up and showed me. It was a revolver. "The big fucker tried to shoot me," Peter said.

My eyes fixed on the weapon. When I approached Peter, he gave me a sudden violent shove that knocked me back through the open door behind me. As I fell, a thunderous blast of gunfire sent a ringing pain in my ears. The sharp sound faded and gave way to a biting odor of gun smoke.

Peter kneeled and shook me. "You okay?" he asked.

"What happened?" I said.

Peter grabbed my hand and pulled me to my feet. "Let's get the fuck outta here," he ordered.

I was dazed as I gazed into the semi-darkness, awed by Peter's quick, decisive moves as he rushed to the end of the hall and snatched the weapon from the hand of the fallen old woman.

He stuffed this weapon in his front pocket, while the other weapon still remained in his left hand.

He scurried into the hall bathroom. I tagged behind, watching as he washed the revolver handle with painstaking thoroughness.

A groan from the hall ignited quick action from Peter. He knocked me aside as he charged at the black man, who had raised his head and leaned on an elbow. My body cringed in disbelief as Peter raised a fist and cracked him with a vicious blow that slammed his head against the wall.

I held my breath as Peter stood ready to strike at him again. One blow was enough. The man's head flopped to the side and thumped on the floor. Peter waited to make sure he remained still.

I exhaled a breath of relief as Peter returned to the bathroom. After he finished cleaning the revolver, he carried it on a washcloth to the old woman, avoiding the puddle of blood on the threadbare carpet. Peter deftly squeezed the old woman's limp fingers around the revolver handle.

After sustaining this position for several minutes, he released his grip. Her fingers slowly opened.

My muscles twitched. Peter calmly rose to his feet.

"We better call the police," I said.

"NO WAY!" Peter snarled, as he rushed into an adjourning room. There, he kneeled down and picked a wallet off the floor. "The fuckers," he said as he looked inside before stuffing it in his pocket. Turning to the man lying on the bed, Peter pulled his legs off the mattress and raised his torso. My body slumped as I recognized our father. Peter hoisted Dad over his shoulder. I tried to help, but Peter had the task accomplished before I could lend assistance.

"Let's get the hell out of here," Peter said.

Events were moving so fast that I couldn't think straight. I followed Peter as he carried Dad like a sack of flour. This was no small feat. Dad was a big man.

As we emerged from the Burlington Hotel, the outside air was a refreshing contrast to the nauseating stuffiness inside. The sudden jarring crash of coupling railroad cars made me shudder. We returned by the same route that had brought us on this strange adventure. As we crossed the Central Avenue Bridge near St. Anthony Falls, Peter removed the revolver from his pocket and flung it into the swift current of the Mississippi.

"Why'd you do that?" I asked.

"So nobody can find it."

"You got me confused."

"Just wait. It'll make sense." His actions disturbed me. Peter sensed my concern and stopped to explain: "I killed that old woman. The gun that killed her is the gun she holds in her hand. The police are gonna assume she got in a scuffle and accidentally shot herself."

"Why not tell the police the truth?"

"That I killed someone? Fuck that noise. I ain't trustin' no police. I don't want my ass locked in a cage."

My head was muddled. "Want some help with Dad?" I asked.

"I'm doin' fine," Peter answered, breathing heavy.

Several times I offered to help, but Peter was adamant. The truth was that Peter knew I wasn't strong enough to carry Dad's 190 pounds. Why should he embarrass me? All I could do was tag along.

When we arrived home, Peter hauled Dad upstairs and plopped him on the bed. Dad let out a muffled groan as he landed like a dead fish. Instantly, he was snoring, oblivious to the world. I leaned over to unbutton his shirt and caught a whiff of his whisky breath. The putrid smell backed me off.

"Fuckin' disgrace," Peter said. "Let him sober up." Peter started toward the bathroom, removing his sweat-soaked shirt. "I need a shower," he said.

"Sure you don't want me to inform the police?" I asked again.

"Forget it!" Peter snapped back. "I don't want the police to know shit."

"Don't you think they'll find out?"

"How?"

I couldn't answer. My thoughts remained confused as I tried to sort out the events at the Burlington Hotel. I was tempted to call the police despite Peter's objection. Several times I made a move toward the phone, but held back, worried about what Peter might do.

I was convinced that Peter's anger was the driving force in all that happened tonight. Anger propelled him to go out in search of Dad. Anger fueled the assault on the black man. The shooting of the old woman was an impulsive outburst of violence. Peter acted without thinking.

I envisioned Peter as a powerful steam engine charging down a mountain toward disaster.

He moved so fast and forcefully that all I could do was sit by and watch. My presence had been of little value. I was too slow and indecisive.

My worry was that the police would find out and Peter would be in serious trouble. I curled up in bed like a helpless puppy. Mom had been dead one day and already I let her down.

Chapter 3

My first waking thought the next morning was to talk with Peter about what happened the night before. He was sound asleep.

It was still too early to awaken him, so I meandered down to the kitchen. Old feelings of love and warmth emerged, feelings associated with the cheerful, uplifting presence of Mom. It was a pleasant moment, but soon the reality of her absence hit me, and the emptiness returned.

I wished that somehow, by magic, she could still be with us.

Realizing her absence forced me to sit down, close my eyes and visualize her being here in the kitchen. I reached out to touch her, but came up empty. I lost track of time as I grieved.

I didn't notice when Peter entered the kitchen.

"What's to eat?" he asked.

Startled by his arrival, I opened one eye. "Haven't checked the refrigerator."

"Let's get with it, little brother. I'm hungry." Peter plopped a loaf of bread on the table in front of me. "You toast the bread," he ordered. "I'll get some eggs fryin'."

Peter's enthusiasm rubbed off on me. Together, we soon had a breakfast that was intended to compare with what Mom would have prepared.

"Pretty damn good," Peter said as we ate.

I nodded, and then said, "I been thinking we should go to the police and explain what happened." Peter glared at me. "You still caught up in that bullshit?"

"They need to know the truth."

Peter abruptly shoved his chair back from the table and blurted out, "The truth is I shot and killed that old lady."

"It was self-defense, Peter. She had a weapon."

Peter started pacing. "I made my decision," he said. "I fired the weapon that killed her. I don't want the police to have it. I don't want the police to know it."

"But, Peter. It was self-defense."

"I don't trust the police. I ain't tellin' them shit."

"If you don't tell them and they find out, you'll be in big trouble."

Peter came to my side of the table and grabbed my arm, fear in his eyes. "I ain't takin' no chances. Who knows what the police will believe?" His lower lip quivered as he said, "I ain't goin' to prison. Understand?

Dad always screamed at me that I'd end up in prison someday and I ain't gonna let it happen."

I was shaken by the intensity in Peter's voice and the power of his grip on my arm. I could understand his thinking, but not going to the police was a bad mistake.

Peter released his grip on my arm and backed away. He went to the window and gazed out, like Mom used to do when something troubled her.

Now, I was not only worried about Peter's anger, I also realized how much he mistrusted authority. I truly believed that going to the police was the best way to protect him. If we didn't, I feared it would lead to disaster.

Suddenly, Peter turned away from the window, stamped out of the kitchen and went upstairs to our bedroom.

As I stood in silent thought, I heard a thump on the front porch. Sudden fear stiffened my body. I stood rigid, thinking it was the police knocking on the door. I held silent, sweating; then, realized it was the paper boy who had tossed the paper on the porch.

I went to retrieve it, unfolding it as I walked back into the house. Again my body stiffened at sight of the headline: MURDER SUSPECTED IN DEATH OF ROSY REDMAN.

I clutched the paper and started reading: "Dr. Lawson, Chief Surgeon at Hennepin County Hospital, concluded that the gunshot wound that killed Rosy Redman did not occur as the result of a physical tussle as originally surmised. The bullet that killed her was fired from an estimated distance of 25 feet." I stood in shock, my hands trembling as I resumed reading:

"As a result of Dr. Lawson's report, what initially appeared to be a routine accidental shooting will now be escalated to a full-scale police investigation."

With the newspaper in hand, I headed upstairs to share the news with Peter. I entered the bedroom, tossed the paper to him and said, "Read this."

He brushed it aside and said, "I'm not interested."

I grabbed the paper. "Okay, I'll read it to you." I read while Peter remained silent.

Then, I asked, "What do you think of that?"

"I ain't gonna let no newspaper change my mind," Peter said firmly.

"The odds are the police will find out we were in that hotel," I said.

Peter responded, "I heard what you read about Rosy Redman. She was no Sunday school teacher. She pulled more than a few tricks in her day. I can't see the police bustin' their ass on a whore."

Peter's unyielding attitude frustrated me. If I was going to the police, I'd have to do so against his wishes.

Before noon I'd read the newspaper article three times. With each reading, the burden of my commitment to Mom seemed more formidable. I always knew that Peter had his own way of doing things and I knew that it sometimes got him in trouble. Until now

I didn't realize that distrust came along with his defiance of authority.

To go against Peter would be a serious blow to him. I feared creating a wedge between us and destroying the trust that was the basis of any influence I had with him.

Reason told me it was dangerous to avoid the police. I expected they would discover our presence at the Burlington Hotel on the day of Rosy Redman's death. Of course, I couldn't be certain. I felt trapped. I didn't know what to do.

Disagreement about going to the police now kept Peter and I apart. That was not good at a time when we were mourning Mom's death. The funeral would be tough on both of us. I imagined the police were watching the house. I wanted to go to them and tell the truth, to free Peter from the trouble he was in and end the worry. Each day Peter checked the morning paper for information about Rosy Redman. He read fast, always quick to conclude that his decision to avoid the police was the right thing to do.

To ease my torment, I searched both the *Minneapolis Tribune* and the *St. Paul Dispatch* for information about the murder. I cut out the articles, saving them in a folder, hoping to compile enough facts to convince Peter to change his mind.

The silence between Peter and me lasted one day. It ended the following evening when I heard Peter shouting. Rushing to the scene, there was Peter, blocking the front door, not allowing Dad to leave. Dad looked for a way to slip around him.

"Who the hell you think you are?" Dad yelled at Peter.

"A chip off your old fuckin' block—that's who I am," Peter shouted back.

"You're a punk, a no good punk. That's what you are."

"One thing this punk knows is that I ain't lettin' you out of this house. You're goin' to be sober when you go to Mom's funeral tomorrow."

"Go fuck yourself," Dad yelled, lunging at Peter. Peter deftly stepped aside, causing Dad to lose balance and crash into the wall.

Knowing how quick the anger could build between Peter and Dad, I rushed between them.

I took Dad's arm and helped him to his feet. "C'mon, Dad," I urged, "Peter's right. You can't go drinking the night before Mom's funeral."

"Who says I'm going out drinking?" Dad responded, jerking his arm free from my grip.

"That's all you ever do," Peter said.

"Shut your mouth!" Dad shouted as he tried to crack Peter upside the head.

Peter avoided a direct hit, and caught a glancing blow on the shoulder, setting off an explosion inside him. Peter shoved me aside. I reeled backward and landed on my rear end. In a flash, Peter had Dad in a corner, ready to let loose on him. Dad cowered into a defensive posture. The slightest provocation or gesture from Dad would have unleashed Peter's anger.

Thank God, Dad was sober and wise enough to restrain himself.

I placed a hand on both Peter and Dad, turned to Dad and said, "We better take you to your room."

"Keepin' him in his room ain't gonna be easy," Peter responded.

"What else can we do?"

Together we escorted Dad to his upstairs room. It surprised me that Dad was so willing to comply. He entered the room and closed the door.

"Where's the key?" Peter asked.

"Lock him in?"

"How else we gonna get any peace?"

With reluctance I found the key and Peter locked the door. "Maybe now we can get some rest," Peter said.

During the next hour Peter and I got our clothes ready for the funeral. We pressed Dad's military shirt and trousers and shined his shoes. "This will be the first time I'll be goin' to a funeral for somebody I really care about," Peter said.

"Mom was everything to you and me."

"Wonder if I'll get through it without cryin'?" Peter asked.

"I cried about as much as I can, but I haven't really seen you cry."

"The first night I cried in bed. The more I cried, the more angry I got. I had to stop myself. I was gettin' so pissed I wanted to whip Dad's ass."

I gave Peter a gentle pat on the shoulder. "I understand why you get so angry at Dad."

"He made Mom's life miserable. That's bullshit about Mom fallin' down the stairs. It's a goddamn lie."

There was a pause. "Guess Dad's the only one who knows," I said.

"You think he cares?" Peter snarled.

I pondered Peter's question. "Deep inside I think Dad cares, but I doubt if he'll ever be able to show it."

"What's with Dad that he's such a mean fucker?"

"Mom said he learned it from Grandpa Amonovitch. Grandpa used to manhandle Dad when he was a kid."

"Father Sikorski told me once that Dad was still fightin' the Germans in the war," Peter said.

"Did Father Sikorski show you Dad's medal?"

Peter's eyes now shined with pride. "Guess Dad must a been a tough-ass soldier."

"Remember how Dad used to scream and holler at night?"

"I member the night they came and hauled him away," Peter said, sounding remorseful.

"That's the time he escaped from the hospital and the police found him down by the river."

"After that's when Dad turned into a real drunk."

"Remember when we used to go and look for him?" I asked.

"Couple a times he damn near froze to death. Remember?"

"Mom told us we saved his life."

"Mom was so happy when we brought him home. Then a few days later he'd kick the shit outta her. The fucker!" Peter's teeth clenched and the fingers of his hands tightened into big fists.

"She always saw good in Dad," I said.

I was momentarily baffled when Peter's hands started shaking. After a time his shaking ceased. His arms dropped to his sides. The instant our eyes met, Peter's jaw stiffened. "Mom opened her arms to Dad and he beat her." Peter became so intense that it was hard for him to speak. Yet, he was adamant. He had to talk: "That's when I felt like killin' the fucker." As Peter spoke, he covered his face with his hands, his fingers curled and shaking.

Overcome by Peter's emotion, I put an arm around him. After a time his shaking ceased.

His arms dropped to his sides.

"Let's go in and talk with Dad," Peter said calmly.

I didn't know what to say. I followed as Peter unlocked the door. The first thing we saw was the curtain whipping in the open window. Peter shouted. "Let's go after him!" He knocked me aside as he charged out the door and down the stairs.

It hurt deep inside to think that Dad would sneak out the window when he knew how much Peter and I wanted him home the night before Mom's funeral.

Peter raced off into the darkness, heading in the direction of Central Avenue. I stood in the yard near the road, immobilized by this sudden turn of events. I glanced off in the direction of Peter's flight, attempting to see in the darkness.

Unable to see Peter, I turned and looked up at the open window from which Dad had escaped. A sudden dark cloud came over me and I couldn't move as my eyes fixed on the sight of Dad hanging beside the house, his feet several inches from the ground. I tried to shout, but the words wouldn't come out.

The ambulance siren blared into an ascending crescendo that started at Hennepin County General Hospital and ended with sudden silence at the curb in front of our house. Before the ambulance arrived I pulled the sheet down on which Dad had been hanging, causing him to drop to the ground. Then, I desperately tried to blow air into his lungs.

When the ambulance stopped out front, lights popped on throughout the neighborhood. I felt shame that others would find out what happened. Fortunately, the ambulance crew moved quickly. "You want to ride with the ambulance?" an officer asked.

"Guess not," was my nervous answer. "I need to be here when my brother comes back."

The ambulance had just rounded the corner of St. Anthony and resumed its siren when Peter came charging back toward the house. He was puffing and sweating. "What's all the commotion about?" he asked.

"The ambulance came to haul Dad away."

"What?"

"Dad tried to hang himself."

"Where?"

I pointed. "Beside the house."

"Been a few years since he tried to kill himself."

"Mom's death must a been hard on him."

Peter didn't know what to say. "S'pose so," he conceded.

"We better forget about Dad going to the funeral," I said.

Peter went upstairs to Dad's room. I trailed behind. "Dad was sure desperate to escape," Peter said with a thoughtful foreboding.

"He must have been feeling pretty bad."

"Probably remembered all the times he beat Mom," Peter said.

"Could be." I was concerned that Peter looked so sad.

"Lotta times Mom got beat 'cause she tried to protect me," Peter said in a quiet monotone.

"That's when you were too little to stand up to Dad."

"Between you and Mom, you did a helleva job keepin' Dad from whippin' my ass."

"That's because Dad was always after you. And he had no reason."

"He got me enough times when I was little. After every damn time, I'd vow to get back at him someday. I couldn't wait till I was big enough to get back at him."

I smiled. "The first time was when we were in seventh grade. Remember?"

"Sure as hell do. I put him square on his ass."

"After that you started protecting Mom."

Peter smiled. Then his smile faded, his shoulders slumped as he bowed his head. "I ... I sure as hell wasn't there when she needed me." The set of his jaw became rigid and his big hands curled into tight fists. "Goddamn it!" he shouted. His voice then abruptly mellowed as he said, "And now she's dead."

I gave him a hug. He hugged me back. We had to stick together.

Dad was taken to Hennepin County Hospital where they successfully revived him. Later, he was transferred to the VA Hospital over south on Hiawatha.

The next day Mom's funeral was at Ft. Snelling Chapel. Peter and I kept close. I was absorbed within myself, not seeing much.

Peter gave me a nudge. My eyes widened. There was Dad dressed in military uniform, walking tall, looking proud, a striking contrast to the limp body I saw hanging from the upstairs window.

The people at the VA Hospital took responsibility to shape Dad up for the funeral. It had been years since we'd seen him in uniform. I remember the pride I felt when I saw him back then when he marched in a Memorial Day parade.

On both sides of Dad were men in uniform, hospital attendants to keep Dad in line. Seeing him in uniform, clean shaven, hair slicked in place, and shoes shined reminded me that there was reason to be proud of a man with a war record like Dad.

Peter saw it too, and stood tall, just as I did. This held up until the end of the ceremony at Ft. Snelling Cemetery. Then, when the rifles blasted, well before the volley, I could see Dad's eyes glisten. A moment of silence was followed by "Taps," the eternal goodbye to the woman I knew Dad loved.

I could see Dad fight to restrain his feeling, but the tears came anyway. He didn't move a muscle, standing at rigid attention, his eyes focused on the casket as the bugle held clear and true to its mission.

Peter and I couldn't hold back as we stood along side Dad in saying farewell to the finest human soul we'd ever encounter. My body was numbed by the surge of emotion. I wanted to be alone with my feelings. Peter shared my sentiment. At the first opportunity he turned to me and in a strained voice said, "Let's get the hell outta here."

We ran off through the cemetery, weaving our way among the endless rows of white crosses, ending up near Minnehaha Creek where we meandered in a trance. It was like Peter was with me but not with me. I was alone in my thoughts. All my energy was devoted to one commanding thought: Mom's final message for me to watch after Peter.

We followed Minnehaha to the River Road, over the Franklin Avenue Bridge and on to University Avenue. All was quiet at home. We wandered into the seclusion of the backyard, surrounded by lilacs, dogwood and high bush cranberry. This had been Mom's private sanctuary, where she attended the flowers she loved. We walked among the dahlias, chrysanthemums, geraniums, touching the delicate pedals and kneeling to smell the fragrance.

The backyard and kitchen were our earthly ties to Mom. We wanted to treat both with respect. The backyard must remain trimmed, watered and weeded. The kitchen must remain neat and orderly, just as Mom liked it. Of course, the kitchen would never harbor those exquisite moments when we could smell the baked bread, cinnamon rolls and fried bacon, served to us with Mom's warm gracious smile.

Chapter 4

The following morning our quiet reverie was interrupted by a knock on the door. This was no ordinary knock. It was solid, with a deliberate firmness, a sound of authority that sent a chill through my body. It had to be the police. "Who the hell's that?" Peter asked. Peter refused to budge. Had it been up to him, he would never have answered the door.

I rushed to answer, holding my breath as I opened the door. There stood Father Sikorski.

Having expected the police, it was like a miracle facing the holy man of our church, the church of the Immaculate Conception.

"Andrew, my boy," Father Sikorski said. "May I come in?"

I invited him in, showing solicitous reverence. When Father Sikorski stepped into the front room, he saw Peter who hadn't budged from the couch.

"Thought I better come and see you boys," Father Sikorski said as he watched Peter begrudgingly rise to a more respectful position.

Attempting to be apologetic, I directed Father Sikorski to what had always been reserved as Dad's chair.

Father Sikorski smiled. "With your father still in the hospital, I was worried about how you boys were getting along."

"Me and Andrew can take care of things just fine," Peter answered.

"I visited your father at the hospital. He asked about his military pension that comes in the mail."

"S'pose he's wantin' money so he can sneak off and get drunk," Peter responded.

"You can't be so quick to condemn your father," proclaimed Father Sikorski with a ring of authority.

Worried that Peter might explode with an angry response, I stood to face him and glared into his eyes. Without a word, he knew my message. He slid back from his battle position at the edge of the couch.

"I hope Dad's pension check comes soon," I said. "We need money for food."

"I called the welfare office about that," Father Sikorski said. "They asked me if I'd watch over the money for you boys. I agreed to do it for now."

"Should we let you know when Dad's check arrives?" I asked.

"Yes, and I'll go with you to the hospital to have your Dad sign it." Father Sikorski reached in his pocket and handed me twenty dollars. "This is from the congregation. Let me know if you run out of money."

Father Sikorski rose to leave. With the expectation of his departure, Peter for the first time presented a respectful smile.

As if waiting for this to happen, Father Sikorski turned to us again. "Son of a gun," he said, snapping his fingers, "I almost forgot to mention that a family from our parish who live out in Anoka expressed interest in having you boys live with them."

Without hesitation, Peter responded, "Tell those people to forget it! We got a home."

"We must not forget that you boys are at an age when you need a strong hand to guide you."

"We can take care of ourselves," Peter snapped back.

"I plan to visit these people in Anoka tomorrow. I'll let you know more about that later."

As he departed, he made a sign of the cross and said, "God be with you boys."

Before Father Sikorski reached the street, Peter sounded off. "To hell with that Anoka business. I ain't goin' nowhere."

"He's just trying to help."

"Bullshit!"

"Wouldn't it be nice to move in with people who have plenty of money?"

"Sure as shit, Andrew, you move in with somebody and they'll be tellin' ya what to do all the time."

"There's always adults telling kids what to do."

"No stranger's tellin' me what to do."

"What you think it will be like when Dad comes home from the hospital?"

"I can take care of Dad. Long's he's got money for booze, he'll be happy."

"You seem to forget Dad can be hard to live with."

"You worry too much, little brother."

"I worry about keeping you out of trouble."

Peter laughed. "Don't you worry, little brother. I can take care of myself."

Father Sikorski's plan for Peter and me to move to Anoka weighed heavily on us. Although Anoka was a suburb only twelve miles away, to us it was as if we were leaving the face of the earth. Peter and I talked with our friends at school about the possibility of moving to Anoka.

Father Sikorski also announced it to the church congregation. He sounded determined to find us a new home.

During the last week of the school year at Northeast Jr. High School, Peter and I were invited again to the counseling office of Mr. Hayes. I worried that he had more bad news for us.

When we arrived at his office, we were surprised to see Woody Watson, the Edison High School football coach. Mr. Watson greeted Peter and me with enthusiasm.

"It appears you've met these young men before," said Mr. Hayes.

"Oh yes. I've watched them play football several times. I also had the pleasure of honoring Peter with the most valuable player award after the park board championship game last fall."

"Mr. Watson called to ask if we could get together here at school to talk about your future," Mr. Hayes said. "Isn't that right, Mr. Watson?"

"Exactly. I heard that you boys may be moving out to Anoka. To tell the truth, I considered that mighty bad news."

"Is it true you're moving?" Mr. Hayes asked.

"I ain't movin'," Peter said.

There was a pause. "How about you, Andrew?" Mr. Watson asked.

"To tell the truth, Peter and I don't have a say about moving."

"Hell we don't," Peter insisted.

"Let's hold down our tempers," Mr. Hayes urged. "Maybe you better explain to the Amonovitch brothers about what you were planning for next year."

Mr. Watson gave Mr. Hayes a sharp look, like he didn't appreciate the way Mr. Hayes was trying to take over the meeting. "My plans, of course, have been conceived with the expectation that you fellows would be sophomores at Edison in the fall. I expected you boys would be in my starting backfield."

"Don't worry, Coach," Peter said. "We'll be there."

"I sure as hell hope so," Mr. Watson responded. "You, Peter, have the potential to be the greatest running back Edison High School ever had. And you, Andrew, can block for your brother with uncanny instinct. We need you boys."

"I'm curious," Mr. Hayes said, "How'd you brothers get so interested in football?"

Peter nodded for me to answer. "Our Dad got us into it. Before the war, he used to take us to practice every day."

"Then, when he went to the war he made us promise to never miss practice," Peter added.

"Your father must be mighty proud of your football talent," said Mr. Watson.

"That's about the only thing he's proud of," Peter snapped back.

The quick, sharp anger of Peter's voice caused uneasiness in both Mr. Hayes and Mr. Watson. "Maybe we better change the subject," Mr. Watson suggested. He smiled and turned to Mr. Hayes. "I'd be interested in hearing how these boys do in the classroom."

Mr. Hayes obviously expected this question. He had our school records on his desk, along with a stack of papers with hand written notes. He opened our school files. "First, I want to share important information on how you boys performed in the national-normed wide range achievement tests."

Peter yawned and slid down in his chair, the same thing he did in the classroom when he was bored with a teacher.

"Let me start with Andrew," Mr. Hayes said. "Andrew has excellent scores, ranging from the high eighties to the low ninetieth percentile."

"Can you explain to the boys what that means," Mr. Watson requested.

"What it means is that only ten percent of the kids in the nation, kids the same age, did better than Andrew on these tests."

"That's pretty damn good," Woody responded.

"Now listen to this!" Mr. Hayes added. He turned to Peter, who was about as interested as if Mr. Hayes was reading from a dictionary. Peter did recognize that the attention was now focused on him, so he rose slightly in his chair.

"Your scores on these tests, Peter, are among the highest in the nation. In every category you're above the ninety-ninth percentile."

"That's what I like," Woody said, "bright football players."

"Of course," added Mr. Hayes, "these tests only reflect an intellectual potential. They say nothing about school performance or attitude or self discipline." His eyes were on Peter, and Peter knew it. I sensed the veil of avoidance and withdrawal come over Peter, a protective device he developed in response to Dad's demeaning harangues on him over the years.

As Peter slid down a couple inches further in his chair, Mr. Hayes took pleasure in presenting what was clearly a prepared speech. "You have reason to be ashamed," Mr. Hayes said as he glared at Peter's blatant show of disinterest. Peter didn't budge, but I knew if it wasn't for the presence of Coach Watson, Peter would have told Mr. Hayes where to go and what to do with his reports.

"The teachers tell me Peter rarely completes a daily assignment," Mr. Hayes said.

"Peter reads books on his own!" I blurted out in Peter's defense.

Mr. Hayes glared at me, then, continued. "Peter's attendance is satisfactory, but he's often tardy to class. When the teachers confront him about it, at times he's vulgar and disrespectful.

All your teachers say that if it wasn't for your outstanding performance on final exams, you wouldn't be passing your classes." When Mr. Hayes finished, he was out of breath and his eyes were bulging and riveted on Peter.

I wanted to say something in support of Peter, but at this point I was so emotional that my mind couldn't think straight.

"Looks to me like there wasn't much effort to understand this young man," Mr. Watson said with firmness.

Mr. Hayes appeared uneasy.

Mr. Watson's words made me even more emotional. I liked this man and if it wasn't for his presence, this meeting could have been just one more reason for Peter to be angry at the world.

"C'mon, fellows. Let's go," Mr. Watson said. We stood and walked out with Mr. Watson in the middle, an arm around both Peter and I. We had no parting words for Mr. Hayes.

Before taking us home, Mr. Watson treated us to hamburgers and malts at Polaska's Deli on Central Avenue. He talked football and it was plain to see that we were important to him.

Mr. Watson took us home, walked us to the front door and shook our hands. "Guess it's not certain if I'll see you boys in the fall," he said. "If I don't, this may be goodbye. Wherever you go to school, you should be great ballplayers."

After Mr. Watson's departure, Peter and I rested quietly. Mr. Watson did something to me emotionally. Judging from Peter's response, I'd say he was also impressed.

Peter couldn't remain inactive for long. When I sensed he was becoming impatient, I reminded him today was Thursday, our day to spruce up the backyard. Before I started off for the mower, Peter grabbed my arm and said, "Listen, little brother, there's no way I'm movin' to Anoka. I'm playin' football at Edison."

"That's what I want, too."

"So, what the hell's to stop us?"

"We just turned fifteen. Kids our age need a responsible adult to watch over us."

"Who the fuck says so? We can be responsible."

"Father Sikorski for one."

"That old fart don't know shit."

"Father Sikorski knows more about our family than anybody."

"He's a fuckin' snoop."

"No, Peter. If Mom were here, she'd say, 'Listen to Father Sikorski.'"

Peter walked over and knelt beside the dahlias. I followed. He reached to pull some quack grass from the flower bed, careful so as not to disturb the flowers. With finesse, he plucked out weeds, and with an angry gesture, flung them into the garbage barrel.

"Maybe we should go and talk with Father Sikorski," I suggested. "The least we can do is explain that we don't want to move."

"I doubt that old fart will listen to anything we have to say."

"I'll call and tell him we want to talk with him tomorrow."

Peter and I arrived early for our meeting with Father Sikorski. He was waiting and greeted us with a tense smile, then directed us to chairs he'd prearranged. Peter was to sit on his left and me on his right. "I'm glad you boys came today. What we have to discuss could be the most important event of your lives."

Before we sat down, Peter took the chair designated for him and moved it over beside my chair. Father Sikorski's face reddened.

The instant we were seated, Father Sikorski started to speak. "I got great news. I had a long talk with John and Tracy Higgins from Anoka. They've agreed to have you boys move in with them."

"Forget it!" Peter snapped back.

Father Sikorski forced a smile, his face showing sarcastic self satisfaction. "I've talked with the juvenile authorities and with the welfare. They give full blessing to my plan."

Peter bolted from his chair, charged out and slammed the door so hard it shook the room.

Father Sikorski waited; wanting to make sure Peter was far enough away before speaking. "I worry about Peter," he said. "He harbors such defiance."

"I'm with Peter. I don't want to move to Anoka."

"Surely, Andrew, you must realize that your brother has a tremendous need for adult guidance."

"I agree. But Peter isn't easy to handle. It won't work."

"Threats like that won't deter me. Peter needs strong guidance and that's exactly what the Higginses' home can provide for him."

"We belong at Edison."

"Andrew, let me remind you that you're in a unique position. Your mother told me, and I fully agree that you have more influence with Peter than anyone. One might say you're in the powerful position of being your brother's keeper."

I wanted to leave. Father Sikorski tried to give me a conciliatory pat on the back, but I moved away to avoid him. I could tell he felt hurt. "I'm sorry, Father," I said.

For the first time I noticed that he appeared tired and there was a look of compassion in his eyes. "Listen, Andrew. I know how you boys feel about Northeast and about Edison. I know you don't want to move to Anoka, but I assure you, it's the wise thing to do."

"I just don't think it'll work."

"You can make it work, Andrew. You're a sensible young man and I'm counting on you to assert your influence on your brother."

"My heart isn't in it, Father."

"The decision is made, and I'm sure your mother would approve. A truck will be coming to your place at eight on Saturday morning."

Father Sikorski's words made me uncomfortable and worried. I didn't want to hear or believe the words he was saying.

Chapter 5

I was up early Friday morning to begin preparation for Saturday's moving. I thought about waking Peter, but decided it would be less of a hassle to let him sleep and remind him later about getting ready for tomorrow.

I hurried with breakfast, and then started packing. When Peter opened his eyes at 10:00 AM, he gave me this strange look as he watched the hustle and bustle of my preparation. "Don't forget that you need to pack," I reminded him.

Peter rolled out of bed and went off to the shower. When he finished, he went down for breakfast. I remained upstairs, deliberating over what I should and shouldn't take along to the Higginses'. I forgot about Peter.

At 11:30 I became curious why Peter hadn't joined in packing for tomorrow's move. I went downstairs to check. He'd disappeared without a word of where he was going. The day passed without any sign of him. By evening I became worried, wondering if he'd come home at all. My worry turned to anger. His absence was deliberate. I'd be mighty embarrassed if he wasn't here when the truck came tomorrow morning.

At 10:00 PM I was tired and frustrated with waiting. I crawled in bed, turned out the light and tried to sleep. I remained awake, alert to every little sound, hoping it was Peter. I must have fallen to sleep because I was awakened by a strange noise. I bolted to a sitting position and groped in the dark for the light switch. I squinted at the clock, finding it hard to believe it was 2:30.

I heard singing. It was Peter, sounding happy and jovial in the middle of the night. As he climbed the stairs, I could hear the lyrics:

> "*It was in the month of June,*
> *When the flowers were in bloom,*
> *Never dreamin' she would do me any harm,*
> *When out behind the barn we went,*
> *Without gettin' her consent …*"

The door opened. Peter peeked in, saw me sitting up and said, "How pleasant seeing you so wide awake, little brother."

"Where you been?" I asked.

Peter strutted in as if he were on a mid-day stroll through the park, and resumed singing:

"It was nine months after that,
In the 'lectric chair I sat,
Never dreamin' she would do me any harm,
When the guy behind the glass, shot the juice
square up my ass,
Just for rollin' out that eight pound ball of
yarn."

"PETER!"

"You say somethin', little brother?"

"You're drunk."

"It was in the month of June ..."

"SHUT THE FUCK UP! I want to get some sleep."

Peter smiled. "Little brother. Ain't like you to use curse words like that."

I snapped out the light. It was quiet. A while later I heard mumbling. It was Peter singing again, soft, so all I could hear was the melody. I was about to shout at him again, but before I could, the mumbling ceased. At last, we could sleep.

I opened my eyes to the bright light shining through the window, and checked the clock. Not bad, five minutes late. I glanced over at Peter's bed. It was empty.

Flying down the stairs, three-four-five steps at a time, I searched the downstairs, ending up in the kitchen, where I found Peter.

"My goodness, little brother. That's no way to be dressed for breakfast."

"What you up to?" I asked.

"Fixin' for a celebration."

"What you talking about?"

"Ain't this the day they haul us off to Anoka?"

"The truck comes at eight."

"I don't 'spect to be in Anoka for long, but I thought it fittin' we celebrate what should be an excitin' adventure."

"We owe it to Father Sikorski to give it a fair try."

"We don't owe him nothing'. We don't need anybody messin' in our lives." Peter busied himself with preparation of breakfast.

"How long you been up?" I asked.

"Time enough for me to fix one of those famous Amonovitch breakfasts. Check it out, little brother. Mom would be real proud of me."

I couldn't believe it. Peter had everything. "Get your butt upstairs and shower," Peter ordered. "This is a special event and ya can't be in your underwear."

Peter had a way of coming up with surprises. Leaving home was not an easy thing to do. Peter's decision to celebrate gave it special meaning. He was right. Mom would have been proud of him.

After eating I volunteered to clean up the kitchen, to give Peter time to pack his belongings.

Peter insisted on helping with the clean up. He wanted the kitchen spotless. "I think that's how Mom would want us to leave it," Peter said.

At 8:05 the truck driver knocked on the door. "You the Amonovitch boys?" he asked.

"That's us," I answered.

He pointed to his Chevy pickup truck. "There she is, boys. Load on your things. I'll sit over here and wait."

Peter helped me load my belongings, then grabbed his one small bag.

"That's all you're taking?" I asked.

"I don't 'spect to stay long."

We arrived at the Higginses' home at 9:10 AM. Their house was at the top of a hill, a big mansion that must have cost a heap of money. Everything about it looked trim and neat and expensive.

A man and woman approached us at a brisk pace. The man was tall and slim, with ramrod straight posture, graying hair and mustache. He had an official look about him, like Mr. Snippet, the eagle-eyed grumpy old principal back at Northeast Junior High School.

The woman was pretty, younger than her husband, with blond hair. She appeared surprised, as if we were remarkably different from what she expected.

The man moved toward Peter, inviting a handshake. Peter brushed him off with sober defiance, like when invited to shake hands with an opposing captain before a football game.

Peter was never one to pretend.

Embarrassed, I stepped forward. "I'm Andrew Amonovitch and this is my brother, Peter."

"This is my wife, Tracy, and I'm John."

"When Father Sikorski told us you were fourteen-year-old twins, I expected, you know, two frail teenagers who looked pretty much alike," said Tracy Higgins with an uneasy smile.

"We're not identical," I said. "We looked more alike when we were little."

"Did you boys have breakfast?" Mrs. Higgins asked.

"Yes, we did," I said.

"How about if we help you carry your things into the house?" volunteered Mr. Higgins.

They showed us to our room, which was large with all new furniture. There was two of everything, arranged so that each of us had a defined area at opposite sides of the room.

"We hope this will be comfortable," said Mrs. Higgins.

We had hardly caught our breath when John Higgins made an official announcement: "I'll give you boys half an hour to get yourselves settled. At ten o'clock I want you to report to the rec room. There's some important information I want to present to you."

When Mr. Higgins departed, Peter plopped down on his designated bed. "Pretty fancy place," I said. Peter didn't respond. He rested while I unpacked. "Wonder what Mr. Higgins wants to talk with us about?" I said.

Peter responded, "I 'spect mustache man is gonna unload some bullshit."

"I suppose he'll lay down a few rules."

"Sounds like a waste of time to me," Peter said. "I'll stay here and rest."

"You need to be there!"

Hearing the urgency in my voice, Peter said, "If you say so, little brother. Just thought I'd save Mr. Gestapo from wastin' his breath on me."

The rec room was huge, with a fire place, oak ceiling beams and patio doors leading to a plush, landscaped backyard. John and Tracy were waiting when we entered. Tracy seemed tense as they waited for Peter and me to take our places. John began, "Guess you boys should know that I'm an old military man. I was in the marines twenty years."

"He retired a full colonel," Tracy said with childlike pride.

"The most important thing I learned in the military is that for people to get along, they need to have a common understanding." Peter's mischievous smile bothered me. "First of all," John continued, "Let it be known that I'm in charge here. Father Sikorski warned me that maintaining order will be important, and I assure you, I'm in full agreement with that thinking." John Higgins proceeded with a detailed explanation of the house rules. He was only a few minutes into his presentation when Peter calmly stood and sauntered toward the door.

"Young man!" John Higgins blared out.

Peter kept walking. Tracy looked alarmed as John charged toward Peter. Mr. Higgins grabbed Peter's arm.

Peter whipped a hand upward, freeing his arm from Mr. Higgins's grip, and forcing John to lose balance. Mr. Higgins quickly recovered and again charged toward Peter.

Impulsively, I rushed between Peter and Mr. Higgins. Mr. Higgins glared at me with stony, fiery eyes. Frightened and shaking, I held my ground. A tense, uneasy silence cemented everyone motionless. Peter shrugged his shoulders, turned aside and departed.

Mr. Higgins stood red faced and twitching with anger as he watched Peter walk away.

When Peter was out of sight, the tension eased. "Could we talk?" I asked with a shaky voice.

John Higgins motioned for me to sit down. "Thanks for coming between us, young man. I'm not one to back away from such defiance."

"It's happened before, Mr. Higgins. Peter and Dad used to face up to each other."

"I got no patience for such insubordination."

"Maybe our being here isn't such a good idea."

"I won't tolerate such talk, young man. Surrender to the enemy is not my style."

"Peter can be mighty stubborn."

"I've broken some powerful wild horses in my day."

I didn't like his referring to Peter as a wild horse, but this was no time to object. "You folks have a nice peaceful home. I feel bad if we bring you trouble."

"Don't worry, young man. I can handle that brother of yours."

When I returned to our room Peter was lying in bed reading *God's Little Acre.*

"Cheer up, little brother," Peter said. "You look like doomsday."

"The least you could do is let Mr. Higgins explain the rules."

"I ain't interested in his rules."

"It's their house and we're guests."

"Mustache John thinks he's a general and you and me's his soldiers."

"The guy's strict. So, maybe that's what we need."

"Speak for yourself, little brother."

"What's so bad about being in bed at ten o'clock?"

"I don't need anybody tellin' me when to go to bed."

"So what will you do? Go out drinking every night and come home after midnight, like last night?"

Peter flung his book across the room. "You some kind a lieutenant? Brown nosin' up to the general and tryin' to tell me what to do?"

I'd pushed Peter too far. I'd forgotten the soft words that gave my ideas a chance to be heard. All I could do now was back off and allow the angry dust clouds to settle.

I heard the revving of a car engine. I looked outside the window, and Tracy was waving as John backed down the driveway.

Twenty minutes later there was a knock on our door. It was Tracy Higgins. "You can come down now for lunch," she said.

"Thanks," I said. "We'll be there."

Peter was lying on his bed with his eyes closed. "Mrs. Higgins has lunch for us," I said.

The sound of his breathing told me he was asleep. I backed off.

When I arrived in the kitchen, Mrs. Higgins asked, "Where's your brother?"

I hesitated. "He's not hungry."

She gave me a questioning look. "Oh, I see," sounding disappointed. "Well, we can't let your brother stop us from eating. It's all set up on the patio." She motioned for me to follow her.

Mrs. Higgins had obviously given considerable thought and effort in preparing this lunch.

Since it was her first meal for us, I could tell she wanted it to be a success. The setting was flawless. The backyard was immaculate, too perfect, but it didn't have the intimate touch like Mom had created at our home.

We sat beneath the shade of a huge umbrella. "I'll miss that big handsome brother of yours."

"Me too."

"I thought it would be easier for your brother if John wasn't here. He went to play golf."

I didn't want to tell her that I'd be more comfortable if John was here with us. I felt uncomfortable alone with such a pretty woman.

"Don't be afraid," she said. "Help yourself."

The sandwiches looked too fancy to touch. I tried to be delicate, taking small bites. There was a spicy, unfamiliar, unappealing flavor. I worried that she might detect my distaste. "Real good," I said.

Mrs. Higgins was more interested in talking than eating. "You must think John is being too tough on your brother?"

"To tell the truth, Mrs. Higgins, Peter doesn't take a liking to any authority."

"He does have respect for you."

"Peter and I always been close."

"Being twins, that seems natural."

I sat my sandwich aside. Mrs. Higgins filled my glass with lemonade. "Father Sikorski says your brother is filled with anger. Is that true?"

Talking about Peter like this with a stranger seemed improper to me. "Peter has reason to be angry," I said.

"Why?"

I sipped my lemonade. "I don't want to talk about it."

This cooled the discussion. Except for an occasional polite comment, we quietly gazed out at the scenery. I was eager to return to our room.

When I got back to our room, Peter wasn't there. He left a note on the bed:

Little brother,

Hitchhiked back to Northeast to spend evening with friends. Don't sweat it ...
Peter

I dreaded going to supper without Peter. I had the notion to take off myself. I couldn't do it. John Higgins had made it clear that he expected us to be at every meal and be there on time. Supper was at 6:00 PM.

At five minutes to six I entered the empty dining room, feeling embarrassed and nervous.

The table was adorned real fancy, all ready for us to eat. Preoccupied and jittery, Tracy gave me a quick wave of her hand as she rushed in with a steaming casserole.

When John Higgins entered, it was one minute to six. I sensed his scrutiny as he stood tall in his white shirt and tie. With abrupt, crisp movements, he took his place at the head of the table. "Where's your brother?"

I wanted to crawl under the table or run out. "P ... Peter went to Northeast. T ... to be with his friends."

"Tracy! Did you give permission for Peter to leave?" John asked.

"No, sir. This is the first I heard of it."

"Remove his plate!" John ordered. "Late for supper here and you don't eat." Tracy hastened to remove Peter's place setting. John sat down first, and we followed. "Let us pray," John said. He bowed his head and placed his folded hands on the table. I did likewise. John prayed: "Dear Lord. Bless this food. Bless this house. Bless our new family and bring the lost sheep back to the fold. Amen."

The food was plentiful and delicious, but not that enjoyable for me under the circumstance of Peter's absence. Tracy Higgins had made another extraordinary culinary effort, but a silent foreboding prevailed, conveying to me that these people had feelings that cast a tainted shadow upon us.

"Can I help with the dishes?" I asked when we finished eating.

Tracy sought John's approval. John turned to me and said, "I want you to accompany me to look for your brother."

"I can take care of the dishes," Tracy said.

John drove to Northeast, going to our home first. Peter was not there. I gave direction to the homes of Peter's friends. "Your brother sure has lots of friends," John said after we had gone to six of their homes.

"Peter needed friends to get out of the house and there's lots of kids who loved being Peter's friend. He's loyal and likable."

"Peter ran off like this when he lived at home?"

"If Dad was home, Peter always stayed there to watch after Mom, except to go to school. but when he had opportunity to go out and have fun, no way could you keep him home."

"Sounds like you have high regard for your brother, despite his defiance of authority."

"Peter's defiant for a reason. He took the brunt of Dad's anger, anger so strong it took hold of Dad's life. Mostly, that anger was directed at Peter. I'm not sure why, except maybe Dad sensed that Peter was stronger than Mom and I, and could handle it better."

"Sounds like excuses to me," John said.

His words bothered me. I had opened up to John, trying to explain about Peter, but it was like he didn't hear a word I said. Defiantly, I blurted out, "Peter's got reason to be angry inside!"

John didn't answer. I could tell he thought I was making another excuse for Peter. By 10:00 PM we hadn't found Peter. John asked me for directions to the Northeast Police Station.

There, John explained Peter's absence to the police and directed me to give them information on names and addresses of Peter's friends.

John mumbled and brooded all the way back to Anoka. His threatening attitude had me worried. Through clenched teeth he made the menacing promise: "Whatever it takes, I'll teach that brother of yours to follow orders."

The next morning Peter had still not returned. John Higgins called the police at 6:00 AM.

They had no information on Peter. John then called Father Sikorski, explaining in a gruff voice,

"We have us a serious problem. Peter took off and we can't find him."

There followed a silent interlude as John listened, then he said, "That's up to you. You can come over if you want, but it isn't really necessary."

After breakfast I had to go out for a walk, to ease my tension. I had to get away from the house. The walk caused me to think thoughts that had me even more worried. There were so many forces beyond my control. Eventually, I felt a pressure to get back and face up to the problems.

Upon my return, I saw Father Sikorski's car out front. I entered quietly. Immediately, loud voices from the kitchen heightened my anxiety. I scampered upstairs and entered our room. A familiar smell struck me. My heartbeat elevated.

There was Peter crashed out on the bed. I sensed that it was best to let him lay. I hurried downstairs to the kitchen. They were surprised by my abrupt arrival.

"Good morning, my boy," said Father Sikorski.

"Good morning, Father," I answered nervously.

"We're talking about Peter," Father Sikorski said. "We're concerned about his whereabouts."

"Whereabouts?" I said with surprise.

"You must know the police haven't been able to find him," Father Sikorski said.

Timidly, I said, "Peter's upstairs—sleeping."

"Upstairs?" Tracey asked.

"I thought you knew."

"He must have snuck in," John said, attempting to conceal his resentment in the presence of Father Sikorski.

"It's imperative we talk with that young man!" John Higgins demanded.

"He's sleeping," I said with urgency.

John Higgins glared at me with disgust. I sensed that again he viewed my comment as an excuse for Peter. He took off toward the stairs. Father Sikorski followed. I hurried to catch up.

They charged into our room like storm troopers. When I got there, John Higgins hovered over Peter's bed and ordered, "Rise and shine, young man!" Peter didn't budge. John shouted, "RISE AND SHINE!" There was no way Peter could fail to hear this angry command, but he didn't budge.

John grabbed Peter's arm. In a flash Peter spun around and caught John off guard. John instinctively lunged backward. Seeing the entourage of visitors, Peter calmly stretched and yawned.

"You been drinking!" John Higgins growled.

"Is it true?" Father Sikorski asked Peter.

Peter yawned. "I'm tired and I'd 'preciate if you'd leave and let me sleep."

Peter's composure disarmed John Higgins and Father Sikorski. I couldn't resist smiling.

Father Sikorski motioned John Higgins aside to confer privately. Peter turned over to resume sleeping.

This set John off. He made a quick move toward Peter, but Father Sikorski was quicker as he positioned himself between John and Peter. "Relax," Father Sikorski urged. "Let's go out in the hall and talk this over."

Reluctantly, John yielded. "I can't blame you for being angry," consoled Father Sikorski. "You have to realize that Peter can try the patience of Job."

"What he needs is a damn good session in the woodshed."

Father Sikorski pleaded. "I agree that the boy needs firmness and consistent discipline, but he doesn't need more violence or physical force."

John had that familiar look in his eyes, clearly indicating that he believed Father Sikorski also made excuses for Peter. John raised a hand, rubbed his forehead and said, "Don't you worry, Father, let me take care of this. I've handled some tough customers in my day and I'm not about to let a fourteen-year-old whippersnapper tarnish my record."

Father Sikorski appeared uneasy. "You sure you want to take this on, John?" he asked.

John forced a laugh. "When I agree to do something, that's what I intend to do."

"I just want to make sure you don't lose control with Peter. He isn't an ordinary kid."

"Don't you worry, Father. He's just like another stubborn recruit. Give me some time. I'll shape him up."

Father Sikorski studied John's face, seeming unsure if he could trust John's judgment, then said, "Well, I guess you deserve the chance to give it a try. But promise not to let your anger get the best of you."

"Don't worry, Father. I know what I'm doing."

Chapter 6

Father Sikorski's plea for restraint was of little comfort to me. John Higgins was exactly what Peter didn't need. John was a hard-nosed military man with an attitude. He took pleasure in using force and unyielding rules. He had no time for suggestions from me, Father Sikorski or his wife. John appeared to listen, but ignored advice from others.

I considered it useless to try to change his thinking. The sympathetic glimmer in Tracy Higgins's eyes and her reticent body movements revealed discomfort with John's rigid approach. Yet, she went along with his agenda.

Father Sikorski also showed signs of reservation about John Higgins, but wasn't close enough to the day-to-day events to grasp the full intensity of the gathering storm. Besides, John was a strong, outspoken respected force in our church congregation. How could Father Sikorski cast doubt on one of his most devout parishioners?

Peter was the only one with guts enough to confront John directly. A showdown between them was inevitable. I just wanted to keep people from being hurt.

The night after Father Sikorski's visit, I pondered what to do. The next morning I waited for an opportunity to convey a message to Tracy. "I need to talk with Father Sikorski," I told her.

"You just saw him yesterday."

"I know, but I need to talk with him privately."

"Want me to give you a ride to the church?"

"I was hoping you would."

"You arrange the time to see Father Sikorski and let me know."

The tone of her voice indicated that she was pleased with my request to meet with Father Sikorski, but didn't want to tell John about it.

I was tense and quiet during the ride into Northeast Minneapolis. Mrs. Higgins gave me an occasional glance, always about to speak, but each time held back.

We arrived at Immaculate Conception five minutes early. On my walk to the church office, I sensed Mrs. Higgins watching me, causing an unnatural hitch in my stride. Father Sikorski peered out the window as I approached. My tension intensified. I hunched up as if there was a twenty below zero windchill. My breathing came in gasps.

Father Sikorski opened the door well in advance of my arrival. He must have come directly from serving mass, being he was dressed in his black, flowing, officious gown and clerical collar. "Andrew, my boy. Blessed to see you."

"Good morning, Father."

"Never have I seen you so insistent as when you called yesterday. What is it that compels you?"

"Peter and I can't remain at the Higginses."

"You must not let your emotion get the best of you."

"There's about to be an explosion between John and Peter and somebody could get hurt."

"Did Peter put you up to this?"

"Peter doesn't know I'm here."

"This isn't like you, Andrew. You're not one to give up. You try to make things work."

"That's why I'm here, Father. To make things work."

A hardness came to Father Sikorski's eyes. He started to speak with a penetrating resonance that bore into the depths of my soul. "You must realize, my boy, that what you propose could have serious implications for your brother. John Higgins is the one man with the experience and force of personality to mold Peter into a responsible young man." The omniscient tremor of

his voice was unsettling. "Don't you see how important John Higgins can be for Peter?" Father Sikorski
pleaded.

"You don't understand," I responded, trying also to
be forceful, but feeling disappointed because my strong
emotion caused me to falter and come across meek and
ineffective.

"I'm afraid it's you, Andrew, who don't understand," Father Sikorski insisted. "Maybe it's the devil
who's twisted your mind."

This comment was so disturbing I was afraid to
speak, for fear of what I might say. For a moment I
glared daggers at Father Sikorski; then, in a huff, I
stormed out of his office.

"Remember what I said," he called out as I made
my way down the walkway to the car. I refused to
look back. The force and determination of my stride
contrasted sharply with the nervous uncertainty with
which I'd entered his office twenty minutes ago.

My visit failed to change the mind of Father
Sikorski. The one who changed was me. My position
was now the same as Peter's. The battle lines had been
drawn and the war had been declared.

"What happened?" Mrs. Higgins asked the instant
she saw me.

"What happened is that Peter and I will be moving
back home."

Tracy was silent until the traffic thinned out at
the north outskirts of Central Avenue. "I can't believe

that Father Sikorski would have you return home," she said.

"He was adamant that we stay at your place."

"I'm confused, Andrew. You said you were moving home."

"That's right."

Again there was silence. Tracy's driving became unsteady.

"It isn't anything to do with you," I said. "You understand better than John."

"John understands better than you think he does."

"John and Peter are on a collision course. That's why we need to move."

Tracy swerved. A horn blasted. Tracy clutched the steering wheel and settled the car. "All Peter needs to do is to cooperate. Once that happens, John can be a great guy."

"Peter won't cooperate."

"If that's true, I feel sad for your brother."

"It is true and I feel sad about what could happen if we don't move out of your beautiful home."

Our arrival at the Higginses' house ended the conversation. There was an uncomfortable feeling as we went in different directions. I had to find Peter. I'm sure Tracy wanted to talk with John.

Peter was in our room, lying on the bed reading a book on Gothic architecture. As long as I can remember, Peter was interested in buildings and how they were constructed.

"Put your book down," I said. "We need to talk."

"Go ahead, talk," Peter said as he continued to look at the book.

"We need to move back home," I said.

Peter slammed the book shut. "I'll be damned. What happened?"

"You and John Higgins aren't made for each other."

"Actually, Andrew, I'm having fun with John Higgins, but I agree he's a perfect reason for us to return home."

"I talked with Father Sikorski about it. Tried to convince him."

"Thanks, little brother. I 'preciate what ya did."

"My visit hurt more than helped."

Peter smiled, "Me and old hard head is gonna clash. When that happens, they ain't gonna want us here any longer."

"You and I need to find a way to move. Soon as possible."

"My friend, Dart Davenport's got a pickup truck. Want me to ask him?"

"Who's this Dart guy?"

"A friend I met at Andre's."

"You aren't old enough to be in Andre's."

"They never ask my age."

"Going to bars at your age is asking for trouble."

Peter opened the architecture book again and asked, "How about I call Dart to bring his pickup truck here Saturday?"

I glared at Peter, who appeared to ignore me as he looked at his book. "Okay," I said, "Tell him to come early."

Peter laughed. "Dart don't see the light of day before noon on Saturdays."

Peter hardly finished talking when there was a solid knock on our door. I sat up straight on the bed. Peter didn't budge. "C'mon in," Peter yelled.

When John Higgins entered, the first thing he saw was Peter lying on his bed with his shoes elevated and resting on the bottom bed board of the bed. "Put your feet down where they belong," John ordered. He gave Peter time to respond. Peter ignored him. I was about to urge Peter to comply when John shoved me aside and advanced toward Peter with the intention of knocking his legs down.

Peter saw it all the way. The instant John made his move; Peter swung his legs and caught John in the gut by surprise. John catapulted backward and landed on his ass. John was slow to get up. I hurried to help him. "Get your paws off me," he scowled.

Peter raised his feet back up on the bed board. There was a mischievous twinkle in his eyes. I tipped my head to the side, signaling Peter to lower his legs. Peter swung his legs off the bed board and rose to a sitting position.

John's staunch posture eased and the blood-red shine of his face faded. He turned to me and said, "Tracy told me what you said today."

"It's for the best," I responded.

"Forget it," John said.

I saw anger in John's eyes. "We plan to leave as soon as we can," I said, my voice quivering.

"We'll see about that," John snapped back. After one last menacing glare, John stormed out of the room.

At noon on Saturday I heard the blast of a car horn. I looked out and saw a pickup truck in the driveway. Peter was still sleeping. The horn blasted again. I grabbed Peter's shoulder and shook him. "Your friend's here with his truck."

Peter rubbed his eyes, "Run down and tell 'em to hold on. I need some time to get percolating."

Dart Davenport looked to be in his mid-twenties, grubby looking and bow legged. Must a been several days since he'd shaved and his bloodshot eyes stood out against the blackness of his disheveled hair and whiskers. His jeans were dirty enough to stand on their own and when he walked, he swayed from side to side, his weight teetering on the outer edge of his lopsided cowboy boots.

"So you're Peter's twin brother?" Dart said. "Guess ya do sorta 'semble 'em."

"We're not identical."

"Thank the Lord for that. The world couldn't handle two the likes of Peter."

"Peter can be different at times."

"You tellin' me. When Peter 'rives on the scene, da girls pretty up and the guys run for cover."

"You exaggerate."

"Shit no! Ya seen dat big dude when he's boozed up? Hell, man, he's one mean son of a bitch. 'Notha thing, he's a real ladies man. He can get all the ass he wants."

"Suppose you seen all this yourself?"

"Damn betcha," he said. "Me and Peter's like this." Dart held up his right hand and crossed two fingers. "We're drinkin' buddies." He winked. "He 'tracts the chicks and I buy the booze."

"Don't you know Peter's only fifteen?"

"Who the fuck cares? He's big enough to fool anybody."

Before Peter came out, a familiar car pulled up behind the pickup truck. It was Father Sikorski. Father Sikorski showed intensity the moment he got out of his car. He hardly noticed me as he rushed into the house.

A short time later, Peter shouted from the upstairs window. "All ready, fellows. You can come up now."

When we got to the bedroom, Peter had already moved several of my larger boxes near the door. "Grab the other end of this big one," Peter said. "Let's get this outta the way first."

We carried the box toward the door. I was moving backwards, when a stolid voice from behind me said, "That's far enough." Father Sikorski blocked the door. "You may as well sit that box down," he said. "You boys aren't leaving."

My attempt to stop was useless as Peter plowed ahead, forcing me into Father Sikorski, knocking him backward. There was a loud gasp from Tracy. John Higgins rushed to help Father Sikorski, who had fallen to the floor.

"You okay, Father?" I asked.

Peter directed me to resume carrying the box out to the truck. Seeing this, John lunged at Peter with fists clenched.

"NO! NO! JOHN!" Father Sikorski shouted. Peter lowered his end of the box and prepared to defend himself. John froze in mid-action. Father Sikorski scrambled between them and raised his right hand with an open palm to Peter and said, "God forgive you for what you've done here today."

Peter motioned for me to take the other end of the box. Numbly, I lifted it up and we carried it out to the pickup truck. Father Sikorski, John and Tracy stood quietly aside as we finished loading.

Chapter 7

My hands were still shaking when we arrived at home. Dart Davenport parked his truck out front while Peter walked to the house at a pace I couldn't match. I tagged behind. Peter waited and held the door open for me. "You first, little brother," he said.

Peter did most of the work as he hurried to carry my belongings up to our bedroom. When finished, Peter said to me, "Dart and me are going out to celebrate. Wanna come along?"

I hesitated. "Think I better stay and unpack."

"It's your life, little brother," he said as he took off with Dart.

Now that we were home, Peter went out every night, returning in the darkness of early morning. Sometimes he'd sleep only a few hours, other times, he'd sleep until noon.

Soon, we were without money for food. As if antici-pating this, the Hennepin County Welfare Department sent out a pretty lady. "My name's Gladie Summers," she said. "I'm from the welfare department and need to talk with you and your brother."

"Peter's sleeping."

She smiled. "Does Peter always take a noon nap?"

Trying to be friendly, I said, "Peter's unpredict-able."

"We got a call at our office last week from a Father Sikorski. He was concerned about you and your broth-er. I believe he's the priest at your church."

"He's known our family for years."

"He had some great things to say about you and your brother."

"About both of us?"

"Why not?"

"Usually he favors me. Sort of like our father fa-vored me."

"You don't seem too happy about that."

"It isn't fair to Peter."

She seemed unsure how to answer. "Fact is Father Sikorski talked a good deal about your brother. He had good things to say about him, but also expressed grave concern about him."

"What did he say?"

"Well, several times he mentioned Peter's physical strength and athletic ability. He also said Peter could be smart when he wanted to be."

"Suppose he told you what happened at the Higginses' place?"

Her eyes showed curiosity. "No, what's that all about?"

"It's no big deal," I was quick to respond.

"Sounds like there's something I should know about. It's important that I understand you and your brother."

"It didn't amount to much," I said quickly.

She knew I was covering for Peter. "Maybe we can talk about it another time," she conceded.

"What else did Father Sikorski say about Peter?"

"I'm the one who is supposed to ask questions," she said in a congenial manner.

I liked Gladie Summers. She knew when to back off. "I suppose Father Sikorski told you that Peter's been known to get into mischief once in a while?"

Her face turned serious. "I'm glad you brought that up. Father Sikorski told me about your father, about the war, your Dad's depression and about how he took his anger out on Peter." She hesitated. "He told me about Peter's sensitivity and defiance of authority. This defiance was of grave concern to him."

"People need to understand. If they treat Peter right, he can be the greatest guy in the world. He's smart and can accept reason, but people can't lord over him or be pushy in telling him what to do."

"Father Sikorski told me that you understand Peter better than anyone."

"Peter and I are real close."

"We decided it was best for now that you boys stay at home. We'll arrange for a housekeeper to take care of the house and keep an eye over you boys."

"What about Dad?"

"The doctors at the VA Hospital think it best that he live at the Veterans Home over on Minnehaha."

"How about his pension check?"

"That will come to our office. We'll pay the house-keeper and the house expenses. You boys will get a small weekly allowance."

Gladie Summers extended her visit, hoping Peter would wake up. I offered to awaken him, but she said, "That's not necessary. I'll meet him another time." She assured me that she'd come back next week with a housekeeper, then left. Our wish had come true. Peter and I would be able to live at home and attend Edison High School.

The following Tuesday Gladie Summers returned with a little old lady named Amy Pritchard, our house-keeper until they could find someone permanent. Wanting Peter to be present for this introduction, I excused myself and hurried upstairs to fetch him. Once again I found Peter absorbed in a big old book. He was now reading THE SEVEN LAMPS OF ARCHITECTURE by John Ruskin. It took some diplomatic persuasion to separate him from a favorite activity.

Before we entered the living room, I gave Peter a stiff punch on the shoulder, so he'd present a civil image as we entered the room.

The instant Gladie Summers saw Peter, she showed obvious surprise and I sensed an attraction to Peter. "I'm so happy to meet you," she said, extending a hand to Peter.

Peter refused to respond to her friendly gesture. I glared at Peter and felt embarrassed. Gladie Summers appeared hurt by Peter's coldness, but she smiled and proceeded with her introduction of Amy Pritchard.

After laying down some guidelines for our relationship to the housekeeper, Gladie Summers excused herself, explaining she had to rush off to a court hearing downtown.

Following her departure, I invited Peter upstairs to our room, where I felt more comfortable talking with him. "Why did you give Gladie Summers such a hard time?" I asked.

"She's just like Tracy Higgins," Peter said. "A pretty lady with a smile. I ain't fallin' for that shit."

"She was just trying to be friendly."

"I know the game," Peter responded. "First, comes the pretty smile and next comes the orders telling me what to do. I ain't gonna play that shit. She needs to know right off that I'm onto her game. I don't need anybody tellin' me what to do."

Peter's attitude was no surprise. It made me feel sad and disappointed. It also made me angry and critical of him, feelings that later would be followed by guilt.

Amy Pritchard was a neat freak. The sight of dirt or disorder was painful to her. Except for the kitchen and backyard, the remainder of the house and outdoors had been neglected since Mom's death. Amy Pritchard became vibrant with enthusiasm as she prepared to do battle with what she deemed a "horrendous mess." She expected Peter and me to join forces with her in this all-important battle.

Peter quickly analyzed what was happening and began cleaning with a blustery slovenliness. Amy looked on aghast, hovering over Peter, and then got carried away as she picked, picked, and picked at him. Peter whistled a sprightly tune as he persisted in his slipshod eagerness.

Amy appeared about to explode as Peter whistled with ever-gleeful delight. "Don't you understand?" she screamed. "You are not to touch the silver with your germy fingers and you must hold the silver up to the light to inspect for spots."

Peter smiled as if joyful of being enlightened. Carefully grasping the handle of a tablespoon, he held it to the light and said, "Oh my God. There's a spot." He frantically attempted to wipe away the blemish, then raised it again, and said, "Damn it. I'll fix it." He turned to Amy with a solicitous smile, raised the spoon to his mouth, spit on it and rubbed at it ferociously. "OH MY GOD," Amy screeched as she grabbed for the spoon and said, "Hurry. Toss it back into the hot soupy water!"

Peter playfully held it high and let it drop into the dishpan, splashing water in Amy's face. She groped for a towel to wipe the soapy water from her eyes as she transformed into a screaming banshee. "Can't you ever learn?" she shouted, shoving us aside with the tips of her fingers, careful not to expose herself to our germs. "Go and play," she ordered. "Get out of here."

Peter smiled. "C'mon, little brother," he said. "You and me ain't got the talent for housework."

It would have been hard living with Amy Pritchard for long. Our clothes couldn't have withstood her daily washing. She used Hilex with a passion and our clothes were turning white. Fortunately, Miss Hilex, as we came to call her, got a call to move on. I'm sure the welfare had other messes for her to clean up.

The permanent housekeeper arrived the Monday after the Fourth of July. Her name was Emma Burbank. She had gray hair but didn't look that old. She let us know from the beginning that she loved to go dancing on Friday and Saturday nights at the Prom Ballroom on Nicollet Avenue in Minneapolis. She wasn't much for cooking or anything that required work. She did the minimum to get by.

She had orders from Gladie Summers to keep a close eye on Peter and me, and report when we got out of line. Emma preferred that Peter and I take care of ourselves, and we made a deal with her: If she didn't tell on us, we wouldn't say anything about how little she did.

In the beginning Gladie Summers came every week. The day before Gladie was scheduled to visit, Emma would give the house a casual uplift and wash the laundry. She'd also bake cookies and insist Peter and I take a shower and dress in clean clothes.

Since all seemed to be going well, Gladie cut back her visits to once a month. Either we or Emma could call her if there were problems.

Emma was perfect as far as Peter was concerned. She let him do his own thing. Peter loved when she went dancing on the weekends. She came home at all hours of the night, on occasion not until morning. Some man would always bring her home, but no man ever came into the house.

I saw Emma as selfish. She cared about herself, not us. There was a relaxed atmosphere in the house, but it worried me that she didn't discipline Peter, and much of that burden fell on me. I could go to Gladie Summers or Father Sikorski, but I preferred to avoid them.

I was better off doing the job myself, aware of the challenge Peter could present and forever mindful of my commitment to Mom. As long as I didn't squeal on Peter for anything he considered petty, my credibility and influence with him could be maintained. If a serious issue presented itself, I'd calmly discuss it with him, and if he didn't respond with attentive concern, I told him I'd discuss it with Gladie Summers. Peter knew he had a good thing going and wanted to keep his behavior below the radar, so he'd shape up just enough to hold off my threat.

Peter and I were excited about going to Edison High School in the fall, especially about playing football. I was also excited about the academic challenge. I had done great at Northeast Junior High School and was eager to show off my intelligence to the Edison teachers.

Edison had a mystique throughout Northeast Minneapolis. There wasn't much talk about academics, but there was plenty of talk about football. Football players were celebrities.

Among our male friends there was frequent talk about the wild escapades of the "jocks" who attended Edison. Most of the stories floating around involved the drinking crowd. I worried about Peter becoming a part of this group. He was already into going to bars with older guys. Drinking, chasing girls and having fun were big on Peter's agenda. In Peter's mind playing football and having fun were synonymous with Edison.

I had great hope for our future. Going to Edison was a new phase of our life that had me feeling enthusiastic, but also uncertain.

Peter's expectations were dominated with thoughts of enjoying today. He thought little about how what happened today could influence tomorrow. This attitude made my life difficult, but I never expected fulfilling my promise to Mom would be easy.

Chapter 8

In the fall of 1948 the country was excited about electing a new president. The blue-collar population that dominated Northeast Minneapolis was expecting a Truman victory.

On the world scene the headlines were influenced by events growing out of the big war. Congress passed the Marshal Plan to provide seventeen billion dollars to war-ravaged Europe, though the threat of conflict persisted. Each Sunday at mass Father Sikorski prayed for peace in the world and he always made a point to remind parishioners of the growing dissent between East and West. I likened this to the warning he gave about Peter. Of course, world events were far away and I could conveniently remove them to the back of my mind, but his concerns about Peter were with me much of the time. Each night before going to sleep, I had an uneasy feeling about what the next day would bring.

Peter and I reported for football practice on the last Monday of August. Our first team meeting was in front of the school auditorium. Head Coach, Woody Watson, previewed our season and laid down some rules. "There are three rules that Edison football players have always lived by," Woody explained. "Number one: no booze. You drink booze, you're off the team— like yesterday." The guys were stone silent. "Number two: no smoking." He made slow, intense visual contact with every ballplayer. "And number three." His voice snapped like a whip. "My ballplayers are in bed by ten o'clock. Hear me?" There was a long silence to let his words sink in, and then he took a deep breath and shouted, "ANY QUESTIONS?" It was quiet. The guys were too afraid to breathe. Peter and I stuck close together at Edison. We had all the same classes. Walking the halls with Peter that first week gave me a strange sensation. I could tell the new faces in the building, the sophomores, by the shy reticence in their stride through the halls.

Peter didn't have the sophomore look. He moved with ease and had a quick smile for a friendly face or a pretty girl. Peter's size, stature and handsome presence drew attention. The guys sized him up with a wary look, for good reason.

They could see that Peter drew attention from the girls. If Peter saw a girl that appealed to his eye, he had no qualms about introducing himself, then me, and striking up a conversation. To Peter, a girl was a girl.

He didn't care if she was a junior, a senior, or if some upper classman had a claim on her.

I sensed the tension brought by Peter's presence. I sweated the jitters as I watched the reaction of the upper class guys. "You need to be careful who you talk to," I said, pulling him aside.

"You worry too much."

"Can't you see the guys don't like it when you talk friendly with their girl?"

"That's 'cause they don't know me." Peter took off down the hall, heading for our next class. I tried to relax while following him.

Our football season opened with a game on Friday of the first week of school. We played West High School and defeated them 28 to 7. Peter scored three touchdowns and became an immediate hero. Wherever he went in school, he drew the attention.

Each game brought another victory and each victory enhanced Peter's rising star. As Peter's blocking back, some of the light shined on me. I didn't like the limelight and tried to shy away. Peter liked the attention of the girls, but was uncomfortable when they got gushy over his football exploits. If it got too heavy, he turned away and joined me.

The drama was building as both Edison and Roosevelt High Schools remained undefeated. Edison had two games remaining. Our next game was with Patrick Henry High School. It was our homecoming and we expected to win big. The way things were shaping up, our final game with Roosevelt would be for the city championship.

Peter was being heralded by Sid Hartman of the *Minneapolis Tribune* as the most outstanding running back in the history of Minnesota High School football.

All this fanfare distracted me. It was hard to concentrate and be myself. On the Wednesday before homecoming, a problem had surfaced that involved Peter. On the way home from football practice, I was eager to talk with him, but he walked so fast my tired body couldn't keep up with him. "Slow down," I said. "I need to talk with you."

Peter stopped and waited. "Sorry, little brother. Sometimes I forget that being a blocking back is more tiring than carrying the ball."

"About time you recognized the real talent in the family."

Peter gave me a brotherly pat on the back. "So, what's on your mind, hot shot?"

"You can't be so friendly and think you can go out with any girl you want."

"What ya talking about?"

"You can't cozy up to girls who have boyfriends, especially upper class boyfriends."

"Who says so?"

"It's like an unwritten rule. When a guy's got a girl, you don't butt in."

"C'mon, little brother. Nobody owns anybody."

"That's not the way it is. There's rules and they were at Edison long before we came along."

"That rule's bullshit."

"There's your downfall, Peter. You don't respect rules."

"That ain't true. Most rules I respect."

"This is one rule you better start respecting."

Peter clicked his heels and gave me a Heil Hitler straight arm. "Ya! Mien Fuhrer!" he said.

I smiled. "Listen, Peter. I'm serious."

Peter draped his arm over my shoulders. "I know, little brother. I'm listening."

"I want to talk to you about Cindy Hawkins."

"Everybody says she's the most beautiful girl in the school."

"Everybody knows she's Andy Givens's girl and that you been playing up to her. Sophomore guys don't mess with senior girls that got boyfriends. Especially when the boy is Andy Givens."

"You tellin' me it's against the law?"

"Hell no! It's just a rule and you better wise up."

Peter smiled. "She's somethin' special."

"That's right. And you better back off."

"This is a free country, little brother. I pick my own girlfriends."

Andy Givens's claim on Cindy Hawkins was considered a fact of life at Edison High School. Andy was a big guy, six-two, two-hundred-forty pounds. He was a tackle on our football team, All-City the past two years, and considered one of the finest linemen in the state.

When it came time to select an All-State football team, there would be only one tackle from the Metro area. Tradition commanded that the other tackle position come from out-state. The selection of the All-State tackle from the Metro area was dependent on the outcome of the Edison-Roosevelt game. If Edison won, Andy Givens would receive the honor. If Roosevelt won, Eddie Elmore would get it.

Andy Givens had no doubt that Edison would win the game and that he'd be selected All-State. He considered himself the greatest. He swaggered as he walked the halls of Edison. When he came down the hall, he was given plenty of room. The guys were careful what they said or did in his presence. They knew Andy was quick to challenge anybody who didn't suck up to him.

The girls were even more afraid of him. The word was that Andy had no qualms about smacking girls around. Since he latched on to Cindy Hawkins, the other girls were more relaxed, believing he'd leave them alone since he had his woman.

Cindy was not only considered by the students and school staff to be the most beautiful female student in the school, they all understood that Andy Givens had total claim on her. The least indication of interest in her by other guys could bring swift and painful reprisal from Andy. Edison students viewed Andy as a mean ass and a real threat.

On the Thursday evening before homecoming, like every other night, Peter was preparing to go out, and I was worried. Peter had little respect for the rules set down by Coach Watson and considered the 10:00 PM curfew, "total bullshit." He did give some respect to the drinking rule: "Don't worry, little brother," Peter said, "I'll be careful how much I drink." The smoking rule was no problem. Peter didn't smoke.

Tonight he was more fussy about his appearance than usual. I asked him, "What's the big deal? You got a special date?"

"You better believe it, little brother. Me and Cindy Hawkins is having some fun."

"Cindy Hawkins!"

"Right on, little brother."

I struggled to control my anger. "Listen, Peter," I said, shaking, "you can't go out with Cindy Hawkins." Peter continued getting ready. "Did you hear me?"

Peter smiled. "Don't worry, Andrew. I know all this bullshit about Cindy being Andy Givens's woman. Big deal. We need a little excitement at Edison High School."

"This is serious, Peter. Can't you see what you're doing?"

Peter's voice was calm and soft as he said, "I'm not worried about any silly rule." He took a final look in the mirror and departed.

Coach Watson was worried about the homecoming game with Patrick Henry. "Keep your minds on the Henry game," he warned us. "Don't let all this homecoming hoopla get to your heads."

During the week before homecoming, word spread through Edison that Peter Amonovitch had dated Cindy Hawkins. Most everybody considered it a false rumor. They couldn't believe any guy would go out with Andy Givens's girl.

The truth was that Peter had been seeing Cindy every night for the past week. The previous Friday and Saturday nights he'd been with her until the wee hours of the morning. As we neared homecoming, there was talk about Peter going to the homecoming dance with Cindy.

The dance was scheduled for eight on Friday night. Preceding that at noon was the parade on Central Avenue and the game at three.

An ominous hush swelled through the halls of Edison on the morning before the game. Cindy Hawkins wasn't in school. Word spread that Andy Givens had slapped her up, giving her bruises and a black eye.

After our first-hour class Peter and I were walking in the hall when Andy backed Peter to the wall and stuck his nose in Peter's face. Peter shoved Andy backwards, a bold response that Andy didn't appreciate. A fight would have exploded if it hadn't been for me and

Andy's friends. I backed Peter off and Andy's friends did the same with Andy.

Within seconds a crowd gathered. "Listen to me, 'Monovitch," threatened Andy as he waved a big fist at Peter, "You take my woman to the dance tonight and your pretty snoot will be hamburger. Hear me?"

Peter smiled, a mischievous twinkle in his eyes. He loved the excitement. Andy lunged toward Peter, but Andy's friends restrained him.

"C'mon," Peter said to me. "Let's go to class." We made our way through the crowd, leaving Andy and his friends standing in the hall.

Tension hung heavy throughout the school. The teachers sensed the students had other things on their minds. They were tolerant, assuming that the homecoming festivities diverted student attention. Among the students there was whispering, an excited expectation that a big fight was brewing. It was building up to a David-Goliath spectacle, everyone assuming Andy Givens would kick the shit out of Peter. Most guys hoped Andy would put Peter in his place. They thought Peter was getting too big for his britches, that he considered himself God's gift to women.

The girls felt differently. Not only did they consider Peter handsome, they admired his belief that girls had a right to choose any boyfriend they wanted. They saw Andy Givens as mean and domineering. If a boy like Andy laid a claim on a girl, she had no choice but to go along with his wishes. If she refused, she could expect to get slapped around.

The guys on the football team had mixed feelings of loyalty toward their two teammates. They realized that Peter was the big reason for the team's success. They liked his friendliness, but were jealous of all the girls he attracted and resented his avoidance of football drills at our daily practice.

Everyone, including Coach Watson, knew Peter's attitude about training drills. Peter described the drills as "boring and stupid." He found clever ways to avoid them and when he did do them, he did the minimum.

There was also mixed feelings about Andy Givens. Although the football players recognized Andy's value to the team, they knew his contribution had more to do with meanness than talent. He was a dirty player who would do anything to win. He created fear with his intimidating, ruthless tactics. It was important for him to dominate by threat. Though the guys resented this, they were too afraid to do anything about it.

In a bet on who'd win in a fight between Andy and Peter, none of the players would put their money on Peter. "Peter'll get killed," said Herb Wilkins, the guard who played next to Andy. Everyone on the team agreed.

I kept my thoughts to myself. I'd seen Peter duke it out with Dad, and Dad was a tough ass. Peter had talents only I had witnessed. The ballplayers had seen Peter's speed as a running back, but never had they seen the quickness of his hands or the power of his punch. My bet was on Peter. Andy was a windbag.

If I truly believed it would actually take place, and was afraid for Peter, I'd have wanted to stop it. I could have gone to Coach Watson or Mr. Lucus, the school principal. I didn't think this silly talk would come to anything. Andy's friends showed that they wanted to prevent a fight. They'd done that in the hall on Wednesday, and surely they'd be even more cautious in the future.

I asked Peter, "Do you want to fight with Andy Givens?"

"Why should I fight him?" Peter said. "I ain't got anything against him."

"I heard he slapped Cindy up pretty good."

"If Cindy tells me that's true, then I got a score to settle with Andy."

"That could be big trouble."

"Who cares? If Dad hit Mom, Dad got his payback from me. If Andy hit Cindy, he'll get his payback."

"You can't get yourself suspended for fighting!"

"I ain't stupid enough to fight on school grounds."

"You think Andy Givens will stand around and let you take his girl?"

"'Bout time somebody faced up to him."

At half-time of the homecoming game we were behind by ten points. The slant play over Andy Givens's right tackle position had been our bread and butter all season. Today, the Henry defense was stopping it cold. Andy's mind wasn't on the game.

Andy played like a wild man on defense, making tackles everywhere on the field, but he got called for three unnecessary roughness penalties, one of which resulted in a Henry touchdown.

Despite Woody Watson's harangue during half-time, we were still unproductive the third quarter, trailing by a score of 17 to 0. In the break after the third quarter, Peter pulled me aside. "Let's forget about going inside the defensive end on the slant play," Peter said. "If you can bump the end to the inside, I'll bounce out to the flank and try get into the secondary."

Who but Peter would take it upon himself to change the coach's playbook? Though I was real uncomfortable going against the coach, I had to admit that Peter's idea made sense. The off-tackle play had got us nothing for three quarters.

Amazingly, as soon as we went on offense in the final quarter, Coach Watson showed confidence in Andy by calling the slant play that hadn't worked all day. I was so nervous thinking about Peter's idea that I moved too quick and got us a motion penalty. The next play, with first down and fifteen to go, Coach Watson called the same play. My heart pounded. What a stupid call, I bitched to myself. The coach should have called a passing play. Our running game wasn't working.

When Alfredo, our quarterback, barked off the signal, Peter gave me a crack on the rear end to remind me of his defiant challenge to Coach Watson's stubborn refusal to change his play calling. Angry and frustrated, I stumbled off the mark, but joined Peter in defying

Coach Watson's decision. I smashed the defensive end to the inside.

The defensive end was totally surprised with my slashing change of procedure. It was just enough to free Peter around the flank. Peter sidestepped the linebacker and hit the secondary going full speed. There wasn't a defensive back in the conference that could stop Peter in the open field. Peter scored a touchdown. Our kicker made the extra point and we were charged with renewed energy. Our defense came on like gangbusters, holding Henry on the next series of downs.

On our next offensive play, Coach Watson again called the tackle slant play. Peter and I pulled the same shenanigan as before. By the time the Henry defense figured out our changed blocking pattern, Peter had broken around the end for two more touchdowns.

That was the game. We won and were still undefeated. Later, in the shower, Andy Givens gave Peter a bump on the shoulder and said, "Remember, hot shot, Cindy Hawkins is my woman."

Peter didn't say a word as he brushed his hands through his dark curly hair and walked out of the shower. The instant Peter was out of sight, Andy smashed his right fist with three quick blows into his left palm. Then, he made like a prize fighter, crouching, jabbing, and whipping out with vicious haymakers, a menacing grin on his face.

This display of anger by Andy had me alarmed. I hurried from the locker room and was stopped by Coach Watson. Sternly, he said, "Here's some homework for the weekend." It was a copy of the off tackle slant play. "By Monday, memorize the assignment of every player on the team!"

"Yes Coach," I said, feeling guilty.

Chapter 9

After the game Peter and I walked home together. I chose to ignore telling him about Coach Watson's reprimand for failing to follow his directions on the off tackle slant play. I wanted to talk with him about Cindy Hawkins. "Andy's sure worked up about you and Cindy," I began. "You think it's worth fighting over?"

"Depends if Andy got rough with Cindy."

"Do you think it's wise to go to the homecoming dance with Cindy?"

"If you're sayin' I should buckle up to Andy Givens, you're full of shit."

"So, your mind's made up?"

"That's right."

I didn't know what to say, so we walked in silence. Peter slowed the pace, his way of giving me more time to talk. "I don't want you to get in trouble," I said as we neared home.

Peter gave me a serious look. "Thanks, little brother, but I ain't lettin' Andy Givens run my life."

My date for the homecoming dance was Kathy Amundson. She seemed the shy type, like me. I knew her from Northeast Junior High School where we'd gone to several dances together. Kathy wasn't popular in school because she studied more than most students. She earned straight A's. She even looked intelligent with her dark-rimmed glasses. I liked Kathy more than I let her know. I was too bashful to tell her. The excuse I gave myself was that I had my hands full with Peter and school work and football and didn't have time to get serious with a girl.

Since I didn't have a parent who could drive us to the dance, Kathy's father offered to give us a ride. He picked me up at our place at 7:30, mighty early.

The dance was at the clubhouse of the Columbia Golf Course. To my surprise, when we arrived, many students were already there. Tickets had sold like hotcakes and if you wanted a place to sit down, it was wise to come early.

Finding a place to sit down was no problem for the football players. There was a long table up front reserved for the team and their dates, with name cards designating our places.

I was the first ballplayer to arrive. Kathy and I bashfully took our places up front. Being alone up there with Kathy, I felt self-conscious with the eyes of our classmates focused on us. I wanted to appear sociable with Kathy, but couldn't think of anything but the Henry victory to talk about. Kathy patiently listened to me, although obviously disinterested. She'd gone to the game, but apparently paid little attention to the play on the field and could care less about who won.

Yet, she knew exactly what was going on between Peter and Andy Givens. "Do you know who your brother's bringing to the dance?" she asked.

I gave her a stern look. "Is that all anybody can talk about?"

"I assumed you'd know who your brother is bringing to the dance."

"I sure hope he doesn't show up with Cindy Hawkins."

"I thought you'd stick up for your brother."

"I do stick up for him. That's why I don't want him to show up here with Cindy Hawkins."

"Why can't girls date whomever they want?" Kathy snapped at me.

"You don't understand, Kathy."

She glared at me. "You guys are the one's who don't understand. I think Cindy should go to the dance with anyone she wants."

"Calm down, Kathy. You make it sound like a big deal."

Kathy grabbed my wrist, scowled at me with her big blue eyes, her glasses sagging half way down her nose and exclaimed, "You think Cindy Hawkins should give in to Andy Givens? You think that creep's got the right to beat her up?"

By now several of the ballplayers had arrived with their dates. I was embarrassed by Kathy's exuberance over Cindy Hawkins. "Can't we change the subject?" I pleaded.

"You guys always want to tell us what to do."

Fortunately, one of my teammates, Larry Olson, a second string center, and his date, Alice Hoverton, had sat beside us. Now, I had someone who could talk football, and Kathy could talk with Alice. Kathy was quick to engage her in talking about Cindy Hawkins.

By 8:00 PM the clubhouse was packed. At 8:15 the bustling crowd was silenced by a disturbance at the entrance, a loud, angry exchange of words. Peter had arrived. I excused myself and tried to rush to the entrance, but it was crowded and hard to move.

The instant I saw Peter standing beside Cindy Hawkins, tension grabbed me. Close by were a policeman and Mr. Lucus, the Edison principal. They were talking to Andy Givens, trying to calm him down.

When Peter saw me, he came forward, "Where ya sittin'?" he asked.

"C'mon, I'll show you."

When we arrived at the long table, Peter noticed that his designated seat was six chairs down the line from mine. He asked Larry Olson if he and his date would trade places so he could sit beside me. Larry was not eager to move, but yielded to Peter's celebrity status.

I became self-conscious again as Peter and Cindy sat next to us. The eyes of everyone were focused in our direction. I, too, was curious, wanting to see if Cindy's face showed signs of having been bruised by Andy Givens.

I discreetly peeked in her direction. The first thing I noticed was the sadness in her puffy eyes, which were heavily covered with facial powder. A brief involuntary shudder shook my body as I realized the story about Andy Givens was true.

"What was all the commotion at the entrance?" I asked Peter.

"Andy was tryin' to act big and tough."

"That guy's gross," Kathy said. We all glanced over at the usually quiet Kathy Amundson.

"Let's forget about Andy Givens," Peter said. "I want to have some fun."

I didn't expect the homecoming dance would be much fun. I was too worried about a big blow up between Peter and Andy. Kathy was eager for something to happen.

It amazed me that Peter could relax and enjoy himself. The threatening presence of Andy Givens and his friends didn't appear to bother him. Peter danced and socialized, uninhibited by the events taking place around him. Peter and Cindy were mighty cozy together. To see them dance was proof enough that Cindy was love struck, swept away by Peter's bold, affable attention. But she also appeared uncomfortable with people watching. It was like she couldn't wait to be alone with Peter.

Andy Givens's presence was strange and captivating. For him to be at the homecoming dance without a date was most unusual. To see him and his friends lurking around the edges of the crowd created a weird uneasiness. At times, Andy and his friends would disappear briefly. "What they up to?" Kathy asked.

No one answered her, but later in the evening Andy and his friends became more careless and Kathy and I caught a peek of them sipping from a bottle. We hastened to inform Peter and Cindy. "You need to get out of here," I said. "Andy and his buddies are boozing it up. There could be trouble."

"You crazy, little brother?" Peter responded. "I'm not leavin'. I'm having too much fun."

"This is one time you better listen to me," I urged.

"You worry too much."

I grabbed Peter's arm. "Listen, Peter. This is serious. Let's leave."

Peter gave me a hug. "No offense to you, little brother, but I ain't runnin' from Andy Givens."

Peter's eyes showed respect for me, but there was also a determination that told me he wouldn't leave the dance because of a threat from Andy Givens.

When it came time for the last dance, Peter and Cindy were eager to make the most of it. They were the first couple on the dance floor, and soon were entwined in a passionate embrace. Andy Givens and his friends charged toward Peter and Cindy, catching them by surprise. Before Peter knew what was happening, Andy's friends grabbed him, pulling him away from Cindy, restraining him so that he couldn't break free. Andy then seized Cindy by the arm and forced her across the dance floor toward the exit.

Peter was desperate to escape. He turned to me with his eyes pleading for help. I couldn't resist. Bound by a sense of duty to my brother, I faced his abductors, obsessed with setting Peter free.

Andy's friends recognized immediately that it would be too much for them to hold off both Peter and me, so they released their hold on Peter. Just like that, he was free. I was dazed by this sudden turn of events and faced a hushed crowd, whose eyes were all on Peter.

Peter motioned for me to follow as he rushed toward the exit. The instant he did, the crowd surged forward and created a log jam at the door. The policeman and supervising school staff hastened to gain control of the unruly students.

The students were quick to cooperate. A scene of potential havoc instantly became one of order and discipline. It had to be baffling, yet appreciated by the school authorities in charge of the homecoming dance.

If only they recognized that the students knew of a hidden agenda, one that had been building for several days. It had to do with power, the desire of Andy Givens to dominate and control, like World War II was all about power, just like the current Cold War conflict building between East and West. With such power tactics forever being played around the world, why shouldn't they take place at Edison High School?

Once outside the clubhouse, the crowd drifted toward the west end of the parking lot. From there they flowed up and over the hill, joining the throng of students already gathered at the base of the valley beyond. It was a quiet, anxious crowd, out of sight and hearing of the clubhouse.

When Peter and I arrived at the base of the hill, Erik Smithson met us. Erik was Andy's most loyal friend. "Follow me," Erik ordered. We followed as did the crowd behind us. Soon, we were joined by more of Andy's friends, who led us to a remote location of the golf course, away from the presence of police and school staff.

The pace increased as we moved further out over the hills and valleys of Columbia Golf Course. I glanced back at the huge mass of students, a faceless, dark silhouette of bodies, hungry for excitement, expecting a big showdown.

Moving swiftly, Peter and I walked side by side with Erik and his friends. I saw Erik taking a swig from a bottle, which he passed to his boozing buddies. I knew the smell. It was whisky.

The movement was toward the north end of the golf course, which was like an amphitheater with high ground rising on three sides. As we entered the valley, I saw a small gathering in the distance. It was too dark to distinguish who they were.

"Get the fire going so we can see," I heard some-one say. As we waited, the only sound was the hushed murmur from the whispering crowd, punctuated by the sharp slapping of hands against flesh, a desperate lashing out to kill the feasting mosquitoes.

Within minutes the fire was glowing, revealing the presence of Andy Givens and Cindy Hawkins. Cindy was holding her hands to her face.

Seeing this, both Peter and I rushed to her side. Blood trickled from the corner of her mouth. Peter wiped the blood from her face with his hand, and then nudged me to take a look at Andy Givens guzzling from a bottle of booze.

Andy tossed the bottle aside and started toward Peter, accompanied by his friends. Andy bullied up to Peter, nose to nose, provocative and threatening. Peter didn't flinch. Andy grinned with clenched teeth and said, "I'm gonna mess up your pretty face." Peter remained silent. Then, Andy spat a wad at Peter, hit-ting him below the left eye. Andy's grin widened as he raised his fist, preparing to strike.

Peter calmly wiped the spittle from his face, and then struck so fast I couldn't see exactly what happened. Apparently, Peter had pumped Andy in the gut with his left fist, causing Andy to bend forward. Swiftly, Peter followed with a smashing right to Andy's jaw with a revolting crunch that knocked him to the ground.

Peter's flurry caught everyone off guard. I bolted toward Peter to restrain him from hitting Andy again.

At the same time, Andy's friends hovered over their disabled comrade.

A hush settled over the crowd. They knew something dramatic had taken place, but what exactly happened was a mystery. Collectively, the crowd held their breath. It was spooky. All I could hear was the crackling of the fire and the thumping of my heart as I gazed at Andy on the ground.

"Let me go," Peter insisted, pulling away from my hold on his arm. Peter kneeled down beside Andy. He shook Andy's arm, trying to rouse him. All he got was a muffled whisky smelling groan. Peter turned to me. "C'mon, give me a hand." With my help and the assistance of Andy's friends, together we lifted Andy and carried him off in the direction of the clubhouse. The crowd followed.

When we reached Central Avenue, two officers in a roving police car sighted the mob of kids. Andy's friends made a mad dash for the anonymity of the crowd, and then disappeared. Peter approached the police, "Our friend needs help."

Without questions the officers loaded Andy in the police car. "Can one of you come along to the hospital?" an officer asked. "The doctors will want to know what happened."

There was a brief search for Andy's friends. They had vanished. "You ride along," Peter said to me.

"Do you know what happened?" the officer asked me.

"I think so, but I'm not sure," I said.

"Okay. Climb in."

Andy was taken to the emergency ward at Hennepin County Hospital. While he was being checked by the doctors, the police took me into a small room and asked questions. They were more concerned about the smell of booze on Andy's breath than they were about the fight over the girl. "Were there other kids drinking at the dance?" they asked.

"I don't know," I lied.

The questioning was brief. Leaving me waiting, the officers went to check on Andy. Half an hour later they returned. "Come with us," they said. "We'll take you home."

"What about Andy?"

"They'll keep him overnight. He had a concussion and they want to play it safe."

Chapter 10

Andy Givens was not at football practice on Monday, and Coach Watson started asking the ballplayers questions. After practice he invited me into his office. "The guys tell me you know what happened to Andy," he said.

"They know as much as I do."

"I need to know about Andy," Coach Watson demanded. "We got a championship game on Friday. We need him." I sat quietly, my hands sweating, my heart pounding. "Listen, young man, one way or another I'll find out what happened to my star tackle."

I held my silence, with Woody glaring at me. Afraid and stammering, I asked, "Can I leave now?"

Woody turned away in frustration and said, "Okay, get the hell out of here."

Moving slow and cautious, I eased up from my chair and cowered out of his office. I was glad to escape further questions.

The next morning at school there was an announcement that the football players were to report to the gymnasium promptly after school. At 3:05 the team was in the gym waiting.

Coach Watson entered, looking somber. His assistants, who usually hovered close to him, kept a distance.

Woody stood ominously before us, checking to see if anyone was missing. He began: "Yesterday after practice I paid a visit to one of our friends." He paced back and forth, unsure how to proceed. "Right now Andy Givens is sitting home with a broken jaw. He can't play Friday." He paused. "Andy's a senior. His football days at Edison are over." Woody moved closer to where we were sitting. He stalked slowly, making eye contact with each of us, then shouted, "You guys know how Andy's jaw got broken and I intend to find out what happened. You're not leaving here until somebody tells the truth. UNDERSTAND? I'll be waiting in my office for someone with guts enough to be honest."

Woody dashed briskly away, the force of his heels striking sharp on the hardwood floor, projecting a pounding echo through the huge gymnasium.

No one dared move. Eventually, Woody's assistant, Herb Beckel, came forward. He looked nervous. "You heard the coach. He'll wait in his office for you guys to give him the story."

Before Herb Beckel finished speaking, Peter was heading toward Woody's office. It took several seconds of heavy breathing on my part before I could pull myself together. I hurried off to join Peter, who was already in Woody's office. "What's the story?" Woody asked as Peter and I stood before him.

"I broke Andy's jaw," Peter said.

"It was Andy who wanted to fight," I added.

"What the hell were you guys fighting about?"

There was a long silence. "Andy beat up Cindy Hawkins," I said.

"Fighting over a girl! FOR CHRIST'S SAKE!" Woody shouted. "Here we are with a football championship on the line and you damn leather heads are fighting over a girl." After what seemed an eternity of pacing, he came to a halt and gave an order: "Get your asses out on the practice field. We got a big game on Friday that I expect us to win. Goddamn it!"

Monday and Tuesday we had our most grueling and productive practice sessions of the season. Wednesday morning Peter and I were called out of class and told to report to the to the office of the principal, Mr. Lucus. When we arrived at his office, two other men were there also. Principal Lucus introduced them: Mr. Owen Lindblad, associate superintendent of the Minneapolis Schools and Lieutenant Gary Olson of the Minneapolis Police Department.

Mr. Lucus spoke, "Mr. Lindblad and Lieutenant Olson are here to investigate rumors about what happened on the night of our homecoming. Since your names have come up in both the school and police reports, you're the first to be questioned. I expect you to cooperate with these gentlemen."

"What about Andy Givens? Can you call him down too?" asked Mr. Lindblad.

"Andy Givens hasn't been in school all week. I understand he's got his jaw wired shut and has trouble eating and talking," Mr. Lucus said.

"Give me his home address," said Mr. Olson. "I'll go to his home. I also want to hear his story of what happened."

Peter was seen first, alone. It lasted fifteen minutes. I was next. They rushed me in, so I had no opportunity to talk first with Peter. Before I sat down, Mr. Lindblad began, "We've had several calls at the central office, with information that would indicate there have been serious violations of the school discipline policy. There are claims of drinking and fighting at the homecoming dance."

I assumed Mr. Lindblad had given Peter this same information. "Do you know anything about drinking or fighting on the night of the homecoming?" he asked.

Loyalty to my friends commanded one answer, "No, I don't," I said.

Mr. Lindblad responded with inquisitive eyes. He handed me a card. "Here's my phone number. If you have anything more to say, I'd appreciate a call."

"Okay, sir."

Before excusing me to return to class, Mr. Lindblad spoke to me clear and deliberate, wanting to make sure I heard him. He said, "I'll be in the building all day to question as many students as possible. Let me know if you have anything more to say."

Following the next class, I talked with Peter. "I didn't have any information for the man," Peter said.

"Me neither." My voice was shaky. I wished I could be as relaxed as Peter.

The Thursday morning *Minneapolis Tribune* had a news report about the Edison homecoming. I was shocked by the story. It wasn't totally accurate, but basically covered everything. Word about the news story spread quick among the students. Soon rumors started about who squealed to the authorities.

Of greater concern was the *Tribune* announcement that the superintendent's cabinet would be meeting to consider disciplinary action against those who had violated the district's disciplinary code.

There was no mention of specific reprisals, but the implication was that any action taken would have a significant impact on the outcome of the Edison-Roosevelt championship game. They expected an announcement of the cabinet decision at 11:00 AM the following day.

Tension hung heavy in the air that next day. At 11:15, classes were interrupted by a message on the intercom: All students and faculty were to report immediately to the auditorium. It sounded like an emergency.

Mr. Lucus and Assistant Superintendent Lindblad were on stage. As soon as the audience was settled, Mr. Lucus approached the microphone. "I'm sure most of you have read the morning paper," he began. "The superintendent's cabinet has made a decision. Here, to give us that report is Assistant Superintendent Owen Lindblad."

Peter, Cindy and I were standing at the back of the auditorium. Cindy took Peter's hand as Mr. Lindblad came forward to speak. "This is indeed a sad day for me," he said, his words causing an instant foreboding silence. "After hours of questioning Edison students, the true story has been revealed. I want to commend those students brave enough to withstand the social pressure to cover up what happened."

Many of the audience glanced around, as if they could determine those students Mr. Lindblad was referring to. Mr. Lindblad saw what was happening and responded sharply, "I assure you, those who provided information will remain confidential."

A swell of disruptive chatter emerged. Mr. Lindblad raised his voice, "Let me report now on the action taken by the cabinet."

There was a swell of obtrusive chatter. Obviously embarrassed, Mr. Lucus stood and raised his arms, "Quiet! Quiet!" he ordered. With the influence of the faculty in the audience, the noise slowly abated.

Mr. Lindblad's voice trembled as he continued, as if this was a proclamation from God. "The cabinet learned that a core group of six to eight students were guilty in varying degrees of violating the district's disciplinary code. Many spectators were involved through their presence, but they were enticed by this core group, led by two students. The cabinet has decided to direct their disciplinary action to these two students. Their names are Andy Givens and Peter Amonovitch."

Chatter again broke out, too obtrusive for the speaker to continue. Once more Mr. Lucus and the faculty had to quiet the students. As soon as reasonable calm was restored, Mr. Lindblad continued: "After considerable deliberation, the unanimous decision has been made to disqualify Andy Givens and Peter Amonovitch from participating in inter-high school athletics for the remainder of this school year. This action will become effective immediately."

Before Mr. Lindblad could finish, many students started to walk out. Mr. Lucus shouted, "SIT DOWN AND WAIT TILL YOU'RE EXCUSED!" The students ignored him. They walked out of the auditorium and out of the school.

Most of the students didn't return for the remainder of the day. Those few who did were jeered with threats and catcalls.

Following the auditorium spectacle, I went to the office of Woody Watson. "Does this mean that Peter can't play against Roosevelt?" I asked.

"That's what the man said," responded the dejected coach.

"It isn't fair. Peter didn't start that fight," I pleaded.

"Don't talk to me about what's fair. For the first time in twenty years of coaching, I had a chance to win a Litkenhous Trophy as the top high school football team in the state. Now it's shot to hell."

"I refuse to play against Roosevelt," I said. "If Peter can't play, forget it."

"I can certainly understand your attitude. Maybe you should pass the message on to the rest of the team."

That's what I did. There were eight football players who were ready to join me in my protest. That night the *Minneapolis Tribune* had a bold headline at the top of the sports page: EDISON TEAM BOYCOTT CHAMPIONSHIP GAME.

There was no game. We held tough. To hell with them.

A football season that had held so much promise had ended with bitter disappointment. The students, Coach Watson, the Northeast community and, in particular, Andy Givens, were in a state of despair.

"To hell with it," Peter responded. "Now that football's over, I plan to have some fun."

The only thing that appeared to bother Peter was the fate handed to Andy Givens. With Roosevelt winning the city title and Litkenhous Trophy, Andy lost any chance for the All-Metro and All-State honors, which diminished his value on the college recruitment market.

"Andy got a raw deal," Peter said.

"You can't condemn yourself for that," I told Peter.

"I'm goin' to make peace with Andy Givens," Peter said.

Peter now reached out in a gesture of friendship toward Andy, which Andy found flattering. He welcomed Peter into his circle of friends. This was about the worst thing that could happen. All those guys did was drink and raise hell.

Despite my word of caution to Peter, he had an unusual desire to befriend Andy. "I don't like anybody to be treated like an outcast," Peter said. "Besides, Andy hates rules as much as I do and what I really like about him and his friends is that they like to have fun."

Peter started going out every night with Andy and his friends, causing us to drift apart. He knew my view of his friendship with Andy Givens and he knew I was unhappy with his drinking and the fact that he became more secretive about it.

Throughout the following winter I heard stories about Peter and Andy having contests over who could put away the most booze. I listened closely, searching for the truth, worried about Peter.

I stayed up late at night, hoping my being awake when he returned home would influence him to limit his drinking. My presence made him uncomfortable, so he went overboard trying to hide his drunkenness.

He didn't need to hide it. I could smell the alcohol the moment he entered our room. Almost every night this happened. I felt pain inside. I wanted to help, but didn't know how. I wanted to get angry at him, but remembered how Dad used to get angry at Peter. It only made Peter more defiant. He'd go overboard, doing exactly what Dad didn't want him to do.

Mom had often made a special point to remind me that it was my quiet, positive influence that worked best with Peter. I had to remember this and remain confident that my gentle presence was the only weapon I had to bring some sense to Peter's head. It was hard being patient, but I couldn't chance a battle with Peter. In all likelihood it would end in a rebellious victory for him and a serious setback for me, and the ultimate damage would be to Peter.

The anxiety and late hours drained my energy. It was a strange game Peter and I played. I was pre-occupied with worry that something terrible would happen.

The opportunity for me to influence Peter suffered a blow when he started remaining out all night. As much as it bothered me, I kept quiet. Then, he started staying out all weekend. It reached a point where he was gone more than he was at home. It was no longer worthwhile for me to stay up late.

Despite Peter's night life, he always made it to school and always on time. I made a point to mention this to him. "I'm happy to see you in first hour every day," I said.

"I know you're always watchin' me."

"I worry that something will happen to you."

"You worry too much, little brother."

The latest rumor at Edison was that Andy Givens and his friends were renting a cheap room on Washington Avenue, where they were supposedly enticing Edison girls. Another story told of them picking up a whore on the Avenue and all the guys taking her on.

I admit these stories excited me. Since sixth grade back at Lowry Elementary School, the fellows talked about the whores on Washington Avenue. Back then such comments mostly brought a red-faced giggle. I remember one day Mom overheard us talking about whores with our friends. Later, she called Peter and me aside. "I don't want any more of this whore talk. These girls are human beings and deserve respect like anybody else."

At the time Mom's words didn't mean much to me. Only later at Edison when I was doing some extra credit work for social studies class did it have an impact on me. I came upon an article in the *Saturday Evening Post* that reminded me of her comment. It was an article about prostitution. It told how most of these girls were physically or sexually abused at an early age, and the pattern of abuse continued into prostitution.

My respect for Mom and the hurt I felt because of the physical abuse she suffered from Dad merged with the information from the article in the *Saturday Evening Post*. I got an angry attitude about the stories of Washington Avenue and felt ashamed to think my brother might be part of such activity.

Peter didn't want to hurt others, but his defiance could end up being hurtful to him or others, like when he broke Andy's jaw. Such incidents followed threats from others. I rationalized that Peter hurt others only when he was hurt first.

The Washington Avenue story didn't fit with the picture I had of Peter. It bothered me so much that I felt an urgency to talk with him about it.

It started with my making a big breakfast for us on Saturday morning. "What's the occasion?" Peter asked.

"Let's say it's a tribute to the old days when Mom made this kitchen famous."

Peter seemed suspicious. I tried not to be pushy. We were well into breakfast when I introduced my concern. "There's something I want to talk about," I said, trying to sound casual.

"Kinda figured that."

"It's about this story of you and Andy and his buddies going to Washington Avenue. Is it true?"

Peter continued eating. I waited. Finally, he responded, "I don't think it's any of your business."

The bite in Peter's words angered me. I blurted out, "To tell the truth, Peter, I don't believe the story."

"So, why'd ya bring it up?"

"I was embarrassed about what kids were saying about you and your friends."

"Forget about it, little brother. That talk don't change my way of living."

"You sure sound snippy about it."

Peter held back before he said, "It's just that I'm gettin' tired of your bullshit."

This hit me hard. I couldn't look at him. I sat quiet, as did Peter. It lasted until we finished eating.

"Thanks for the breakfast, little brother," Peter said. His voice was now calm and respectful. "I'll take care of the dishes," he added.

I helped Peter with the dishes. Without a word, we cleaned the kitchen together, both determined that it be spotless. Mom would have been proud of us.

The following Sunday evening I waited up late, expecting Peter to return after being gone all weekend. In the past he'd always come home in the afternoon or early evening. Now at 9:00 PM he was still not back and my imagination created reasons to worry. When the phone rang at 9:30, I snatched it with sweaty hands and with a timid voice said, "Hello."

"It's me, Peter. Thought I better call and tell ya I won't be in school tomorrow."

"What happened?"

"I'm in jail."

"In jail! What for?"

"I was talkin' with this guy's wife and he came after me."

"So, what happened?"

"I swear, Andrew, this guy came after me full bore and I had to let him have it."

"He's in jail too?"

"No."

"Why not?"

"He's in the hospital." I waited in silence, and then Peter continued, "When he came after me, I got pissed and messed him up pretty bad."

"How serious is it?"

"I ain't heard nothin' yet."

"So when are you getting out of jail?"

"Soon's the police get a report from the hospital, they'll plan a preliminary hearing."

"What should I tell them at school?"

"That's up to you, Andrew."

"Sure hope you're not in big trouble."

"Don't worry, little brother. The most they can do is lock me up in Stillwater." Peter chuckled.

"This isn't funny, Peter." My comment brought silence. Then I asked, "Can you call me soon as you find out what will happen?"

On Wednesday morning I was called out of class for an emergency. Peter was on the phone. He explained, "There's a hearing today. I need a responsible adult in court with me."

"Shall I tell Emma?"

"Shit no! She ain't responsible for nothin'."

"How about Father Sikorski?"

"I'd rather have Emma."

"Maybe I should ask Coach Watson."

"He's got classes."

"I can still ask."

I went to Mr. Watson's classroom while he was teaching and knocked on the door. When he answered, he looked angry, but on seeing me he mellowed and asked, "What's wrong? You look mighty upset."

"Peter's got a court hearing today and needs a responsible adult there."

"What did he do now?"

"Got in a fight."

"Peter's middle name is trouble. I swear that brother of yours will never make it through high school."

"Peter needs an adult to come to the court."

"So you're asking me to be there?"

"Don't know who else to ask."

"What time's this damn hearing?"

"At 2:00."

Woody brushed his hands through his hair with an anguished look in his eyes. "I'd have to find someone to take my sixth hour."

"Can I meet you after fifth hour?" I asked.

Woody hesitated, studying me with what looked like compassion and said, "Guess Peter needs my help."

I rode with Woody to the courthouse. We worried about being late. The juvenile hearings were held on the third floor of the Hennepin County Courthouse.

It was a scene of confusion. We were told to sit and
wait. Ninety minutes later we were still waiting.
Woody constantly glanced at his watch and checked
with the officer who monitored the entrance to the
judge's chamber.

At 3:45 we were called forward. We entered this
huge room with empty seats, arranged in a semi-circle,
facing an elevated throne where this gray-haired man
officiated in his black robe. Inside a wood railing in
front of the seats sat Peter and some guy in a blue suit
and a red tie.

The judge started by reading the charges against
Peter, which included underage drinking, disturbing
the peace and assault. The man in the suit and tie
stood. "Your Honor," he said, "I object to the assault
charge. Peter Amonovitch was merely defending himself from a twenty-three-year-old man who was coming
after him."

"I'll rule on your objection after I receive the hospital report," the judge said. "All I want to do now is set
a date for a disposition hearing." The date was set for
Tuesday, May 3, 1949.

"That's it?" Woody asked.

There was no answer. The judge gathered his papers and disappeared through the door in the back. The
man in the suit and tie came toward us. "I'm Sidney
O'Conner," he said. "I'm Peter's public defender."

Mr. O'Conner invited us to sit down, and instantly started talking. "Before the disposition hearing the
judge will order an investigation by the juvenile depart-

ment. The worst that could happen would be for Peter to be ordered to the boy's state reformatory in Red Wing. The least would be probation." Mr. O'Conner gave us a hurried look. "Any questions?" he asked.

We were too stunned to answer. Mr. O'Conner rushed into a quick round of handshakes and sped off to his next case.

Two days later when I came home from school there was a car parked in front of our house. I thought it was one of Emma's boyfriends. Inside I found Emma sitting at the kitchen table with a young man, sipping coffee and munching cookies.

The man greeted me. "You must be Peter," he said. "I'm Harry Humphery from juvenile probation."

I smiled. "I'm not Peter. I'm Andrew, his twin brother."

"Where's Peter?" he asked.

"I don't know. He usually doesn't get home this early."

"That's okay. I'll catch him at school. I came mostly to talk with a parent."

Emma gave me an uneasy smile. "I explained," she said.

"The court wants to know about a kid before they make a decision," Mr. Humphery explained. "My job is to gather information on Peter."

"Care for a cookie?" Emma asked me.

"No thanks. I'm not hungry."

"So, you and Peter are twins. Do people get you mixed up?" Mr. Humphery asked.

"We're not identical. Peter's a couple inches taller, with twenty pounds more muscle and his hair is more dark and curly."

"I heard your brother's quite the football player."

"That's for sure."

"You play too?"

"I'm Peter's blocking back."

"How'd your brother get in all this trouble?"

This question caught me of guard. "Guess he must be running with the wrong crowd," I said.

"What you think, Emma?" Mr. Humphery asked.

"I agree with Andrew," she answered.

"What about your father? What's he think about Peter's situation?"

"Dad's got his own problems," I said. "I think it best we keep him out of this."

"Doesn't your Dad have any influence over Peter?" Mr. Humphery asked.

"He has a way of making Peter more angry and defiant," I answered.

Mr. Humphery gave me a serious look. "Your father incites defiance in Peter?"

"Peter doesn't like anybody that gets pushy," I said.

"So there's more to this than Peter going with the wrong crowd?" Mr. Humphery asked.

"That's right, sir," I responded.

Mr. Humphery jotted notes on his pad. "Guess I better be going now," he said, "You been real helpful." I walked Mr. Humphery to the door. "Tell Peter I'll be coming to the school to talk with him."

I wasn't sure what to think about Mr. Humphery. He seemed to make things sound more simple than they were, but I did feel that he wanted to help Peter.

Chapter 11

The possibility of being sent to the boy's reformatory in Red Wing didn't faze Peter. He continued going out almost every night and coming home late, smelling of alcohol. Knowing how much Peter needed his freedom, the thought of him going to Red Wing seemed about the worst thing that could happen to him. On the other hand, maybe the strict rules of a boy's reformatory would be good for him. Father Sikorski would probably consider it a valuable experience for Peter.

I asked Peter, "Aren't you worried about being sent to Red Wing?"

"I'm too busy having fun," he answered. "I learned long ago that I can't worry about what other people do."

Those many incidents of unfair abusive discipline and criticism from Dad had made Peter disrespectful and mistrusting of any authority.

Two days later Mr. Humphery came to Edison to talk with Peter. After the meeting, Peter volunteered no information. "How'd you come out with Mr. Humphery?" I asked.

"He thinks I'm a nut case."

"What?"

"He said I need a psychological test. He claims it could help my position with the juvenile court."

A week later Mr. Humphery arranged for Peter to be excused from school for the afternoon, to take him to the Hennepin County Mental Health Center for psychological testing.

The date of Peter's court hearing was delayed because the psychologist was having a hard time with Peter. Peter viewed the test as a challenge that he was determined to win. He couldn't accept that it was a serious effort to understand him.

It took the psychologist three sessions attempting to accomplish what should have taken only one. A new date was set for Peter's hearing, May 10.

On the evening of May 9, Peter was preparing to go out for the evening. "You can't go out tonight," I said. "You need to be in bed early. Your hearing is at 8:30."

Slowly, Peter rose to his full height, his fingers forming tight solid fists. His arms and body stiffened, his jaw muscles beneath his ears twitched. I was afraid I'd gone too far. I could sense the tension in Peter. He seemed to look through me, like he was searching for something to hold onto, to keep him from falling off the edge. I'm not sure what I felt, perhaps a combination of fear and compassion. I tried to give Peter wise advice, but he proceeded with his preparation to go out. "Where you going?" I asked.

Peter didn't answer. He hurried from the room and out the door with a loud slam. This was his way of handling the pressure of tomorrow's court hearing. He wanted to get away and try to forget about it.

I went to bed early, but couldn't sleep. At midnight I got up and went to the window, gazing out into the night. With Peter still gone, I knew there was no point in trying to sleep. I sat in a chair beside my bed, eyes open, alone in the darkness. My ears became super sensitive to the sounds of the night. There was a crash of railroad cars in the distance. It brought back memories of the Burlington Hotel, of Dad and Mom. A sharp pain tightened my chest, a vision of Mom's dead body flashed in my mind.

The memory of Mom brought a warm pleasant feeling. I thanked God that Peter and I had such a great mother, who left no doubt of her love for us. My chest tightened once again as I recalled the hurt she felt when Dad came home drunk and turned on Peter. I pressed my hands to my eyes, squeezing to restrain the tears that swelled inside me.

I heard the back door open. Peter had returned. I dived into my bed and scrambled under the covers. The bedroom door opened. I waited for Peter to snap on the light, but he didn't. I inhaled, sniffing for the smell of alcohol. I didn't smell it. I smiled, and soon the silence had me falling into sleep.

I was not allowed in the courtroom during Peter's disposition hearing. Woody Watson served as the parental representative. Mr. Humphery represented the probation department. Mr. Michael Lawson was the public defender. The juvenile judge was Hershel B. Atwater.

During the long wait I paced the hallway outside the courtroom. As soon as the door opened, I rushed forward to hear the result. The serious demeanor of the participants, including Peter, had me worried.

Mr. Lawson motioned for me to follow as he led us into a small room. As soon as we were seated, Mr. Humphery spoke to Peter. "Well, big guy, it's up to you. You heard the judge. You get in trouble again, he won't be so lenient."

"You better be careful, young man," added Mr. Lawson. "Maybe you should take the advice of the psychologist and get some counseling help. He thinks you got a problem with controlling your anger."

"Hell, that's nothin' new," Peter responded. "People been complaining about that shit for years."

"Maybe it's time you started listening," Mr. Humphery said.

I could see the emotion building in Peter. All this advice coming from so many directions wasn't going over well with him. I could tell he brushed off every word they were saying.

Once Mr. Lawson and Mr. Humphery had finished taking turns hammering advice at Peter, they got ready to leave. Peter was also quick to make his exit when Mr. Humphery tossed out one more word of caution. "Remember, Peter, you'll be on probation for a year. I'll be checking on you."

That very night after this encounter with authority, Peter went out and came home late, smelling of alcohol. After that he started coming home earlier, was more quiet and no longer turned on the light when he entered the room.

Two weeks after the court hearing, Woody Watson started an initiative to make Peter eligible for football in the fall. He sought the support of Mr. Humphery. Their plan was to present an appeal to the Discipline Committee of the Minneapolis Public Schools. Mr. Humphery asked Peter for written permission to present the committee with a copy of his psychological evaluation. His intention was to convince the committee that playing football was healthy for Peter's mental well being.

Peter refused permission. "I don't trust those people," Peter said. "Somehow they'll find a way to use it against me."

The appeal appeared doomed, but then Woody Watson came up with an idea. He approached me and said, "What we need is student support on behalf of Peter. How about if you stir them up? Tell them to call the School Board."

My immediate decision was to go to Kathy Amundson and explain Woody's idea. Besides being super intelligent, Kathy had become a spokesperson for social justice. Now a junior, she had gained self confidence and with her tenacity she could be a formidable force.

Her first big move was to convince the powers of the Minneapolis Schools that Peter Amonovitch deserved to be "pardoned" from the injustice imposed upon him. Kathy wrote letters to the school superintendent, Dr. Herbert B. Bruner, to the mayor, Eric G. Hoyer, and state governor, Luther W. Youngdahl.

She told the story of Peter's fight with Andy Givens, pointing out that it was provoked by a drunken Andy Givens, and although Peter's response was inappropriate, he had little choice but to defend himself. She also presented it as a fight for women's rights. In her view, Peter was fighting for the right of female students to make their own decisions about whom to date.

Her cause made the pages of the *Minneapolis Star Tribune*. Peter was portrayed as a hero who was being condemned by the authority of a male dominated school administration.

It felt great having Kathy on my side, both of us helping Peter. I called to thank her. There was more I wanted to say to her, to tell her how much I liked her, but I held back.

"Was there something else you wanted to say?" she asked.

After a long hesitation I answered, "Guess not."

The Northeast community wanted to see their football star back on the field. To my surprise, Father Sikorski got in the act. He was impressed by Kathy's plea for justice and urged parishioners to call the Minneapolis School Board, asking that they allow Peter to play football.

It was mid-August when Woody Watson informed Peter that he'd been declared eligible to play football in the fall. I was present when Woody talked with Peter. Peter thanked Woody, but actually he appeared unhappy about the news.

"What's wrong?" I asked Peter afterward.

"Won't be free now to have as much fun," he said. "Be even worse with Andy leavin' town."

"Where's Andy going?"

"He's gone. To Wahpeton." "North Dakota State? He got a scholarship?" "The whole package."

"That's great." "Probably a good time for him to be leavin' town," Peter said. "Kathy Amundson stirred up some bad publicity for Andy."

"She brought out the truth."

"She spread lot's of bullshit, making me out like a hero and making Andy out like some kind of a monster."

Peter's criticism of Kathy bothered me, but I chose to withhold comment.

There were many reasons to feel good in the fall of '49. Truman was elected president and there were signs of the Cold War easing. The Berlin blockade was officially lifted and the US completed withdrawal of occupying forces from South Korea.

On the local scene Peter was back playing football and the Northeast community, the Edison students in particular, were fanatically enthused over Peter's running wild on the football field. So far we'd won all our games.

Amidst this joyful atmosphere, Peter continued to be discontent. He seemed preoccupied. Every so often, he got a distant gaze in his eyes, as his thoughts were totally removed from the festive events surrounding him.

Peter went out most nights, but I knew he missed Andy Givens. When he stayed at home, he kept to himself, reading. If he liked what he was reading, he'd stay up most of the night. The next day he'd take the book to school and read it in class.

The nights Peter went out, he came home earlier, but seemed to be drinking more. I was worried about his drinking and his brooding. I waited for the right moment to talk with him. With homecoming approaching, I was curious about his plans.

Because of the problems at last year's homecoming, this year's dance was to be held in the school cafeteria. Security and student discipline were major concerns.

With Cindy Hawkins graduated and in college, Peter was quiet about who he was taking to the homecoming dance. Two days before the dance, I asked about his plans.

"Don't you worry, little brother," he responded.

"Who you taking?"

"Not sure yet. All I know is that we'll go some place more excitin' than the school cafeteria."

Peter scored five touchdowns in the homecoming game, running for a total of 320 yards, as Edison defeated Roosevelt by a score of 60 to 6.

Peter's absence from the homecoming dance became a hot topic of discussion among students and staff. I got tired of the questions about his whereabouts and it embarrassed me that I couldn't give an answer.

Peter didn't come home Friday night after the homecoming celebration. He showed up the following day, Saturday, at 4:00 PM. "How'd your homecoming celebration go?" I asked.

"Had a blast," he responded.

Peter's manner told me he wasn't in a mood to talk. Aside from a few comments about the game, he had nothing to say.

The following Monday morning I was called out of class and asked to report to the principal's office. Mr. Humphery and Mr. Lucus were waiting to see me.

"We want to talk with you about homecoming," Mr. Lucus said.

"Peter got in trouble again?" I asked.

"We hope not, but we need to find out."

"Have you talked with him?" I asked.

Mr. Humphery smiled. "Yes, we did. He told us it was none of our business."

"He's a private kind of guy."

"He's more than private. He's sensitive as hell about sharing anything," Mr. Humphery added.

"Peter's got his reasons."

"True. But he doesn't have the right to break the law or violate his probation," Mr. Humphery emphasized.

"Who said he broke the law?" I asked.

Again Mr. Humphery said, "That's what I'm here to find out."

The curiosity over Peter's homecoming night activity fed on the force of Peter's popularity and the memories of last year's dramatic events. Peter's silence only added to the gossip. Since Peter had the reputation of doing unusual exciting things, it was natural that there was curiosity. Being Peter's brother, my interest was stronger than anyone. This was fueled by fear that once again he was in serious trouble.

Within a week the story unfolded. The talk was that Peter and Luke Sherwood, past member of Andy Givens's drinking crowd, had celebrated homecoming at a nightclub on Highway 61, north of the city. They supposedly had been accompanied by two Edison girls.

The girls had been kept out all night and one of the parents called Mr. Lucus, complaining that the school hadn't reported her daughter's absence from the homecoming dance. The girls, Emmie Southland and Lisa Tabor, had lied to their mothers, claiming they were going to the dance in the cafeteria when actually they went with Peter and Luke to a nightclub.

Mr. Lucus wanted to determine the truth, and discovered that Emmie and Lisa had not signed up for the dance in the cafeteria, and thus were not included in the attendance check.

Mr. Lucus had little difficulty pressuring the two Edison girls into telling the full story. It was determined that Peter had violated both his probation and the school discipline code. He had stayed out beyond his curfew, had been drinking alcohol, and had shacked up all night in a motel.

The Discipline Committee acted quickly in declaring Peter ineligible to participate in any high school athletics. When Mr. Humphery heard the full story, he was duty bound to report Peter's violations to the juvenile court.

I arranged a meeting with Mr. Humphery. "Peter needs help," I said. "Remember what that lawyer guy told us about counseling for Peter?"

"I sure do," Mr. Humphery responded.

"How about it? Could Peter do that?"

"It's a great idea, but Peter resists counseling."

"Could you give him an ultimatum, either he accept counseling or go to Red Wing?"

"I don't have that kind of power. Only a judge can issue such an order."

"Can you ask the judge?"

"I admire your determination to help your brother."

"I'm not doing a very good job."

"I like your idea about counseling. It can't hurt to give it a try."

"I'd rather have Peter get help here at home than go to Red Wing."

"I understand," said Mr. Humphery. He checked his watch. "Tell you what I'll do. I need to report Peter's recent violations. I'll include a recommendation that Peter be given an ultimatum: participate in counseling or go to Red Wing."

When I got home, Peter wasn't there. I went to our bedroom. On the floor was a half filled duffel bag. Lying open on Peter's bed was last year's Wizard, the Edison High School yearbook. It was open to the sport's section, displaying pictures of Peter and me in action.

I took the book in hand and soon my mind was in a trance, reliving those beautiful memories. I didn't hear when Peter entered the room. "How'd practice go today?" he asked. I was slow to answer as my preoccupied mind adjusted to his abrupt arrival. "Not so great," I said. "Started out running twenty laps for getting there late."

"Ain't like you to be late, Andrew. What happened?"

I turned my attention to the Wizard, pretending not to hear his question. Then, I placed the Wizard back on Peter's bed and said, "I had a meeting with Mr. Humphery."

"Suppose he pumped you for information?"

"We talked about how to keep you out of Red Wing."

"Don't worry, little brother. I can take care of myself."

"Is that why you packed your duffel bag?"

"I ain't goin' to Red Wing. No way."

"You plan to run?"

"Better believe it, little brother."

"Humphery and I had a good talk. We came up with a plan to help you."

Peter gave me a suspicious glance, and then resumed packing his duffel bag.

"Humphery's working out a deal. He plans to ask the judge to let you to go to counseling instead of going to Red Wing."

"I ain't seein' no shrink."

"What you afraid of? Afraid of finding out the truth?"

"I know the truth, little brother, and I ain't askin' favors from anybody."

I grabbed Peter's arm and spun him around. "Listen to me, big guy!" Peter glared at me as he was forced to cease his packing. "I bust my ass to do you a favor and you don't even listen. This counseling is a good deal and you damn well better go along with it."

I could see in Peter's eyes that my words had touched him. "Okay, little brother. Who's this fuckin' shrink you want me to see?"

On Tuesday morning Peter was scheduled to go downtown to the Mental Health Clinic to meet with Dr. Stewart Masloff, an adolescent psychiatrist. Peter was quiet about the visit. I respected his silence, viewing his contact with the doctor as private.

My hope was that some magic would happen, that Peter would be transformed into my image of how great he could be. The reality was that Peter kept his duffel bag packed, ready for a quick getaway at any time.

Every night Peter violated his probation. He stayed out well beyond his 10:00 PM curfew and when he came home he smelled of alcohol. Peter knew my attitude about his violations, but my words of caution always brought the same answer, "Nobody's tellin' me how to live my life."

"Does Dr. Masloff know you violate your probation?"

"Masloff don't know shit about what I do."

"Maybe that's why he wants to talk with me. Did he tell you about that?"

"Sure he did. He asked my permission."

"And you agreed?"

"Why not?"

"Aren't you worried I'll tell the truth?"

"Hell no. I trust you."

Dr. Masloff must have been eager to talk with me. His secretary made numerous attempts to reach me. Finally, when we made a connection, she pressed for a meeting that same day.

Dr. Masloff was younger than I expected. He was friendly and gentle in his manner. I could tell right off that he wasn't Peter's type. He was soft looking, the kind of guy who sits around reading books and wasn't much for using his muscles.

"Thanks for coming in today," Dr. Masloff began. "I need your help. I'm having a hard time getting to know your brother."

"I expect he don't talk much."

"Your brother has extraordinary command of himself. That's quite a contradiction for someone who's reported to have trouble controlling himself."

Dr. Masloff's statement confused me. I didn't know what to say.

"Let me put it this way," Dr. Masloff said, "Peter talks mostly about you and your mother. He thinks you're both the greatest. He avoids talking about himself."

"Doesn't he talk about Dad?"

"He refuses. He doesn't think it's fair to rip his father."

"That's the way Peter is. He's got a sense of loyalty and don't like knocking people behind their back."

"The truth is the court's worried about Peter hurting someone."

"Peter doesn't hurt anyone who doesn't hurt him first."

"So you don't think his anger is a problem?"

"Only if someone hurts him or those he cares about."

"If that happens, he gets physical?"

"Only if they get physical."

"How about if people insult him or call him names?"

"You can call Peter names all day and it won't bother him."

Dr. Masloff jotted notes on his pad. "It does seem intensely important to Peter that he does his own thing," Dr. Masloff said.

"That's for sure. He's got strong ideas about what he wants to do."

Dr. Masloff smiled. "I don't think a shrink will have much influence in changing that attitude."

"Peter's mighty strong about what he wants to do."

"I'm impressed with his respect for you. It would appear you're the one person in a position to influence him."

These words hit me hard. My hope had been that Dr. Masloff would do wonders with Peter. Instead, it sounded like he was only reinforcing what Mom had asked of me on her deathbed. He was also placing the burden of Peter's defiance on my shoulders.

Then, Dr. Masloff added to that burden when he said, "You're a great young man, Andrew. Peter's damn lucky to have you for a brother."

I was deep in thought during my walk home, comparing the words of Dr. Masloff with Mom's. For Mom to make such a request had seemed a natural outgrowth of our family history, but for Dr. Masloff to do essentially the same thing, it was like the whole world was giving me the same message.

There was no way I could escape the fact that I was Peter's twin brother. Not only did I love him as a brother, I loved him in a special way. I'd seen most of what happened to him over the years and my response had always been to stand by him with support and understanding. Mom saw this more than anybody, and Dr. Masloff wanted me to be proud of performing this responsibility.

It was no surprise that Peter trusted me more than anyone else. He had obviously conveyed this truth to Dr. Masloff. This showed me that Peter had been more open and honest with Dr. Masloff than the doctor realized.

Hearing Dr. Masloff's assessment of my relationship with Peter made me want to charge ahead and assume a more aggressive heavy-handed approach with Peter. Fortunately, this idea lost favor following a day of afterthought, realizing such an approach would have been a blind expression of love, without remembering the unique characteristics of Peter and the continued need to temper my presence with an intuitive touch.

When I got home, I was eager to talk with Peter. He wasn't home. Late that afternoon I heard a vehicle screech to a stop in our driveway. The horn blasted.

I rushed to look out. It was Dart Davenport's Ford pickup truck. He was alone and persisted in leaning on his horn. It embarrassed me that he was so loud and disruptive to our quiet neighborhood. I hurried to inform Dart that Peter wasn't home.

"Where the hell is he?"

"Haven't seen him since he left yesterday."

"Dat sons a bitch disappeared on me again. Betcha anything he shacked up all night."

"That's twice this week that Peter hasn't slept at home."

Dart ripped off his baseball cap and slammed it against his dashboard. "Dat fucker's takin' 'vantage of me," he said. "I had it. He can buy his own fuckin' booze from now on."

"Want me to tell Peter you were here?"

"Goddamn right. And tell 'em he can get his own fuckin' summer job."

"Okay, I'll tell him."

Dart slapped his cap back on his head, snapped his fingers with a sharp crack, smiled with a mischievous glare in his eyes and said, "Come to think of it, I got a better idea. You tell Peter I got jus' the place for him to work." Dart's smile got as wide as the tires on his pickup truck. "Tell Peter this job pays the best road construction wages in the Twin City area."

"What job's that?" I asked.

"Carson Construction."

"How about me? Could I get a summer job there too?"

Dart put a hand to his mouth to cover his slinky smile and said, "Shit yes. Youse guys'll love workin' for Hunker Hanson."

"Who's he?"

"He's the boss man at Carson Construction. And ah tell ya, he's da sweetest ass sons a bitch dat ever laid eyes on road construction." Laughing, Dart pulled off his cap and repeatedly slammed it on his dashboard.

"You look mighty happy," I said.

"You better fuckin' believe it. Ah'm helpin' dat lover boy brother of yours find a job. Maybe then he can buy me some drinks."

The idea of Peter finding a summer job sounded good to me, but I had a hard time believing Dart Davenport. He seemed like a big bullshiter. "How you know about these jobs?" I asked.

"Shit, everybody knows Carson Construction won the bid for dat big St. Paul job and they's havin' a bitch of a time findin' 'nough men to work for 'em."

"You sure they'll give Peter and me a job?"

"What da fuck ah jus' say? Ain't ya listenin'?"

"It's hard to believe. Jobs are hard to come by."

Dart gave me a sly look. "Not for me," he said. "I been 'round road construction a long time. Tell Peter

I'll come after youse guys tomorrow. We'll go out and talk with Hunker Hanson. He'll be eager to hire a couple ah fresh recruits."

Chapter 12

High school guys considered road construction a great summer job. The wages were the best you could get for summer work and you could work long hours and earn a bundle. It was tough work, the kind that proved you were a man. Our young pride made us naïve to the demands of the job.

When Carson Construction won the bid for a big highway project in the Newport-St. Paul Park area, the company had a hard time finding experienced help. Men who knew about road construction didn't want to work for this outfit. The word got around that they were looking for "young studs."

I'd never worked full time. Peter had worked full time for two weeks, helping at the downtown post office during the Christmas rush. This opportunity to earn five bucks an hour working road construction, no experience needed, sounded too good to be true.

I was in favor of Peter working. So was Mr. Humphery. There would be a problem with Peter missing his appointments with Dr. Masloff, but the doctor conceded that Peter might accomplish more working than in counseling. Dr. Masloff believed a full time job would be a valuable experience for Peter and it might keep him out of trouble.

Peter was excited about the job, and grateful to Dart Davenport for alerting us to this opportunity. When Dart saw our eagerness, he seemed guilty and obligated to give us a warning about Hunker Hanson. "To tell the truth," Dart cautioned, "da guy's an Adolf Hitler type."

Since Dart was known as a bullshiter, Peter and I didn't take this Adolf Hitler talk too seriously. Even if there was some truth to it, Peter saw Hunker Hanson as a challenge. I was so eager to land my first job that I ignored any worry about Hunker Hanson.

When Dart came to get us on Saturday morning, it was obvious that he was tipsy. He was either still drunk from Friday night or he was drinking already Saturday morning. Probably some of both.

He drove like a wild man, shouting a greeting to Hunker Hanson long before Hunker was anywhere in sight. He sipped from a pint of Jack Daniel's while speeding over bumps and through water puddles, dodging huge elms and cottonwoods as he plowed through the heavy underbrush.

"Helleva place to be building a road," Dart complained as he swerved to miss a monster oak by inches.

We reached a small elevated clearing with a thirty-foot Winnebago parked in the middle. "Dat's Hunker's castle," Dart announced, showing a seriousness that seemed strange with his heretofore carefree attitude.

Dart screeched the brakes and splashed yet another layer of mud on the dilapidated trailer. Dart banged on the door, but there was no answer. He banged again, harder.

"Get the fuck outta here!" shouted the voice from inside.

"Dat's Hunker. Ain't he sweet?" We waited while Dart fired up a cigarette, sucked hard on it, inhaled, blew it out, coughed up some goop and let it fly. Then he turned to the door again and yelled. "Hunker! Got some new men here." We stood quiet and listened. "Got some tough asses. Good workers."

There was a loud crash as something struck the door from inside. "Sounds like he's waking up," Dart said.

The trailer rocked and the door flew open. "What you fuckers want?" Hunker snarled.

"Look what ah got cha," Dart said.

It felt like I peed my pants as I peered at the whiskered face with the bulging red eyes, sizing us up like we were a couple of lambs on the slaughtering block.

"Ever work road construction?" Hunker growled in his deep gravel voice. We shook our heads. Hunker walked around us. "Look strong enough, but dat don't mean shit." Hunker came up close and peered in our eyes. "So you young farts think you can work for Hunker Hanson?"

"It's the money," Peter said. "We heard you pay good."

"Goddamn right. And ya sweat for every fuckin' penny. Ain't that right, Davenport?"

"Dat's for damn sure," Dart agreed.

Hunker smelled like a nauseating combination of whiskey and body sweat. As much as my nose prompted me to back away, I stood motionless as my eyes widened in amazement at his physical stature. Most impressive were his thick muscular arms, hanging low to the ground, with huge puffy gnarled fingers, perpetually curled like claws. His neck tapered from his trapezoids such that his head seemed to sit directly atop his heavy shoulders. His hair was clipped in a crew cut. When he walked he leaned forward from the waist, giving the impression that he would fall on his face at any time.

"I need men on Monday," he growled. "Be here at six." He defied us to disagree.

"We got school till the end of May," Peter said.

Hunker took a step toward Peter, eyeing him close up. Peter glared back, leaning forward in a mimicking gesture. Hunker's cracked sunburned lips twisted to a smile, showing a mouth full of chipped gold-rimmed teeth. "See you guys the first Monday in June," he grumbled. "You look like a smart ass," he said to Peter. "I think you and me's gonna have some fun together."

Hunker extended a hand to Peter. They clasped hands. Hunker squeezed, as did Peter. There was a brief tussle between them before Hunker released his grip and bent forward so his face was inches from Peter's face. "I can't wait till June," Hunker said.

"We'll be here," Peter responded.

Hunker gave Peter a sharp slap on the back and laughed, his resonant voice echoing through the trees off to the west.

As we walked to Dart's pickup truck, I glanced back. Hunker stood rubbing his hands together. On his face was a bizarre smile that gave me the creeps.

"Ain't he sweet?" Dart said.

That night after our meeting with Hunker Hanson a foreboding came over me as I foresaw an inevitable conflict between Peter and Hunker. The more I thought of this possibility, the more active became my imagination. As darkness came on I attempted to sleep, but couldn't relax as wild visions flashed through my mind.

At such times my reasoning became elusive. I learned long ago that the best strategy was to forget about trying to sleep. I'd remain awake and wait for Peter to come home. I had to talk with him about the job at Carson Construction. I had to convince him it was not the place for us to work. There had to be other jobs that presented less of a threat.

It was after midnight when Peter came home. He smelled strong of alcohol. This wouldn't be a good time to talk. I preferred to approach him when he was sober and well rested. There were still seven days before we were scheduled to start work for Hunker Hanson.

During this time, I felt an urgency to find another job that would pay comparable wages. I knew I had my work cut out for me. With the likelihood of a military draft starting soon, lots of young men were looking for work.

The next day I skipped school to go job hunting. I'd never job hunted before and had a lot to learn. The first thing I discovered was that it took time and patience. I had to wait around for the chance to talk to people and I found rejection to be the norm.

Many young men were desperate to land the few available jobs. The only way I could compete with these job seekers was to take off school each day that I didn't have final exams. Peter explained to the attendance office that there was an urgency for us to find work for the summer.

During this week I became acquainted with some of the competition, young men from poor families, who heard the rumble of war in Korea and strong rumors that Uncle Sam would soon start drafting soldiers. These young men wanted jobs to earn money for college. Once in college they could attain a deferment and avoid the draft like the rich boys, as long as they maintained passing grades. These young men were desperate. They'd take any job, to get money for school.

Some of them carried newspapers to keep up to date on events taking place in Korea. This sparked my curiosity about Korea as I realized that what was happening there could have an impact of Peter and myself.

I read some of the news articles. One in particular made a strong impression on me. It was titled: THE REAL KOREA, and was comprised of comments made by American soldiers who had served there in the peacetime Army. One soldier told of the smell of Korea—the human excrement—field fertilizer. This soldier was quoted: "It reeked with an overpowering fragrance that etched an unforgettable memory in my mind."

I then associated Korea with the smell of shit.

I realized by the end of the week that we would not find another job. At that point, I approached several young men, informing them that Carson Construction was hiring. I gave an honest appraisal of the job. Despite my ominous portrayal of Hunker Hanson, these men thanked me and were eager to check out the opportunity.

The following Monday at 5:45 AM, Peter and I trudged across the wet grass, heading toward a group of men who were waiting for the start of the work day.

They stood in hushed conversation, all facing the same direction, their eyes on Hunker Hanson.

Hunker was some fifty feet away, moving rapidly, inspecting the work site. What a stride he possessed, such big steps, that forward lean, his arms hanging motionless off to the sides, spread wide to maintain balance. His eyes focused downward at a point about twenty feet ahead, giving the impression of deep thought, seeming out of touch with events taking place about him.

At precisely 5:55 Hunker made a quick change of direction and headed toward us. Before arriving, he shouted, "Get your asses in gear. The weekend's over." He stopped and pointed at Peter and I. "You new guys, come with me. The rest of you—start where ya left off on Saturday."

We rushed to keep up with Hunker as he led the way to the tool truck. Hunker pulled out two grub hoes. He tossed them, handle first, to each of us. Then, he took off with a quick start, yelling, "Follow me." We ran to catch up. He led us to a path beside an old road, to an area marked with a long line of red flags. "There's a gas pipe under here," Hunker explained. "Too damn dangerous to put the big cats in here." He stood back to check the line of flags. "Toss me a grub," he ordered.

Peter let fly and Hunker whipped up a big hand to snatch it. He then demonstrated the technique for digging with a grub hoe. With perpetual motion, he tore away at the roots and weeds, his powerful arms and hands manipulating the hoe like an orchestra conductor with a baton.

He didn't stop until he reached a rusty old pipe that lay four feet underground. As soon as the pipe became visible, Hunker shouted, "Catch!" He flung the grub hoe at Peter. Peter swiftly raised an arm to protect from getting hit. The hoe struck Peter's arm with a glancing blow and fell to the ground. Hunker laughed.

"Show me what you can do," Hunker ordered. Peter stood for a minute and glared at Hunker. "Get the fuck moving," Hunker ordered.

Peter grabbed the hoe, took a solid grip and attempted to emulate Hunker, tearing away dirt with a vengeance. I was amazed at his command of the hoe as the soil flew aside at an astonishing speed.

Hunker watched in silence, caught up in observing Peter, like myself entertained by this display of strength, agility and endurance. Suddenly, Hunker spun away from Peter and glared at me. "Who the fuck's paying you to stand around and watch?" he growled.

I stood motionless and speechless, too discombobulated by his intimidation to make my body function.

"Get that hoe flyin'" Hunker ordered.

With hands that were shaking and sweating, I raised the grub hoe overhead, intending to rip it into the soil. I let loose with every once of my strength, crashing the metal hard to the earth. At the point of contact, the flange of the hoe struck something solid, reverberating like a bolt of electricity that sent a shock up through my hands and arms as the grub hoe catapulted off to the side.

Hunker laughed and laughed. "JESUS CHRIST!" he shouted. "What the hell we got here? You handle that hoe like a pansy ass." He shook his head in disgust. "You better get with it, young man," Hunker threatened, "or you won't make it working road construction for me."

It took half a day before my muscles and mind worked together. By then my hands were so blistered and sore that it hurt to breathe hard on them. The job was torture. The only thing that kept me swinging that grub hoe was pride. The monster Hunker Hanson had insulted my manhood and I'd show him I could do the job if it killed me.

Within a week I became a new person. You might say I became a man. I discovered a strength and tenacity beyond what I thought possible. I had a style all my own, showing that I was a steady performer with the guts to endure.

Peter was all different. He worked in spurts, at times performing like a wild man, producing at a level beyond everybody. Then he'd rest. He didn't rest like me or the other crew members. When we rested, it was nothing but a phony change of pace. It was pretend work, intended to placate Hunker. When Peter rested it was honest. He'd sit down or even lay down on a hot day. Hunker didn't like it, but held off saying anything. Whenever I saw this happen, I became tense, my hands sweating more than usual, forcing me to take a firmer grip on the grub hoe. I'd never again lose my hold on the hoe.

The other men saw when Peter rested, and watched as Hunker's mood got bitchier each day. More and more he was getting on our ass for little things. If Peter would have been an all out goof off, the guys would have been on him to shape up. The truth was that every guy on the work crew knew, including Hunker, that Peter got far more work done than any of us. Furthermore, none of the work crew had the guts to say anything to Peter. Anyone who saw the way he could work had to know that he was one mean ass. Hunker was smart enough to realize Carson Construction was getting more then their money's worth from Peter. The problem was that Peter's rest periods made Hunker look like a soft touch. Every time it happened, Hunker's movements got jerky as he saw the men watching for his reaction.

When Peter rested, tension at the work site escalated. It brought a lull in the performance of the men, including myself, as I throttled down to slow motion and kept a wary eye on Hunker, watching to see what he'd do.

With each passing day pressure was growing over this silent conflict. Peter appeared oblivious to what was happening. I attempted to alert him, but he gave me his typical casual response, "You worry too much." It reached a point where I considered it urgent that we discuss this threatening problem.

We were working ten hours a day, from 6:00 AM to 4:30 PM, with thirty minutes for lunch. It was in the early evening, about an hour after quitting time that I chose to talk with Peter. By then he'd have showered and eaten and be content to sit quietly and chat. It was a time when I was too tired to do much but sit around and wait until it was cool enough to go to bed.

For Peter this was his time to recharge his battery, in preparation for another night of drinking and chasing women. Now, with a paycheck coming in, he had more money for fun. How he did it, I don't know. Working all day in the hot sun with four hours of sleep at night would do me in. I had to hit the sack by 9:00 PM, and still there were days when I struggled to make it to quitting time.

I had to approach Peter now before he went out for the evening. "I need to talk with you about what's happening at work," I began.

"I can tell by your voice and the way you been looking at me that something's got ya upset," he responded.

"Don't you see what's happening at work?"

"What ya talkin' about?"

"It isn't only me that's worried."

"What the hell you talkin' about?"

"Hold on a minute, Peter." I sensed anger in his voice and it bothered me. "Listen closely. All I want to do is help. Understand?"

"Okay, little brother. Give me the word."

"I know you get more work done in a day than any of us on the work crew. By rights, you have reason to rest like you do."

"You better believe it. And there's no reason for Hunker to get pissed."

It surprised me the way Peter put it so straight. Trying to be calm, I said, "Have you noticed how Hunker looks ready to explode when you're resting?"

"That's his fuckin' problem," Peter snapped back.

I forced a smile and raised my hands to urge calm. Peter was in no mood to smile. I continued, "We both know that Hunker's a weird one. There's nothing we can do about that." I paused. "It's you I worry about, Peter. I don't want you getting fired or worse yet, having Hunker come after you with his fists."

Peter stood silent, his eyes darting to and away from me. He then spoke softly, "Listen, Andrew. I ain't about to let Hunker Hanson threaten me with his bullshit."

"All I'm saying is use your head. Don't incite something foolish to happen. Okay?"

"You worry too much, little brother." Peter turned and walked away. He went out for the evening, out for another night of celebrating.

Hunker Hanson was a strange, unpredictable man. For several days he appeared on the verge of exploding. Then, on Thursday, his demeanor changed. He had a smile on his face, a weird, disconcerting smile that for some reason was directed mostly at me. It was like he was trying to befriend me.

Later in the morning on Thursday, Hunker approached me. "Come with me, young man," he said.

"I got a special job, just for you." He led me to the tool truck where my grub hoe was exchanged for a shovel. He motioned for me to follow. His pace was slow, like he was trying to accommodate me. He led the way to a swampy area in a valley between two hills. "We need to dig a drainage ditch through here," he said. He pointed. "The river's that way. The water will drain down here to the river."

It wasn't like Hunker to discuss engineering strategy with his work crew. I hardly heard a word he said. I was too worried about his intentions.

"You're the best man for this job," he said. "You work steady and I can depend on you to do good work." Hunker gave me brief instructions and then he was gone.

I was alone. It didn't take long to realize I'd been granted the honor of working in a hellhole. The soil was a soggy tangle of roots and sticky clay that clung to the shovel like glue. The location between the hills blocked off the breeze, making the air humid and stiflingly hot. It was ideal for bugs and mosquitoes, and with my presence, they had a captive blood supply.

Twenty minutes of working here and my clothes were soaked with sweat. There was a constant buzz about my head, a diversionary tactic intended to draw my attention while their silent sucking companions searched out vulnerable areas of my body.

These little beasties had an amazing loyalty to their mission. To me, they were Hunker's air force, out to get me. Some, I envisioned as having orders to taunt me with their buzzing; others were kamikaze pilots on a death defying flight to strike at me where I could swat them, splotching them and my siphoned blood on my sweaty skin. While I gleaned an eerie pleasure from such brief moments of victory, their slinky comrades quietly snuck up to strike at me in locations where I couldn't get at them, leaving mementos of bulging itchy red bumps.

Most oppressive was the depletion of my stamina. To merely exist in this swamp was a challenge. To work and make a favorable impression of my manhood, to live up Hunker's expectation was a big order. It was my nature to do my best. So I stuck with it.

My production was slow, but it was the best I could do. My arms felt heavy. It took great effort to concentrate. To simply grip the shovel was a major undertaking. I had to squeeze hard to keep it from slipping. So hard, that my hands were starting to cramp up, as if paralyzed, fixated in a tense and painful grip on the slippery handle. Sweat oozed into my eyes, blurring my vision. The mosquitoes were relentless. By now, the victory was theirs. I didn't have the spunk to fight them.

I was in a trance-like state, semi-blinded to what was going on about me. Still, something forced my body to move with a semblance of working.

"MONOVITCH! What the hell's wrong with you?"

My entire body was jolted by Hunker's threatening voice that seemed to come from all directions. I was shaken by what I envisioned as Hunker's omnipotent presence.

"Time to quit for Christ's sake. It's 4:45."

I stood dazed, blinking and wiping my eyes, struggling to see Hunker. He appeared to smile, but I couldn't tell for sure.

"You can stop working now, Monovitch," he said. "I know how much you love working here, so you better save some energy for tomorrow." My mind was too foggy to comprehend what he was saying. He gave me a solid slap on the back to get my attention, and then ordered me to follow him. I stumbled along behind, unable to keep up, guided by his repeated urging to "get your ass in gear." Somehow, I made it out of the valley.

The instant Peter sighted me, he rushed forward. "Where the hell you been?" he asked. "I been lookin' for you since quitting time."

Feeling dizziness, I kneeled to the ground and lowered my head. "What's wrong?" Peter asked. "You okay?" I didn't answer. I remained kneeling, rubbing my forehead, gasping for air. Peter placed an arm around me. "What the fuck happened?" he asked. "You look like hell."

I was too dazed to answer. With Peter's support he directed me to a shaded area. He had me sit down by a tree, my back leaning against the trunk. Peter got me water. I sipped. It made me nauseated. I had to lie down.

Not until the nausea diminished did I rise up and blink my eyes. I became aware of Peter gazing down at me. I smiled as soon as we made eye contact.

"Tell me, little brother," Peter asked in a voice that conveyed serious concern, "How'd ya get so damned dirty and how'd ya get all those mosquito bites?"

I searched the horizon until I sighted Hunker off in the distance and then said, "It's a long story. I'll tell you about it on the way home."

Peter listened real hard, looking intense and stern as I told my story. When I finished, he focused his eyes directly into mine and said, "You ain't workin' in that fuckin' valley no more."

After my ordeal, I went to bed that night with the expectation of escaping my distress. I soon discovered that the mosquito bites were with me for the night. They demanded my attention, begging me with maddening urgency to be itched. The heat was even more unsettling. Despite having the upstairs bedroom windows wide open, there was no breeze to cool the hot humid air. I constantly rolled around in search of an escape from the heat.

After a while I started feeling sorry for myself as I thought of Peter out somewhere having fun. The hot weather didn't affect Peter the way it did me. Somehow, I got short changed in the gene pool. I was sensitive to extremes of temperature. Hot weather slowed me down, but it got Peter's motor revved up. He became more energetic, more horny and more thirsty.

I imagined Peter having a wild time and hoped it wasn't so wild that he failed to get home in time for work on Friday morning.

I was half asleep when Peter came home shortly before dawn. Not long after that the alarm went off. Peter was up before me. I was in no mood to face another day of road construction. So, unlike our usual routine, Peter set the pace, and I dragged behind.

When we arrived at the work site, Peter continued to take charge and looked for Hunker. I knew what Peter was up to and it bothered me. "Don't you worry about me," I told Peter. "I'll take care of myself." Peter gave me a look like he didn't believe me.

We heard shouting from the direction of the work crew. "Gather around," said several of the men. "Hunker wants to talk to us."

Everyone hustled to where Hunker was waiting, his eyes glued to his watch. He started hollering before the men arrived. "I want you guys to listen and listen good!" His voice had that familiar threatening loudness. "It's gonna be another hot one today and I 'spect you guys may be wantin' to fuck off and take it easy." He was quiet for a moment as he eyeballed us with his menacing glare. "You can forget about any pansy-ass shit," he shouted. "Carson Construction pays the same wages when the weather's hot as it does any other day, so that means today you work like any other day. Understand?"

The men stood in uneasy silence as Hunker made the rounds of looking each of us in the eye. He had a way of staring a man down, his penetrating, unflinching scowl directed hard at you, not yielding until you turned away in a gesture of submission.

After Hunker's speech about the hot weather, I was afraid to complain about the hellhole. I glanced at Peter and could tell what he was thinking. With reluctance, I drifted off in the direction of my appointed work site. When Peter saw this, he came toward me.

Hunker was quick to respond. "What the hell's this all about?" he yelled.

Peter and I were surprised that he was on us so quick. When Peter stepped toward Hunker, Hunker snapped into a rigid posture, his feet spread wide, hands braced on his hips.

"I decided to trade jobs with Andrew," Peter said.

Hunker's face reddened. "And who the fuck you think you are?" Hunker said.

In a deliberate casual manner, Peter responded. "What's the big deal? All we're doin' is switchin' jobs."

Hunker's face became a couple of shades redder. "Listen, goddamn it. Who the fuck's the boss here? You or me?"

Peter smiled. "Everybody knows you're the boss." Hunker seemed to relax. Seeing this, Peter continued toward the hellhole, still smiling. "There's no need to bust a gasket over such piddly shit. What's the big deal about me and Andrew tradin' jobs?"

Hunker's body started shaking. "Listen, smart ass. Get the fuck over where I told you to work." His voice was so loud it drew the attention of the men throughout the work site.

Peter continued in the direction of the hellhole. Hunker burst at him, grabbed his arm and spun him around. "Where the fuck you going?"

"To the drainage ditch," Peter responded with defiance.

The sound of Peter's voice brought immediate fear to me. I dashed between Peter and Hunker. "How about if we both work on the drainage ditch?" I asked Hunker, my voice meek and shaky.

There was a long silence as Hunker pondered and searched my eyes, seeming suspicious that I was trying to pull a fast one on him. Then, a gradual smile emerged on his face, one that I'd never forget. It was forced and slinky, displaying his chipped gold teeth and the facial wrinkles that stretched up to his bulging eyes.

Hunker accompanied us to set up separate job sites for each of us in the hellhole. Although our locations were in the same vicinity, Hunker saw need to keep us apart. We were close enough to see each other, but too far to talk. We could shout back and forth, but that too would be difficult.

It didn't take long for me to realize that Hunker had pulled a fast one of us. I visualized him laughing his ass off as we slaved in these ungodly conditions.
The weather prediction was for temperatures to exceed one hundred, with humidity above eighty percent. Despite this ominous prediction, it was not until I ac-

tually found myself back in the hellhole that I felt an urgency to share survival concerns with Peter. As soon as Hunker gave us orders on what he expected us to do, he took off over the hill to the major work site. When Hunker disappeared over the ridge, I set out to talk with Peter, a distance of approximately one football field. As I approached, Peter was thrashing away at the muck in his typical frenzied style. He didn't see me until I was close upon him and called out his name. "What ya doin' here?" Peter asked, sweat rolling down his face.

"Thought I better give you a word of warning about working in this place."

"Okay, little brother."

"I intend to pace myself today. I'll work slow and when I get too hot, I'm taking a rest in the shade."

"To hell with Hunker—right?"

"An occasional rest is reasonable working here in this heat."

Peter laughed. "Sounds like my bad habits are rubbin' off on you, little brother."

"Don't get me wrong," I said. "This is just plain common sense. I plan to do my job, but do what's necessary to survive."

"I'm with ya all the way, little brother. When I need a rest, I'll be in the shade right with ya."

"I wanted to make sure you knew my strategy."

"Thanks for the info, little brother."

I had a good feeling as I returned to my work station. I believed I could make it through the day. I had no trouble slowing my pace, though I did find it hard giving myself permission to go off in the shade to rest. It sounded logical and acceptable when I explained it to Peter, but when it came time to do it, I had this uncomfortable feeling of doing something wrong.

At 11:00 AM, with the sun high in the sky, I felt the heat getting to me. It was time for me to go off in the shade. I glanced toward the ridge, looking for Hunker. There was no sign of him. Wiping the sweat from my eyes, I took several cautious steps, my gaze fixed on the horizon. With timid steps I moved slowly toward the shade.

On reaching the wooded area, I maneuvered to a position where I could see the ridge in the distance. I broke off a small tree branch and switched it back and forth like a fan. This was great. If I could take rest stops like this all day, there'd be no problem with survival.

Despite this bravado thinking, I felt discomfort inside. I couldn't convince myself that this was right and had a constant fear of being discovered by Hunker. Each time I went off to the shade, the uneasiness persisted. Nevertheless, I became more bold and careless, remaining for longer periods and becoming less vigilant in watching for Hunker.

Shortly after noon I stood in the shade glancing up at the sun, positioned at its highest point, beating down from directly above, that time of day when we'd face our toughest test.

After twenty minutes in the shade I told myself it was time to go back to work, but in my ever-growing boldness, I lingered, carefree as I indulged in fanning myself with the tree branch.

One second the branch was in my hand, and the next it was gone. Hunker Hanson snatched it, standing close enough that I could smell his alcohol breath and body sweat. There was a quiver in his lower jaw as he struggled to contain his anger. His lips were pulled back tight, showing tobacco-stained teeth, three badly chipped, four with gold fillings, one of which was positioned such that it reflected the sun, casting a glow that made me squint.

Hunker grabbed my arm and squeezed. "Listen to me you son of a bitch," he uttered. "You're getting your ass back to work and you ain't stoppin' 'till quittin' time." He jerked my arm and then let go. "Get the fuck movin'," he ordered.

Hunker walked me back to the work site and remained near by, watching. If I slacked up the least bit, he yelled at me. It wasn't long before my muscles started to ache and twitch. The heat was getting to me.

Suddenly, I heard a commotion and looked up. Hunker had charged off in the direction of Peter. I wiped the sweat from my eyes and squinted. I couldn't see him. He had to be off in the shade. I envisioned trouble.

I hobbled off in the direction of Peter, shading my eyes with my hand, searching for Hunker.

Then came a thunderous echo. "MONOVITCH—you son of a bitch! Get your fuckin' ass back to work."

Peter emerged slowly from the woods, appearing unperturbed by the urgency of Hunker's presence. Hunker charged at him and snatched his shovel, raising it as if intending to strike Peter. Instead, he slammed it hard on the ground. Whomp! Whomp! Whomp! Peter jumped back. Then, in crazed anger Hunker lashed out with the shovel, swinging it in every direction, shouting, "You smart ass bastard."

My lips quivered as I mumbled a prayerful wish that Peter stay away from this wild man. I feared for Peter's life. I attempted to run off toward them, but my rubbery legs collapsed. I stumbled to the ground, exhausted, gasping for air. Desperate to continue on, I tried to stand, but my legs were too weak. I collapsed to my hands and knees and crawled to within twenty feet of Peter and Hunker. They stood face to face. Hunker crouched for battle. Peter appeared unperturbed. Frustrated by Peter's apparent calm, Hunker heaved the shovel off to the side. Peter smiled. Hunker attempted to mimic him, but enslaved by the intensity of his anger, it came out a contorted grimace, the fiendish expression of a madman.

Hunker raised his right hand in a closed fist and motioned with the index finger of his left hand for Peter to come toward him. Peter didn't move. "You're chicken shit," Hunker said. "All you ever do is hide behind that pretty face, actin' like ya ain't scared." Again he motioned with his finger for Peter to come closer. Peter didn't budge. "You and your brother are one of a kind. Couple a shade tree pansy asses."

Peter smiled again.

"Wipe that smile off your face you goddamn smart ass."

Peter couldn't resist giggling.

That did it. Hunker lunged forward and cracked Peter flush on the side of the head. Peter took a quick side step to soften the blow, and then crouched into a ready position, like a big cat about to spring at its prey.

I attempted to shout a warning to Peter to back off, but the words wouldn't come out. I stood stiff-legged and immobilized as Hunker's body trembled into a violent crescendo that erupted with a vicious round house swing at Peter's head.

Lightening struck. Peter's fists lashed out with a combination of blows that crunched on Hunker's face. Jolted and dazed, Hunker teetered on wobbly legs as Peter pummeled him with a furious barrage.

"PETER! PETER! STOP! STOP!" I shouted. My words went unheard. I stumbled forward and tackled Peter, the impact knocking him aside, forcing him to recognize my presence as he glared at me with cold glassy eyes

My attention shifted to Hunker who lay crumpled on the ground. Nausea struck me, shaking as I gazed down at this incapacitated powerful man, struck by Peter's savage fury.

Peter grabbed my arm. "Andrew! You all right? His eyes had changed to compassion.

"Guess so," I muttered.

"Let's move it," Peter urged. "We need to get Hunker some help."

I stood amazed once again at seeing Peter's quick switch from violent anger to compassion. He was now concerned about Hunker. He took the initiative in urging the work crew to assist in loading Hunker into a pickup truck. Peter insisted I ride along with him as Hunker was rushed off to Ramsey County Hospital.

We waited over an hour before the doctors came out to report that Hunker had a severe concussion and would need to stay in the hospital. I was frightened, thinking, *Would this be another Andy Givens incident?*

Peter was quiet on the return trip. He looked sad. "I hope this don't get you in serious trouble," I said.

"I deserve trouble for goin' off the way I did," Peter responded.

"It happened so fast."

"All I remember is Hunker's fist hitting the side of my head," Peter said. "That's all I remember. Next thing I knew, there was Hunker in a heap on the ground." Peter paused, then added, "Thanks for tackling me and knocking me away."

"I was afraid you wouldn't back off."

"Guess I went crazy in the head."

"Hunker more than invited a fight."

The next morning at work we were greeted by a man in a suit and tie. He introduced himself as Carl Abrams, representing the Carson Construction Company. He announced that Hunker was still in the hospital. In his absence there would be no work. The men could go home for the day.

Mr. Abrams wanted to talk privately with Peter and me. He handed each of us a check. "This will take care of the pay we owe you," he said. "As of today, you're both fired." He turned to Peter. "You must be Peter?" he asked.

"That's right," Peter responded.

"Carson Construction has filed charges against you. You can expect a summons in a few days."

Two days later Peter got a call from Mr. Humphery. I was home at the time, and saw an instant change come over Peter as he talked on the phone.

"What was that all about?" I asked.

"Humphery says to get my bags packed."
"Red Wing?"

"That's what he said."

Peter became uncharacteristically quiet and inactive in the next few days. He remained at home, lying in bed, gazing at the ceiling, not shaving, showering or eating.

The following Monday, in the darkness before dawn, Peter awakened me. "Andrew," Peter said. "You awake? I need to talk with ya." He sat beside me.

"What's wrong?" I asked.

"Jus' wanted ya to know I made a decision." There was a seriousness in his face that was quick to draw my attention. "I'm joinin' the Army," Peter said.

"What about Red Wing?"

"I figure the Army's a way to avoid Red Wing."

"Sounds like you made up your mind."

"I'm goin' to the recruiting office today."

"You think the Army's better than going to Red Wing?"

"For me it is. No way could I stand being locked up." We sat quiet for several minutes. Peter then asked, "How about you, Andrew? Want a join with me?"

"Go to Korea? That smelly place."

"It's up to you, little brother. Just thought maybe it was good for us to stick together."

Chapter 13

Peter and I went to the recruitment office together, where we were greeted by Master Sergeant Grady O'Leary. His twinkling blue eyes peeked out from the puffy redness of his cheeks as he told us of his twenty-eight years of adventure. "Great time to be joining the Army," he said. "Lots of benefits."

"How soon can we sign up?" Peter asked.

The sergeant's wide smile made his big round face look like a jack-o-lantern. "You guys pass muster," he said, "I can have you on a troop train to Ft. Riley in three days."

"What we need to do?" Peter asked.

"How old are you guys?"

"Be eighteen in December," Peter responded.

"How about you?" the sergeant asked me.

"The same. We're twins."

"I'll be damned." He gave us a closer look. "By God, you do have a 'semblance." He shoved some papers across the desk. "Never signed up twins before. Here." Peter and I took the papers. The sergeant pointed. "You can go over by that table to fill these out."

While Peter and I worked on the forms, the sergeant played solitaire. Peter finished before me, and flipped his papers on the sergeant's desk, messing up his cards. "Sorry, sir," Peter said. "You sure did that in a hurry," the sergeant said, as he proceeded to check Peter's answers. "Looks like you were expecting to go to college."

"Mostly Andrew and I was wantin' to play football."

"You guys do a hitch in the Army and Uncle Sam will pay your way."

"Here that, Andrew?" Peter asked me.

At least there was one thing I liked about going in the Army. I handed my completed papers to the sergeant.

"The regulation is that I need to give you young guys a couple of days to think about this before signing you up."

"I made up my mind," Peter said.

"You guys come back on Wednesday," the sergeant said. "I need to do some checking. If everything's okay, you can take physicals on Thursday. If you pass the physicals, I can have you on the Friday train to Ft. Riley."

When we got home, Mr. Humphery was inside talking to Emma, eating cookies and drinking coffee.

"Emma tells me you guys went to see an Army recruiter," Humphery said.

"We're joining the Army," Peter answered.

"So you think you can escape going to Red Wing?"

"What's wrong with joining the Army?" Peter asked.

"Nothing, if you don't mind getting your head shot off."

"The war in Korea ain't gonna 'mount to much," Peter said.

"Who knows?" Mr. Humphery said. "According to the morning paper, we could be in for a big mess over there."

"I don't care," Peter said. "Anything's better than goin' to Red Wing."

"Red Wing's like a church picnic compared to fighting a war," Mr. Humphery proclaimed.

"So what happens if Peter joins the Army?" I asked. "What about the court?"

"My bet, the judge will consider the Army a better place for Peter than Red Wing," Mr. Humphery answered.

"Can you check with the judge today?" Peter asked. "We wanna be on the Friday train for Ft. Riley."

Six days into the war, the Army of the Republic of Korea had collapsed. Its capital, Seoul, had been abandoned. The North Koreans, assisted by Russian tanks, were charging south. South Korea appeared doomed.

Truman's decision to "Stop the Sons-of-Bitches. No Matter What!" was bold, but the American military wasn't in a state of readiness to back it up. Truman didn't like spending money on the military and he had little love for its brass. He'd cut the Pentagon budget by a third. News of the Korean crisis created a strong push to strengthen the American military. Young men were needed to back up the president's tough talk.

On Tuesday afternoon, Mr. Humphery excitedly informed us that the judge was happy to hear of Peter's decision to join the Army.

Our enlistment was treated like we going off to some noble crusade to fight those evil Communists. The judge set into motion a collaboration between Mr. Humphery, Gladie Summers, the welfare worker and Father Sikorski to arrange for renting out our house during our absence. At noon on Wednesday Father Sirorski called. "Will you be home this afternoon to talk about the house?" he asked.

"Hold on," I said. "I need to check with Peter."

"Will you be home this afternoon?" I asked Peter. "Father Sikorski wants to come over."

"I don't want any of his religious mumbo-jumbo," Peter responded.

"It's about the house."

Peter hesitated. "Okay, I'll be here."

Father Sikorski was intensely serious from the moment he arrived. First he explained, "I volunteered our church council to take charge of your house when you boys are gone. They'll advertise for a renter and oversee the place."

"Who gets the rent money?" Peter asked.

"The council will get 10 percent for upkeep. The rest will go to the welfare office. They'll take care of the house payments, utilities and insurance. Any money left over will go into a fund for you boys when you return."

"Thanks for taking care of that," I said.

"There's another thing I wanted to bring up," he said. "How about if we go into the front room and sit down?" We all took seats in the front room. "I want to talk about your father. I'm sure you plan to go see him before you leave."

"Maybe we should go see him this afternoon," I said.

Father Sikorski waited for Peter to respond. "It's okay with me," Peter said.

Father Sikorski now took on a serious demeanor, intending for us to do the same as he said with emotion, "This could be a tough experience for your father."

"Our going into the Army?" I asked.

"That's right. Joining the Army with the expectation of going to war will have a special meaning for your dad."

"Did Dad volunteer when he went into the Army?" Peter asked.

Father Sikorski seemed displeased with Peter's abrupt question, but he managed to smile. "Your father was drafted early in the war. You might say he was ripped from the prime of his life. He had a pretty wife and two rambunctious twin boys."

"You've talked quite a bit about the war with Dad, haven't you?" I asked.

Father Sikorski looked uncomfortable after my question. He lowered his head and his eyes became misty. "I tried to. I knew he was hurting inside."

"Guess Dad saw lots a fighting in the war," Peter said.

"Your Dad never talked about the fighting." There was a long silence. "He wanted to forget about the war. Even when he got correspondence from the War Department, he threw it away."

"Didn't Mom find some official document in the garbage?" I asked.

"That's right. Your mother gave it to me for safe keeping."

"What was that all about?" I asked.

"Your father was invited to go to Washington to be awarded a medal."

"Did you ever talk with him about that?" I asked.

"There was a big write up in the *Minneapolis Tribune* about your dad being selected for the Congressional Medal of Honor. I went to your place to congratulate him, but he refused to talk about it. He wouldn't even look at the news story."

"I'd like to have read that story," I said.

"I have two copies. Your mother wanted me to save them to give you boys on your twenty-first birthday."

"Why wait so long?" Peter asked.

"Guess your Mom wanted you to be old enough to understand. She was uncomfortable with the vivid account of shooting and killing."

"Dad must have been in some big battles," Peter said.

The excitement in Peter's voice brought a concerned look to Father Sikorski. His eyes were on Peter as he said, "Your father did more than his share of killing. He had blood on his hands and the memories wouldn't go away."

"Mom said once that's why Dad drinks so much," I said.

Father Sikorski sagged down in his chair, arms hanging limp to the sides. "That's right," he said. "Your father turned to alcohol, desperate to forget the horrors of war."

Peter and I took the city bus to the Veterans Home. It was located east of Minnehaha Creek, sitting on the gentle slope of a wooded hillside, isolated from the mania of the city.

As we made our way up the long walkway to the Veterans Home, we encountered residents out for an evening stroll. Most walked alone, moving slow, seeming aloof. A gray-haired old soldier came toward us, his hands in perpetual motion, accompanied by repetitive chanting. As he came upon us, he raised his hands to shoulder height, fists closed and shaking. His hand movements were synchronized with the singsong of his voice. "Ernie! Ernie! Don't leave me! Don't, Ernie. Don't."

For some strange reason an internal guilt kept me from looking at this man as he passed by. Curiosity did compel me to glance back as he repeated the same refrain, over and over. I also noticed that he had a limp. Looked like he had an artificial leg.

"That's guy's really hurtin'," Peter said as we passed out of his hearing range.

"I wonder if Ernie left him?" I asked.

"I think Ernie left him," Peter answered.

Dad was gazing out the window when we entered his room. "Hi, Dad," I said softly. When Dad turned around, his appearance hit me hard. He looked haggard. Deep, heavy wrinkles mired his face.

Peter gave him a hug and said, "How ya doin', Dad?"

As if not hearing Peter, Dad stood and looked us over, Peter first, then me. "Won't be long till football season. Right, boys?"

Peter responded, "Don't look like we'll be playin' football this season."

"Suppose ya fucked up and got kicked off the team again," Dad grumbled.

I hurried to answer. "We decided to join the Army."

Dad glared at Peter and said with harsh, gruff words, "Was this your doing?"

Peter nodded.

"Stupid decision," Dad said.

I could tell Peter was hurt, but he silently subdued his feeling.

"It isn't as bad as you think, Dad," I broke in. "The Army will pay our way to college when we get out."

Dad's eyes bore down on me. "Dead men don't read books," he snapped back.

"Korea ain't no Battle of the Bulge, Dad," Peter said.

"War's war, goddamn it! I don't want my boys in any war."

"The papers say it's a police action, not a war," Peter responded.

"That's bullshit," Dad said. "You can bet your ass they'll find reason to lash out full bore. Lot's a men'll get killed and fucked up!" He paused, needing to catch his breath, and then added, "Fucked up like me."

I felt pain inside as Dad's body trembled. There were tears in his eyes. When Peter moved to place his arm around Dad, Dad's shaking increased. I took Dad's hand. He started to sob, from deep inside. He struggled to hold back, but couldn't.

We tried to calm Dad down, but it was no use. Supporting Dad on both sides, we assisted him into bed. He turned away from us, facing the wall, curled in a fetal position. We tried say a final goodbye, but couldn't elicit a response from him. We didn't know what to do.

"Let's leave," Peter said. I felt empty inside. Peter gave me a hug. "C'mon, little brother, let's go." Peter gave Dad a gentle pat on the back, as did I. There was no response. Peter then shoved me toward the door.

My mind was in a fog as we headed home. "Looks like Dad isn't too happy about our going into the Army," I said.

"He thinks Korea is like World War II," Peter responded.

The Korean War officially started on June 25, 1950. On June 20, at 5:00 AM we were scheduled to leave by troop train for Ft. Riley, Kansas.

On the night before our departure Peter was preparing to go out for the evening. "Five o'clock's mighty early in the morning," I said. "Maybe you should stay home tonight."

"No way am I staying home tonight, little brother," Peter responded. "There'll be a big celebration. You should be there, Andrew. Lots a people will want to say goodbye to us."

"No thanks. I need my sleep so I can get us on that train in the morning."

"You worry too much, little brother. Tonight will be a night to remember. I wouldn't miss it for anything."

That evening I called for Kathy Amundson. Her mother answered the phone, indicating Kathy was visiting her aunt out east. "I called to say goodbye. Peter and I joined the Army. We're leaving tomorrow."

"I'll be sure to tell her you called," her mother responded. "Kathy thinks a lot of you. She's always admired how you try to hold down that rambunctious brother of yours."

Her comment surprised me. I didn't know what to say. "Just tell Kathy that I'll be in touch."

"Do you want her aunt's phone number out East?"

"Guess not. Just tell her I'll be in touch later."

"I'll be sure to do that."

After hanging up the phone there was a strange and empty feeling inside me, like maybe I should have gotten the phone number out East and called her before we leave. I waited in silence and eventually the thought faded away.

Peter had still not returned home when I awoke the next morning. I had to leave for the train depot alone. Peter had assured me he'd make the train. I had to trust him.

The troop train was waiting in the depot when I arrived. Most of the young men had already said their goodbyes to their families and friends and boarded the train. I paced the loading dock, worried that Peter wouldn't make it. Repeatedly, I checked my watch. The train was to leave in ten minutes. I thought about running off and forgetting the Army.

Suddenly, I heard singing, if you could call it that. A rowdy crowd approached from the north, bellowing out a refrain of the Edison fight song. They yelled, "HIP-HIP—HOORAY! for Peter Amonovitch." They repeated the refrain several times, followed by a loud prolonged cheer.

As they neared the train, Peter rushed forward and gave me a hug. I smelled alcohol. Peter raised my right hand high, shouting to his comrades, "Let's have it for Andrew!" Peter became the cheerleader as the group, many of whom I knew, went wild in a final tribute. I turned away to cover the gush of feeling inside me.

Above all the clamor came the commanding whistle from the train, which started to move. I grabbed Peter's arm, attempting to pull him along. Peter jerked away, caught up in a frenzy of goodbyes to friends.

The train had moved some fifty yards before Peter rushed to jump aboard. I clutched his hand to help him. We stood in the coach's rear entrance and waved as the "HIP-HIP—HOORAYS" faded in the distance. The train picked up speed as it rounded a curve and we lost sight of the cheering crowd. The conductor guided us to our seats.

Before we reached the city limits I moved to a seat across the isle from Peter. I couldn't stand the smell of alcohol and cigarette smoke. Peter ignored my departure. He was already sprawled out and snoring.

The conductor came by selling morning papers. I bought a *Star Tribune* with the bold headline:

NORTH KOREAN 4th DIVISION PLUNGES SOUTHWARD.

The story told of tactical UN failures, command problems, and critical shortages of men and supplies. I glanced over at Peter, thinking about his desperate decision to join the Army. He was oblivious to events taking place in Korea.

To Peter, joining the Army was like a glorious adventure, a big football game across the water. The news article had me depressed. I wanted to forget Korea and the war.

Chapter 14

"Get your ass moving, soldja!"

I yawned and squinted at the tall uniformed black man who stood over me. "What time is it?" I asked.

"Time to soldja. Get your ass up and movin'."

We were herded out to the parade ground where Corporal Witherspoon introduced himself with his harsh threatening voice. "ATTEN–HUT!" I was so nervous that I couldn't make out a word of what was being presented as the battalion commander was being introduced. When I shuffled my feet aside to get a better look at the speaker, my eardrums were once again shattered: "Keep dem feets still!" Whitherspoon shouted. Afraid to move a muscle, I stiffened like a statue.

"Welcome to Ft. Riley," said the battalion commander. "I'm Major Walters. My job is to introduce you to the Army, to dress you men up like soldiers and get you ready for training."

He looked us over. "All I ask while you're here is that you follow the orders of the non-coms. Their job is to keep this operation moving." He turned to Witherspoon. "They're all yours, Corporal."

Witherspoon sent Major Walters off with a flashy salute and click of his heels. Corporal Witherspoon waited until the major was out of earshot before assuming a pompous air. He shouted, "Youse guys fuck wid me, you done had it! When ah say jump, you say how high. Ah say kiss my ass, you say, where's da sweet spot. Undastan'? Ah gives orders, youse all suck up."

Corporal Witherspoon was quite the cat. Twenty-four hours a day he was on a power trip, an immaculate dresser, his uniform starched, pressed, and tailored to fit his lean athletic body, his shoes always shined like the hub caps on Andy Givens' hotshot Mustang. His taunt stretched-out fatigue cap sat well forward on his head, the bill down over his eyes, forcing him to raise his chin to see, giving him a pretentious slither-eyed glare.

There wasn't much that Witherspoon missed and his savvy in reading men was uncanny. Early on he knew who the fuck-offs were and who deserved respect. He had a special talent for smelling out guys who had a thing with authority.

He and Peter were like static before a storm. "What you think of Witherspoon?" I asked Peter when we were alone.

"He's a Hunker Hanson without the balls," Peter responded.

Reville came at 0500 hours. The first morning when I woke up, Peter wasn't in his bunk. My first thought was that he'd snuck off to Junction City to raise some hell, though leaving the post was against military regulations.

When we broke the ranks for chow, he was still absent. My concern about Peter overshadowed any desire to eat. Nevertheless, I dragged myself to the mess hall. The ordeal of a long line, along with the smell of greasy bacon and strong coffee were enough to wipe out the little appetite I had. Anxious to get back to the barracks to see if Peter had returned, I hurried out the exit to discard my uneaten food in the garbage cans.

"Clean off dat tray, soldja!"

Turning quickly to the source of the command, I was surprised. "Peter," I said, "How long have you been here?"

"That fucker, Witherspoon, woke me in the middle of the night and told me to follow him to the promised land."

I smiled. "Looks like you're having fun."

"You better believe it, little brother."

Following lunch and supper, I stopped to chat with Peter as he remained on the KP garbage detail. He didn't return to the barracks until 2200 hours, though the lights had officially gone off at 2100 hours.

"Hey, Peter," I whispered as he started to undress. "You had a long day."

"Those fuckers in the mess hall are crazy."

"To tell the truth, I was happy to see you on KP. I thought you took off to Junction City."

"Sounds like a great idea, little brother."

"They call it AWOL. It's big trouble, so forget it."

Peter went off to the shower and soon the steam was billowing out into the hallway. I thought Peter would indulge in a long relaxing shower, but shortly there was an abrupt shudder of the water pipes.

"That didn't take long," I said, as Peter emerged drying himself. He didn't answer. He was too busy dressing. "What you doing?" I asked.

"Don't you worry, little brother."

"You miss reveille and your ass has had it."

"Want a come along?" Peter asked.

"No way!"

"Calm down. And don't sweat reveille."

Off he went, AWOL on his first night in the Army. I hoped he'd get caught before setting foot off the post, but knowing him, I knew that chance was slim. After Peter departed, I lay awake, worried that joining the Army was the worse mistake we ever made.

At 0430 hours the lights in the barracks flashed on. "Get your asses moving!" shouted the sergeant. As soon as I sat up, my head was throbbing. When I dropped to the floor from my top bunk, the weight of my body seemed enormous. I hit with a thud that rattled my still sleeping brain.

Though I momentarily indulged in self-pity, one look at Peter's empty bunk quickly brought him back to my mind. I promptly dressed and rushed out to the parade ground, looking for Peter. As reveille approached, I became more tense and the throbbing in my head returned. When Peter's name was called out as absent from duty, I tried to shut out the unpleasant reality. When we broke ranks I accompanied the men to breakfast and was soon absorbed in conversation. It surprised me when one of the men laid a hand on my shoulder and said, "Your brother wants to talk with you."

"Where is he?"

"On KP. Garbage detail."

I grabbed my tray and headed for the exit. I was about to dump my uneaten food when I saw Peter kneeling beside a garbage can, reaching inside, scrubbing it with a GI brush. A corporal with a rifle and white arm band stood over him. "Get with it, soldja," I said to Peter.

Peter recognized my voice and peeked around the edge of the garbage can. "It's my brother," Peter said to the guard. "Can I talk with him?"

The corporal was a little skinny guy. He looked to be one of those spit and polish types. "Give ya five minutes," he blurted out.

"Oh you sweet little soldja boy," Peter said as he rose to his feet. Offended by Peter's sarcasm, the corporal made a brash move to step between us. Peter ignored the guard, shifted to the side and motioned for me to join him.

"Soldier!" the guard shouted.

Peter snapped to attention, clicked his heels and saluted the corporal. The corporal didn't know what to do. He held his rifle in a parade-arms position and spoke in a shaky voice, "Okay. Take your five minutes."

We moved several steps further from the guard. "Thank Witherspoon for this guy," Peter said. "Soon's I left the barracks last night the MP's was on my tail. They nabbed me and hustled me to the stockade. Now, thanks to Witherspooon, I go through the induction routine with a guard at my side. All free time I'm on KP. At night I sleep in the stockade."

"You credit Witherspoon for all this?" I asked.

"You better believe it. He put the MPs onto me. Must a told 'em to watch for me."

The guard came toward Peter with his rifle in a ready position. "You talked enough. Get back to work," he ordered.

Peter ignored him and continued talking. "There's one thing I want to accomplish before I leave Ft. Riley," Peter said so the guard could hear. "Witherspoon's gonna get his pay back." Peter clenched and raised his fist so the guard could see it.

The guard saw this as a threat to his authority and shoved Peter away from me with the stock of his rifle.

In a flash Peter whipped out a hand and snatched the rifle so fast the guard stood dumbfounded.

"Peter," I shouted, bringing him to a standstill. The guard's mouth and eyes opened wide, his hands shook. "Give him his rifle," I said to Peter.

Peter studied the look in my eyes, then calmly turned to the guard and gave him back his rifle. The guard now backed off, conceding us the freedom to talk.

The three of us stood in silence, then Peter grabbed the GI brush to resume work on the garbage cans. Slowly I walked way. It hurt inside to see what was happening to my brother. I continued watching from a distance, worried by the anger manifest in his brisk washing of the garbage cans. There was no way I could rest easy.

Strange as it may seem, I was pleased that Peter was kept under close surveillance.

Witherspoon was keen enough to recognize Peter's defiance of authority. I could tell from the gleam in Witherspoon's eyes that he took pride in his power to restrain Peter.

I could only imagine what Peter was thinking about Corporal Witherspoon. My hope was that he could get out of Ft. Riley without more trouble.

Sunday morning reveille came at the usual 0500 hours. The first sergeant presided. "This is the last time we'll see your pretty faces," he said. "At 0700 hours you'll board a troop train that will take you west to Camp Carson, Colorado. They got mountains where you can train and get ready for those sweet little hills of Korea."

There was an attentiveness that exceeded any moment in the past ten days. We were dismissed, with orders to return to the barracks and pack our belongings. "What about Peter?" I asked the first sergeant. "Will he be here on time for the train?"

"Don't worry," responded the first sergeant, smiling, "Witherspoon will take care of your brother."

I didn't trust Witherspoon. He enjoyed making life hard for Peter. The troops were marched on the train well before the 0700 departure time. Our squad was all ready and accounted for, except for Peter.

Still worried, I had to further check on Peter. I went from the squad leader, to the platoon sergeant, and finally the First Sergeant. He smiled, gave me a consoling pat on the shoulder and said, "The Army needs every damn body it can scrape up to send to Korea. Witherspoon won't let your brother off the hook. He'll be on that train to Colorado."

The First Sergeant was right. At 0655 hours, a jeep arrived with an MP escort. Under guard, Peter was marched on the train with his duffel bag over his shoulder. Witherspoon was nowhere in sight. I don't know if he'd ever seen anyone before like Peter, but he sure knew how to keep him in line.

When Peter came on the train accompanied by an MP, he was escorted to a seat and ordered to remain there. The MP stayed at his side. Peter looked intense, a distant glare in his eyes, seeming oblivious to the immediate surroundings. I could tell he was angry and hurting inside.

I sensed this was a time when he needed me. I approached the MP. "I'm Peter's brother. Can I sit here beside him?" The MP looked me over, and then nodded approval. I sat beside Peter. "How you doing?" I asked. Peter didn't answer. He glared straight ahead, like he didn't hear me. "Still thinking about Witherspoon?" I asked.

Peter turned, glared straight into my eyes and muttered, "Witherspoon's a no good bastard."

"He was out to get you."

"That son of a bitch," Peter said through clenched teeth.

"Witherspoon saw you had an attitude and set you up."

"What the hell you mean—attitude?" Peter asked.

I hesitated. "The Army won't let you have your own rules, Peter. They just won't."

"Fuck the Army!"

Again I hesitated. "That's what I mean by attitude. It just won't work, Peter."

"Whose side you on, little brother?"

"I'm on your side, but I can't change the Army. Neither can you. Okay?"

"So you say I was s'posed to suck up to Witherspoon?"

"I say follow the rules, Peter. Then, guys like Witherspoon won't have a chance to fuck you up."

As Peter listened, his intensity diminished, but a glare remained in his eyes, reminding me that although he was my twin brother, his individuality both intrigued and frustrated me.

Chapter 15

We arrived at Colorado Springs at 2100 hours. An endless line of three-quarter ton trucks waited at the train station. The non-coms in charge were in a big rush, for no apparent reason. "Move it!" they shouted. My inclination was to snap shit. Not Peter. He walked at his own pace, not defiant, but clearly not caught up in the pressure.

We hoisted our duffel bags into a truck, pulled ourselves up and took positions on the metal seats. "Slide back!" a shrill voice ordered. They packed us in tight, and the instant the truck was filled the back gate was slammed shut and fastened. We waited, listening to the harsh commands of the non-coms and the periodic resounding clang of a tailgate as another truck was filled.

As we held up in the trucks, I remembered a field trip during my elementary school days, a visit to the St.

Paul Stockyard where we saw cattle being herded and locked in pens.

When all the trucks were filled, a distant order came to: MOVE OUT. The trucks started in unison. A deafening roar of powerful engines and the smell of exhaust fumes filled the night. The troops sat silent as the convoy lumbered along.

Upon reaching our destination, the rush resumed as we were hustled out into a single line. "Keep your mouths shut and stand directly behind the man in front of you." We stood motionless at attention, waiting and waiting, as if they dared us to move.

Then, at last we heard activity at the head of the line. "Name?" came the sharp command. If the response wasn't loud enough, it was followed by another sharp command: "Sound off like ya got a pair!"

Peter was ahead of me. "Name?"

"Peter Amonovitch."

"Barracks. Two. Second platoon."

"Name?"

"Andrew Amonovitch."

"Barracks. Two. Second platoon."

We moved on to our barracks where we met Corporal Williams, the non-com in charge, a short black man with a soft voice and a trim mustache. The corporal showed us to our assigned bunks, handed us a paper with printed instructions and told us to change into fatigues and be ready for duty.

I changed immediately and studied the paper. It was a detailed explanation of how our wall closet, footlocker, bunk, rifle and uniforms were to be maintained. Peter took a brief glance at the instructions and tossed them aside, while I continued to study it.

At 2300 hours, the company was ordered out of the barracks to stand in our first company formation. For twenty minutes, we were drilled on how to stand at attention. "Eyes ahead! Pull back that chin! Suck in that gut!"

When our first sergeant, Master Sergeant Knute Knutson, was satisfied with our capacity to stand at attention, he had a new challenge for us. "Listen up, men. Before we read you little boys your bedtime story, y'all's gonna learn what it's like to sleep in a clean barracks. You're gonna spiff up these quarters like they never been before. When I say clean, I mean soldja clean, none of this pussy-ass civvy shit youse little boys is 'customed to."

We learned how the Army can make life miserable. Over and over we cleaned the barracks, experiencing for the first time what was referred to as "chicken shit." It was 0100 hours when the lights went out. Like at Ft. Riley, I had the top bunk with Peter below. It felt good having Peter back with me.

On July 1, 1950, we began basic training. It started with a meeting of the 2nd Battalion at Theater No. 1, a base movie theater. Presiding was Major Hutchens from Division Headquarters. He started with an introduction of the commanders and first sergeants of each of the four companies in the battalion. Then he introduced General Caraway, the base commander.

General Caraway was here to jack us up and he was damn good at it. He began, "In eight weeks you'll be on your way to Korea. Each of you will be assigned to one of the many proud units serving over there." This was quick to draw our attention. He continued: "These units need well-trained tough-ass soldiers to fill out their numbers. You men have some rough training ahead of you. War's no easy game, gentlemen. You need to be ready."

The general turned the podium over to a Major Rathman, also from Division Headquarters. He gave us the boring details about our eight weeks of training. There were a few facts that impressed me: most of all that the Army had compressed sixteen weeks of training into eight. "Nevertheless," he added, "you will become experts with the M-1 rifle, the 3.5 rocket launcher, the Browning Automatic Rifle and the 35 millimeter machine gun. You will learn to repel down mountains, throw hand grenades and how to sleep on the cold, hard ground."

This meeting was intended to put a spark in our rear ends. It did more than that. I came away feeling overwhelmed and afraid. Most amazing to me was Peter's response. He was exhilarated by the promise of war in Korea. He still looked at it like a big football game, a game he'd always played with the ferocity of a warrior.

As a football player Peter had all the necessary physical attributes: strength, speed and endurance. The rough and tumble aspect of the game is what he loved most—the rougher the better, except for practice. Peter considered most of football practice a waste. He had walked away from many of the drills. Scrimmage was okay as long as the coach didn't repeat the same play over and over. Had it not been for Peter's extraordinary talent, Coach Watson would never have tolerated his insubordination to the practice regimen.

Peter viewed training for war like he viewed training for football. Shooting weapons made sense to him but he gave a minimum of effort to repetitive physical exercise. Yet, he killed the PT tests with scores that exceeded everyone in the company. On the M-1 rifle he scored 245 of a possible of 250, besting everyone in the division.

Peter's performance was the talk of the company. The Army had respect for guys who could shoot, and if they could also run and jump like a wild man, you could command a special reverence. Both officers and non-coms looked up to Peter because of his talents.

Unfortunately, the Army didn't appreciate Peter's other side. The spit and polish types, the chicken shit guys, were annoyed by Peter's disrespect for what he called "bullshit."

To my way of thinking, the spit and polish guys had a distorted sense of values. To them a real soldier was a kiss-ass type who would salute and "Yes, sir!" everything that moved. Most of these guys could be spotted a mile away with their spit-shined boots, starched fatigues and snap-to bearing.

The threat of inspections was a basic training harassment these spit and polish guys loved to hold over the troops. The announcement of an inspection brought anxiety to many of the men. It sure made me nervous. My worry was more about Peter than myself. I could play the spit and polish game if I had to. Peter had little worry about inspections. He just didn't play along.

Many of the men viewed inspections as a waste of time, but the threat of disciplinary action and company pride were enough to force compliance. Peter paid little heed to what he described as a "phony game." While most of us sweated over the minute details for the up coming Division HQ inspection, Peter slipped off to the PX. "I'd rather suck me up a few beers," was his parting remark.

Peter's departure brought a mixed reaction from the men. There was a silent admiration of his defiance, tempered by resentment that a poor performance by Peter in the inspection would reflect unfavorably on them and could result in harsh discipline directed at the total company. This embarrassed me.

I wanted Peter to be respected by the men in the company and I wanted to keep him out of trouble, so I took it upon myself to prepare Peter's equipment for the inspection. The fellows saw me and several of them lent a hand.

I was curious how Peter would respond when he returned and discovered what we'd done. At 2100 hours, when the lights went out, Peter had not returned from the PX. I waited up. He had to be back soon. The PX closed at 2200 hours.

At 2230 hours Peter had not returned. I worried that he had slipped off to Colorado Springs, which heightened my anxiety. At 2300 hours I crawled into my bunk. Reveille would come early. Tomorrow would be an important day, with inspection by the big boys from Division Headquarters. Every few minutes I looked toward the front hall, hoping to see Peter. I couldn't sleep.

We made it through reveille the next morning without incident. Peter was absent, but wasn't reported as missing. That's because the big inspection dominated everyone's mind, causing reveille to be conducted in a hurried careless manner. For now, as least, Peter's absence wasn't officially reported.

Following reveille many of the men skipped breakfast and returned to the barracks to spend extra time spiffing things up for the inspection. I had little appetite for breakfast, but made a point to go to the mess hall, telling myself I wouldn't allow any inspection to keep me from eating.

The inspection was scheduled for 1000 hours. Everything was laid open for viewing: footlockers, wall lockers, latrine, you name it. The big boys could play chicken shit with anything from floor to ceiling.

Thanks to me and several other recruits, Peter's bunk and belongings were in reasonable shape for the inspection. Throughout the barracks, tension prevailed as we awaited this huge event. Peter's absence made me tense to a point that my hands shook.

At 0950 hours we heard the front door slam shut. We snapped to attention, standing tall, brass shining, trousers pressed, our posture rigid and uneasy.

We were shocked at the sight of Peter tiptoeing across the shiny floor, dressed in fatigues, bleary-eyed and sporting a healthy outgrowth of whiskers.

No one spoke a word as Peter proceeded to his bunk area and took a quick look at his belongings, checking to see if everything was in place. He glanced at me and said, "Thanks, little brother," then presented a sarcastic exaggerated salute.

Refusing to smile at Peter's untimely antics, I glared sternly. Peter leaned and whispered in my ear, "I'm goin' to the mess hall. The Army just now assigned me to KP duty." The smell of alcohol on his breath was enough to force me back.

When the brass arrived at the front entrance, Peter scurried out the back door, making his exit within seconds before the first sergeant leading the inspection announced their arrival with a resounding "ATTEN–HUT!"

I stood stiff, not moving a single cell of my body, except my eyes. I watched every move of the head honcho, a lieutenant colonel, who looked pretty young to me. This guy may be okay I thought, but he came across like he was royalty and we were the scum of the earth.

When he came up to me, even the cells of my eyes ceased to move. I was in a trance, not seeing anything. The head honcho made a quick inspection of Peter's area, and then stood before me. "There's a man missing," he said in a provocative monotone.

"Private Peter Amonovitch is on KP, sir," I said, my voice weak and shaky. The lieutenant colonel remained standing before me. I could feel, but not see his eyes as they searched my face with an intimidating thoroughness.

It was not until he moved on that I became aware of my sweating, squirming, wanting to itch my back as the droplets of moisture trickled their way down my spine. When the tension subsided, I still had Peter to worry about. Peter was playing a dangerous game of deception and acting like he was having fun. It was no fun for me. I couldn't relax with the outcome of his latest escapade still in jeopardy.

Peter came through unscathed. He never did report to the mess hall for KP. He never intended to. He simply planted his KP scheme in my head and when the inspecting lieutenant colonel inquired about his absence, my response under pressure of the moment was to report exactly as Peter had stated to me.

Peter's manipulation worked perfectly. He used me, which I resented, but the outcome was so favorable, how could I complain? It was an excellent example of how a big organization like the Army was vulnerable to manipulation from within.

Peter had years of practice as a manipulator. This incident was his most sophisticated thus far. Peter was gaining an understanding of the Army and how the left hand didn't always know what was happening with the right hand. Peter was bold enough to use this understanding to his advantage.

This exploit and the others that followed became topics of humorous interest among the men. These stories became embellished by the telling, making Peter into a basic training folk hero. He was seen as a fun loving, heavy drinking woman chaser who could shoot a rifle and soldier as well as anyone when he put his mind to it.

The officers and non-coms heard most of the stories of Peter's escapades. Fortunately, it was well after the fact. Peter managed to keep a step ahead of them. By August, he knew the Army game real well, both the system and the people. Most of the officers and non-coms looked at Peter as an asset to the Army. He could be an outstanding soldier when he had to be and he could be a hell-raiser when he had the chance. They saw him as good for morale.

Of course, the Army wouldn't be the Army without a few hard-nosed, straight-line chicken shits. The more they saw Peter taking advantage of the system, the more they resented him. Being of a serious nature myself, my eyes were always on these straight-line folks.

I sensed they were watching for an opportunity to nail Peter to the wall.

Peter never worried about being nailed to the wall because he never had the fear, and that made him what he was. I had the fear, which made me what I am, someone who worries, who tries hard to avoid trouble. Since I loved my brother and felt responsible to watch over him, I tried to urge caution.

By late August, as we neared the completion of basic training, Peter became exceedingly bold in his exploitation of the rules. Every night when the lights went out, he'd sneak off into Colorado Springs. Some nights he went as far as Pueblo. Peter never admitted this to me, but I learned of it through the stories that Pueblo had a reputation for being more wild than the Springs, something that would be hard for Peter to resist.

Peter must have been having lot of fun in town. The schedule he followed took enormous stamina, soldering during the day and chasing women and drinking at night. Fortunately, each morning Peter got back to the barracks shortly before reveille.

After a brief rest he'd always make it up for early morning role call. He didn't miss a beat with the training schedule. He survived by taking advantage of the half hour rest periods we had during the day. He'd zonk out, totally, at every opportunity and depend on me to awaken him, so he wouldn't miss the training. Peter's ability to turn himself off and on was remarkable.

Through this period there was one officer who made me mighty uneasy: Second Lieutenant Elvert Bailey, whom the men referred to as the Michigan State ROTC wonder. The men called him Beetle Bailey. Bailey was always pulling out his little note pad, appearing to make entries related to Peter's activity.

My suspicion intensified the night I got up to take a leak and found the mighty lieutenant in our barrack, sitting on a footlocker in the semi-darkness. I was returning from the latrine in my jockey shorts when I caught a glimpse of this man with the shining gold bars. I walked close to confirm what my bleary eyes thought they'd imagined. "Lieutenant Bailey," I said in surprise, whipping off a clumsy salute.

"At ease, soldier," whispered the lieutenant.

I wanted to ask him what he was doing here, but hesitated questioning the intentions of an officer. As I stood speechless in my boxer shorts, I noticed the lieutenant trying to hide his note pad behind him. He looked uncomfortable in my presence, and appeared to recognize my suspicion that he was keeping tabs on Peter.

Without information about Peter's whereabouts, I couldn't see how his documentation could be of much value to his personal investigation. "Is there anything I can do to help you?" I asked.

"No ... ah ... guess not," he said.

Playing on Lieutenant Bailey's discomfort, I found my writing tablet and pen, then took a seat on my footlocker and pretended to begin writing a letter. My manipulation was successful. Lieutenant Bailey left within minutes.

Certain that he would maintain his vigil outside, I was pleased to think that he'd have a long wait. I tossed my writing paper in the waste bucket and went off to bed. I tried to convince myself that this incompetent ROTC wonder presented no danger to Peter. What bothered me was that Bailey was so damn unpredictable. The remainder of the night was sleepless for me as Lieutenant Bailey was on my mind.

As usual, Peter was back from his nightly escapade shortly before reveille. I was still awake when he arrived. I whispered, "Did you see Beetle Bailey out there?"

Peter yawned. "Nope. Didn't see anybody."

"My bet is that he was out there, checking on you."

Again Peter yawned. "Big deal, the Beetle's checking on me."

"Thought you'd want to know."

"Thanks, little brother."

Awaking for reveille was no problem for me since I'd been awake most of the night and seeing Lieutenant Bailey present at reveille was no surprise. I kept an eye on him and when he came strutting our direction, my curiosity escalated.

Lieutenant Bailey didn't fit my image of a soldier. His pudgy build, baby face and clumsy gait were enough to make me chuckle. This morning though there was a noticeable difference in his stride. He had a pompous swagger as he approached Peter. Trying hard to appear threatening, the lieutenant blurted a weighty question: "Where were you all night, soldier?" Peter raised a hand to cover his mouth and prevent the lieutenant from smelling his breath. "Where were you last night?" repeated the lieutenant.

Peter was in no hurry to respond. I didn't think he'd answer at all, so I gave him a nudge. Calmly then, with a voice that had a Father Sikorski-like resonance, Peter answered, "Where I always go, sir, to the church to pray."

The men in the platoon tried unsuccessfully to muffle their laughter, which provoked even more. "Shut the fuck up!" yelled an exasperated Lieutenant Bailey. The laughter instantly subsided, diminishing to sporadic giggling as the men tried hard to restrain themselves. "So, you go to the chapel to pray," Lieutenant Bailey said. "All I can say, soldier, is that you better pray pretty damn hard because sooner or later I'm gonna have your ass."

"Sorry you feel so bitter, sir," responded Peter. "I'll pray for your forgiveness."

This brought another swell of laughter. It was too much for the lieutenant. He shook an angry fist at Peter and again threatened, "I'm gonna get your ass, Amonovitch." He stamped off, taking huge steps and swinging his arms in a brisk exaggerated fashion.

There were two more days of basic training. If Lieutenant Bailey was going to do anything about Peter, he had to move fast. I said to Peter, "Don't underestimate Bailey."

"Don't worry, little brother," Peter said. "Beetle Bailey is a real fun guy. Don't you agree?"

Peter knew my concerns, so there was nothing more to say. When the lights went out that night, Peter proceeded with his usual routine. He showered and dressed. Tonight he wore his Army tans—maybe he had a special date. Most of the time he wore civvies on his unauthorized escapades into Colorado Springs.

When Peter departed, I was mighty worried that something would happen, so I followed him, uncertain how far I'd continue my pursuit. As Peter took off across the parade ground, I was about to enter the open field when Lieutenant Bailey approached from the west. I stopped and waited, allowing some distance between the lieutenant and myself before proceeding. In the middle of the parade field, the lieutenant turned to face the west, raised his right hand and waved. That's when I sighted an MP vehicle parked on Military Road.

I wanted to warn Peter. He could be walking into some big trouble. Peter was headed for the bus stop at the corner of Military Road. Both military and civilian passengers utilized the commercial bus service to and from the post. The military police intervened only when they had reason to believe someone was leaving the post without authorized permission. They'd wait until the bus crossed the base perimeter to apprehend the violating military passenger, because only then would they be legally AWOL.

If Peter got on that bus tonight, I knew he'd be caught AWOL. As Peter neared the corner on Military Road, his pace slowed. It was too far for me to see exactly what was happening, but for some reason Peter changed direction, heading off to the east, toward the PX.

This move had me perplexed. Lieutenant Bailey also appeared baffled by Peter's action. Apparently Peter sensed trouble and decided to go to the PX. This turn of events had me elated and intensified the vigor of my pursuit.

When I could see the entrance to the PX, I stopped. Peter approached the PX, each step raising my spirits, then I couldn't believe it when Peter bypassed the PX. His pace quickened for the next two blocks. Suddenly, he made a quick turn and dashed toward the entrance of Post Chapel No. 1. At the front door he stopped, waited, removed his cap and entered.

I remembered Peter's answer to Lieutenant Bailey when questioned at reveille. I jumped into the air, overcome with joy at the cleverness of my brother.

Eager to see the reaction of Lieutenant Bailey, I turned quick to observe him talking to the military police who were parked in front of the chapel. Their discussion was brief. The military police sped away. Lieutenant Bailey stood alone. For the next half hour he circled the chapel, and then made a move toward the entrance. When reaching the chapel door, the lieutenant peeked inside, then turned and walked off, his pace slow, feet dragging, arms hanging limp.

Chapter 16

On the morning of August 31, 1950, we boarded a train heading for California. After a one-night layover in Los Angeles, we shipped out by military aircraft, destination: Tokyo.

Peter and I sat together. It was my first opportunity to talk with him about his night of prayer in Chapel No. 1. "Best night's sleep I had in a long time," Peter said. "I sacked out on a church pew and rested in peace. Helleva lot more quiet than the barracks."

"About time you had a full night's sleep."

Peter gave me a slap on the back. "Only live once, little brother. Have fun when ya got the chance, that's what I say."

On September 2, we arrived at the chaotic Replacement Depot in Yokohama. Military personnel were coming and going in every direction. Most were awaiting assignment to units stationed in Korea.

Peter and I were determined to advocate aggressively for an assignment in the same unit. We encountered no resistance. The personnel in charge had enough problems in assigning men without taking on a fight with us.

We were assigned to Charlie Company, 3rd Battalion of the 8th Cavalry. We'd be leaving for Korea to join them the following day, totally outfitted and combat ready. We arrived in Pusan on September 4, 1950, where we were immediately loaded in a three-quarter ton truck. Within minutes we were introduced to the rugged terrain and horrendous roads of Korea. This proved to be one helleva ride. We bounced around like ping pong balls as the driver had no sympathy for his passengers.

"Slow the fuck down!" Peter shouted. The driver ignored him. Peter raised the butt of his rifle and pounded on the back of the cab until the driver was forced to stop. The instant the truck stopped, Peter rushed forward to the driver. Expecting trouble, I followed. The driver had also jumped out and was in a huff and charged toward Peter. "What the fuck you tryin' to pull?" Peter complained.

"You telling me what to do, recruit?"

"Damn right I am. You drive like a crazy ass."

The driver pushed close to Peter, who towered over him by a foot. "You don't like how I drive, recruit, you just tipsy-toe down the road in your little combat boots."

Worried that they would come to blows, I moved between them. Peter stepped around me, climbed into the cab of the truck and started the engine. The driver made an attempt to open the door, but Peter reached through the window and shoved back on his ass. "Climb in the back," Peter shouted to me and the driver.

The driver scrambled to his feet, rushed out in front of the truck and held his hands high over his head, yelling, "I surrender. I surrender." He returned to the cab window and gazed with clemency at Peter. In a conciliatory voice, he said, "I promise. I'll cool my heels."

Peter hesitated before sliding aside and allowing the driver to take the wheel. Peter remained up front with the driver until we reached our destination. Thanks to Peter, our ride was now more tolerable.

We reached the location of Charlie Company on Wednesday, September 6, 1950. Peter and I jumped off the truck and waved goodbye to the other men who were moving on to assignments with other units.

Lieutenant Herb Beckel, the officer in charge of the first platoon, introduced himself before escorting us to the hillside position of Charlie Company. As we headed toward the command area in the rear, I noticed the men we passed along the way. I sensed a seriousness among them, leading me to believe these guys had faced some tough shit.

Beyond the introduction there was no talk. Peter and I learned that the way for us to fit in was simply to do what the other men did. The first two hours we walked, and then the lieutenant called us to a halt and directed us off to the side of the road. He motioned to a private who handed him a bottle. The lieutenant held it up for the men to see. "Our whiskey ration," he said. "Pass it around," giving it back to the private.

Each man took a swig. When it came to Peter, he passed it on without taking any. "We haven't earned this yet," Peter said.

We weren't made aware of our closeness to the front line until nightfall. Off to the north there was small arms fire, followed by the roar of F-80s strafing the area. It took a week before Peter and I quietly fit into the routine of Charlie Company. Despite the stand-offishness of the veterans, they did include us in some of the soldier talk. They held back on certain things. New men were never trusted until they proved themselves in battle.

We became part of the daily marches to the north, our objective each day determined by Battalion S-3. Some days we went on level ground, but most days we moved over narrow, treacherous mountain trails. For three days the going had been rough. We inched along, never able to settle in until after midnight. Each night Peter and I were assigned a position on the protective perimeter. One of us would try to sleep while the other kept watch.

On the fifth night of this same routine, Corporal Ortez came around to tell us there was no chow that night. "Chow truck took a hit."

"The bastards," Peter said as we heard the blast of a burp gun some three hundred yards away. Throughout the night the burp guns went off with regularity, making it impossible for anyone to sleep for very long. Towards dawn there was silence. Shortly before sunup I turned my watch over to Peter, and then snuggled into our dugout and pulled my camouflage poncho over me, attempting to sleep.

Soon after, Peter awakened me. "I heard something," he said. I heard it too—the low rumble of tanks. They were Communist T-34s on the road below. I wanted to run. "They'll see us," I said.

"Lay down in the ditch and cover up with the poncho," Peter said. This was my first experience with a feeling of total helplessness. I listened to the rumble and prayed that we wouldn't be seen. A short time later Peter touched me on the leg. I stiffened. "Take a look," Peter said.

My face and uniform were wet with sweat as I pulled off the poncho. I gazed down at a line of tanks accompanied by some 200 North Koreans. They rounded a curve to the east. As we moved back to positions further down the road, we heard heavy fire to the south. A short time later there were Korean soldiers running back around the curve in the road.

When they got close, some fifty yards from our position, we let loose. I couldn't pull the trigger until

I saw Peter blasting away. I managed to let off two rounds in the general direction of the North Koreans.

Many of the fleeing North Koreans were killed. When the battle ceased, there were enemy bodies scattered along the road. The sight of blood and the look of terror on the faces of the surviving North Koreans made me vomit. My body had a hard time handling what I was seeing.

During September there was a push to press north. The word was that the North Koreans were tired and weary and the end of the war was in sight. Recon patrols were sent out every few days to check on their positions. If conditions were favorable, we'd advance further north.

We never knew what might happen on patrol. Except for a few gung-ho types, most of the men preferred to pass up the patrols. Though Peter wasn't the typical gung-ho type, when there was any chance for action, he wanted to be a part of it. This made Peter a favorite of Second Lieutenant Higgins, Charlie Company's commander. Lieutenant Higgins was a soldier's soldier. He had guts to burn. His exploits in the battle for Hill 303 earned him a battlefield commission. When the former CO was demolished by a mortar back in July, Higgins had been a natural choice to replace him. Higgins pushed his men because as he said, "I want to get this damn war finished."

Peter volunteered for every patrol. "What you trying to prove?" I asked him.

"It's better than sittin' around watchin' the sun rise and fall over those fuckin' hills."

"The sun and those hills can look real beautiful," I said.

"Bullshit, Andrew. I know how much you detest being here."

"What's that got to do with you going out on every patrol?"

"I saw how you vomited up your guts the other day."

"I don't have the stomach for seeing bodies ripped apart."

"That's why I go on patrols," Peter said. "If it wasn't for me, you wouldn't be in this fuckin' Korea. Like Higgins says, 'let's get this damn war over with.'"

"I'm here because I wanted to be with you," I said.

"I'd never forgive myself, Andrew, if you didn't make it back to the States."

"What about you?"

"Don't worry about me, little brother. I can take care of Peter Amonovitch."

I hated this war, being away from home, away from the people and the events that had been our lives. I wanted to reach out and touch that world, which only now came to life with a fullness never seen before.

I thought of writing Dad, or maybe Father Sikorski or Woody Watson. My strongest desire was to write Kathy Amundson, to tell her of my loneliness for home, of my desire for news of what was happening back there. Thoughts of writing Kathy made me feel good, but there were emotions I wanted to express that held me back.

Mail call came only when there was mail from home. It didn't happen often, but when it did, those letters had a meaning seen only in the eyes of the men.

So far Peter and I never got a letter. I knew we'd never get one unless someone back home knew where to write. I believed or wanted to believe that Kathy Amundson would write back if I sent her a letter. As I realized my life could end any day, these thoughts intensified, accompanied by a serious search of my feelings.

I had to write Kathy Amundson. I had to tell her how I felt about her. I waited for quiet time, when I was alone. That time came as I lay shivering in a fox-hole on a frigid Korean night as Peter kept watch; it was my turn to sleep. It was too cold to sleep, so I huddled under my poncho, shielded my flashlight over the writing paper and began a letter to Kathy Amundson. It didn't take long before I got carried away. When finished, I had a peaceful feeling inside. At the first opportunity I handed the letter to the mail orderly. An exciting energy swelled within me as the orderly walked away with my letter.

On the morning of September 10, there was an atmosphere of expectancy—something big was brewing. The word came at 0900 hours. Charlie Company had been ordered to send out an attack patrol of fifty men. For this kind of patrol, Lieutenant Higgins preferred men who had proved themselves in battle. He didn't have enough veterans, so he had to call for volunteers. Peter was quick to volunteer. "Great," said the CO. "Now I need two more men."

I reluctantly raised my hand, feeling I should be with Peter. Henry Muelor, a new recruit from Scranton, Pennsylvania, also volunteered. Henry was a braggart, a loud mouth type. Higgins wasn't enthused about him being a part of the patrol, but he made a quick decision and said, "You want action? We'll see what we can do for you."

Lieutenant Grotjon was assigned to command this unit. They called him "the bitching tall man" because he was a lanky former basketball player from Purdue University who was always complaining about something. After a briefing from Lieutenant Higgins, the patrol set out. Our objective was a large hill three miles away. To get there we had to move around or over three heavily wooded hills. Foliage was still on the trees and bushes, and we all knew that we could walk into a North Korean trap and not know it until it was too late.

We were all pumped up by word that the Marines had landed at Inchon. My adrenaline was flowing as we moved slowly through the heavy underbrush. Next to me Henry Muelor carried himself like he was tough and knew what he was doing.

An overpowering feeling of uncertainty paralyzed me. I was tense and jumpy, and the slightest sound caused me to have visions of enemy fire blasting at us. I kept repeating to myself: "If only we knew what to expect."

I could tell Muelor was beside himself with nervousness. I could sense his impatience as he repeatedly rose up above the foliage to take a peek at what was happening.

He looked up once too often. A rippling staccato of machine fire splattered Muelor's brain. The urge to vomit came quickly. Not wanting to admit my queasiness, I swallowed my vomit, then was frantic to squelch the subsequent coughing as I forced myself to present the appearance of being a man.

The incident slowed our advance. Once we neared our objective, Grotjun sent out three of the veterans to check the area. We waited, expecting to hear fire any minute. All was quiet except for occasional explosions in the distance. The three men returned, reporting light resistance. Grotjun made the decision to "charge the hill and flush 'em out." We formed a skirmish line, like in basic training, and I got this knotted feeling in my gut. I joined in the yelling as we moved up the hill, firing like hell.

There were North Koreans who jumped from their holes and immediately drew gunfire. Some raised their hands in surrender; some had potato-masher grenades in their hands, too shook up to realize that having the grenades would draw our fire. They were cut down. We took no prisoners.

Beyond the hill in the valley below, two T-34 tanks sat in a clump of trees. Grotjun called back for artillery, gave coordinates and soon there was a loud blast and a ball of fire.

This war business didn't seem all that tough. I'd passed my first real test under fire. Actually, I was a bit cocky. The sullen veterans gave me a weary look, maintaining that distant and serious glare in their eyes.

On the dawn of September 17 we had a brief Sunday church service conducted in the dark by a visiting chaplain from Division Headquarters. There was a rush to complete the service because we had orders to hit the road at 0500 hours. The big push was to reach Pyongyang.

We didn't get far before we encountered a roadblock and heavy machine gun fire. We faced the east, with the bright early morning sun direct in our eyes. There was a quick call for mortars to knock out the machine guns, but because of our poor visibility, the coordinates were not precise enough to make the mortars effective.

This delay really frustrated the CO. He hated to send out a patrol, which would take more time. He decided to wait and gamble that the mortars would make a hit. That's when Peter pulled on my arm and motioned for me to follow him. He took off before I could respond. I felt the urge to follow even though I was puzzled.

Wild-ass ideas were nothing new for Peter, but this one had me baffled. I quickly got caught up in whatever scheme he had in mind. I had to rush to keep up. There was no time to think. I finally figured that he was circling the North Korean machine gun positions. I now realized he had the crazy idea that the two of us could silence those guns. "This is suicide," I whispered to Peter as we huddled in a crevice to rest. "We better get our asses back to the company," I said.

"You just stay right here, little brother," Peter said. "Cover me. I'm gonna have some fun."

Before I could respond, Peter took off. My position was slightly above the North Korean machine gun locations, but not high enough for me to fire directly at them. The only thing I could do was hold them down with fire over their heads. It was like the wildest of dreams when I saw Peter charging at the machine gun position on the right.

He charged at them from the same direction as the glow of the sun. The only thing I could do was sustain my fire, directed so as to provide effective cover, but cautious not to accidentally strike Peter. I held my breath when I saw Peter leap like a madman into the machine gun nest.

I couldn't see what was happening, but I could hear the desperate sounds of men in mortal combat. I ceased my fire and waited.

A sudden blast of gunfire caused me to shudder. I pressed close to the earth. There came another shorter blast and then silence. Slowly, I raised my head so I could see, only to watch Peter emerging from the machine gun position. When Peter saw me, he waved. I waved back, desperately urging him to take cover. He ignored me and took off toward the remaining machine gun position on the other side of the trail. Peter's quick action forced me into a painful decision. Although in constant fear of enemy fire, I felt an urgency to make my way to the other side of the trail to cover Peter. I told myself that without cover, Peter's chances were slim.

A heavy barrage of mortar fire started hitting our area. I became frantic and disoriented as I scrambled aimlessly for cover. I glanced upon a rocky incline and crawled into it, a position of relative safety. I now recovered my composure enough to realize the danger the mortars presented to Peter. Without hesitation I rushed helter-skelter back to the company area to alert them of Peter's location, so they could call off the mortars. When I reached the perimeter of Charlie Company, I was met by a surprised Lieutenant Grotjun. "Where the hell you been?" he demanded to know, while trying to calm me down enough to understand my frantic message.

Once Lieutenant Grotjun was convinced that my story about Peter was true, he made connection with the CO on the field phone. Grotjun had me explain to the CO what had happened. Fortunately, he knew

Peter well enough to realize that my wild story was probably true. He gave orders to lift the mortars.

We waited for Peter. Fifteen minutes later he was spotted crawling on all fours, heading back toward the company. I rushed forward. "What happened?" I asked Peter.

"Got the sons a bitches," he said.

The machine guns were silenced. The roadblock was clear and Charlie Company moved down the road. Peter became known as the "Wild Man." Though he got a tongue lashing from the CO for going off without orders, eventually this feat earned him sergeant stripes and a Silver Star.

The taste of combat was addictive to Peter. Throughout October he volunteered for every patrol sent out by the CO. His exploits became a frequent subject of discussion. I resented all this talk about Peter. It created an expectation for him to perform ever more dangerous deeds.

It was a nightmare for me as I put it upon myself to be his cover man. I wanted to protect him, to urge him to avoid taking crazy chances. Peter seldom yielded to my words of caution and sometimes got annoyed with my interference.

Each time we went on patrol I feared Peter would be killed. It got to the point where I wanted him to be wounded and forced out of action. With the urgency to push north, our waking hours became lengthened and more demanding. The long days and short nights were wearing on me.

Although I was with Peter most of the time, there was little opportunity to talk seriously with him. I wanted to convey my fear for his safety and quietly challenge him about taking so many risks. I waited desperately for an opportunity when we could be alone long enough for a serious discussion.

It finally came on a rainy day in mid-October. We sat together in a shallow dugout, taking turns guarding the perimeter of an area we had acquired only the previous day. The slow, steady rain persisted. The dirt roads in the Korean hills were tough enough in good weather. When it rained they were muddy and slippery, making travel slow and treacherous. The order had gone out to hold up and secure advantageous defensive positions. All the perimeter watch posts offered no protection from the rain and there was a direct order not to use ponchos for cover because they could obstruct vision. A chill had invaded my bones and the dampness carried a foul earth smell. Raindrops dripped off the rim of my steel helmet as I watched Peter glancing up into the clouds, hoping the weather would clear so he could get into some action. Sitting around was tough on Peter. "How long can this go on?" he asked in frustration.

"Maybe forty days and forty nights so everyone will forget this stupid war," I answered.

"Bullshit!" Peter responded. "Let's fight and get this over with."

"You actually like fighting, don't you?"

"Anyone who shoots at me and my friends is a bastard."

"Don't you worry about getting hit?"

Peter turned to me with a serious look and said, "You know what, Andrew? I learned to ignore fear when I was just a little fart. Remember how Dad used to knock me around when he got boozed up? If I'd been afraid all the time, my life would a been a bitch. So, I learned how to forget being afraid and did what I damn pleased. Know what I mean?"

"You never were one to worry much about consequences."

"Guess that's why I'm the way I am." He smiled and added, "Guess that's why I have so much fun."

"Taking chances in war is a whole different game."

"S'pose you're right. But it don't seem much different to me than kickin' ass on the football field."

"Dodging bullets is a whole lot different than dodging tackles on the ball field."

Peter hesitated, appearing solemn and serious. "I know, little brother. I've seen how the bullets rip people apart."

"Don't you think they can bust you up?"

"Sure they can, but worryin' ain't gonna stop it from happenin'. We got a war to fight, little brother and I want to have as much fun at it as I can."

"If you make it through this war without getting your ass blown off, I'll be one happy Amonovitch."

"Don't you worry, little brother. We're gonna end this war real quick. I figure the more I fight, the sooner we'll make it home. After all, it's me who got us here. You came along just to be with me."

Chapter 17

On November 1, 1950, we had reached a location near Ansung. That evening word filtered to us through battalion command that a patrol from F Company of the 8th Cavalry was in trouble after coming in contact with unidentified troops.

The next day started like so many days before; we were up before dawn, ready to move out at the first sign of daylight. There had been no further intelligence reports on the patrol from F Company. The doubts over this incident created an atmosphere of caution.

We inched along, moving around two rugged hills, following a trail that bordered a small stream. As we advanced, the stream emptied into a river that flowed through a valley, flanked on each side by the hills. Everyone became jumpy. I started sweating and the sun hadn't even shown its face yet. I listened for gunfire from the battalion search patrols that combed the adjacent perimeter.

Before the day started we had strong orders to maintain lateral contact with the units on either side, a task that was rough to sustain on this terrain. As we pushed slowly ahead, we were suddenly shaken with disbelief when a bluster of gunfire erupted from our rear. How it happened, no one knew. Somehow the enemy had infiltrated our line and maneuvered behind us. They probably had slipped through during the darkness of night.

As we engaged the opposition to the rear, additional enemy forces moved in to take positions to our front. Their objective was clear—put on the squeeze.

"We got our asses surrounded," Lieutenant Grotjun yelled.

"What the hell do we do now?" Peter shouted back.

"Hold positions!" responded the lieutenant as he headed back toward the company headquarters area.

"Where the hell you going?" Peter demanded of the lieutenant. There was no answer as the lieutenant continued on without looking back. "This is bullshit," Peter said. "I'm gettin' the fuck outta here."

"Where you going?" I asked, feeling desperate.

"Damn if I know. I ain't stayin' here." Peter took off, crawling, moving toward the rear.

"PETER. YOU CAN'T LEAVE!" I shouted. He ignored me.

I didn't know what to do: follow Peter or hold tight. Peter had stopped and was gazing back at me. I knew what he was thinking. I took off crawling like hell toward him, my rifle over my shoulder, bullets whizzing overhead. Peter waited, but the instant I reached his position, he took off on all fours, moving at a pace that was tough for me to match. Peter was relentless. I couldn't keep up and fell behind. I lost sight of him and became frantic and disoriented.

"ANDREW! ANDREW!" Peter called out. Amidst the constant roar of gunfire, I was somehow able to pick up the direction of his voice. By the time I crawled to his position, the pain in my chest and side was excruciating, my breathing so labored that all I could do was gasp for air.

Within twenty feet of me, an earthshaking explosion erupted. Impulsively, I pulled back and curled up in a fetal ball, my body shaking. A tight grip clutched my arm. It was Peter. "ANDREW," he shouted. "Get the fuck with it. We gotta move."

It didn't happen fast like Peter wanted, but he stuck with me as I slowly regained my composure. During this brief respite we gazed off into the valley below, spellbound by the living hell that was taking place. I uttered in painful words, "Those are our guys down there."

"Ya, I know," Peter said. "Ain't that a bitch?"

"What'll we do?"

"Brace up, little brother; we got a fuckin' fight on our hands." I wondered what he was thinking. "Listen, Andrew. We gotta bust a hole through to Charlie Company. It's the only chance they got."

"That's crazy," I said. "Suicide."

"Fuck you, little brother." Peter took off, running across the hillside.

Not knowing what direction to go, I crawled up a steep incline, seeking to provide supportive fire for Peter. I nestled down between two rocks, peeking out at events taking place below. I could see the positions of the 3rd Battalion, with Charlie Company in the center, directing heavy fire at their southern perimeter, desperate to force a breakthrough that could offer an avenue of withdrawal.

The enemy unit holding this sector remained tenacious in their defense. Their strong and steady firepower prevented any frontal assault by Charlie Company.

The drama in the valley seemed an inevitable tragedy. I felt ashamed as I watched from my position of relative safety, while Peter was risking his life in an attempt to help Charlie Company. I inched forward to a higher elevation, closer to the battle. Despite my resolve to give fire support to Peter, I couldn't control my shaking.

I reached a rocky shelf that faced out over the valley, with an excellent view, but dangerous. The downward side was an abrupt cliff that dropped forty feet. I crawled toward the edge, every second worried about gunfire.

I sighted an enemy outpost where two enemy soldiers with burp guns watched to the south. Glancing to their rear, I sighted Peter. I gasped for air as my fear for him intensified. Suddenly, Peter charged toward the men in the foxhole. There was a flurry of gunfire, accompanied by a chorus of bone-chilling screams that faded to a whimper. An enemy soldier crawled part way out of the shallow hole in a frantic attempt to escape. Peter stood over him, crashing his rifle butt repeatedly to the man's skull. The man's body quivered, then slumped and lay still. Peter gave him a vicious kick back into the foxhole.

Dizziness came over me and I couldn't control my convulsive vomiting. For a moment, I lost awareness of my surroundings. As my eyes began to focus, my attention went back to Peter. That immediately cleared my head.

He was moving toward the other side of the valley. "Goddamn him," I grumbled, angry at his relentlessness. Worried that I'd lose sight of him, I crawled back down to the base of the valley. Too afraid to stand and run, I advanced on hands and knees, cursing and calling Peter names as I rough-shodded over the hard ground. The force of blind emotion drove me in the direction of Peter. Suddenly, I was jolted by a burst of gunfire. I dropped to my stomach and pressed my body hard to the earth. The force of my sudden stop tilted my steel helmet down over my eyes, blinding me. I raised an arm to adjust my helmet and removed my slung rifle from my shoulder. By the time my weapon was in a ready position and pointed in the direction of the skirmish, there stood Peter.

He vigorously brushed blood from the front of his fatigue jacket, glancing down at the bodies at his feet. He kneeled and wiped his hands on their trousers.

"Peter," I called out cautiously, fearful that if I was too abrupt in announcing my presence, he may impulsively blow my ass into the next world.

Peter slowly glanced toward me. "What the fuck you doin' here, little brother?"

"Watching the crazy man."

Peter laughed. "Ain't had so much fun in a long time." There was a bizarre smile on his face and a distant hardness in his eyes as he scanned the battlefield.

"What you up to now?"

"Need to silence that big gun." He pointed. "Over the ridge." He took off, waving for me to follow. We made our way to the ridge where Peter motioned toward the machine gun position. "Fuckin' Chinks," he said.

"Chinks?"

"Shit yes. These ain't NKs. We got us a new war, little brother." We watched the machine gun rattling off, trying to kill our buddies in Charlie Company. Peter waved his hand for me to spread out. From separate positions, forty yards apart, we crawled forward, keeping our eyes on the Chinese gunners, with quick glances at one another.

My mind was focused on the objective before us when a sharp overpowering blow struck my left calf. The force flipped me over. I clutched at my leg. My body stiffened at the sight of blood oozing through a hole in my fatigues.

The sharp crack of another bullet ricocheted off the hard ground at my side. I forced myself to ignore the stinging sensation in my leg as I grabbed my rifle and gazed out over the horizon, desperate to determine the source of the enemy fire. In the frenzy of this threatening moment, I forgot about Peter.

When I remembered him and frantically looked around and didn't see him, I feared he'd been killed. In panic, I scurried forward. There, beyond a slight rise, standing with one foot inside the enemy machine gun position, the other resting on the ground above, Peter leaned on his rifle, the butt resting on the back of a dead Chink.

Peter was gazing into the valley, wiping sweat from his face with his sleeve. He turned to me, "Those sons a bitches got ya in the leg." He lifted me up and pulled my arm around his neck as he helped me hobble to the relative safety of the just conquered enemy machine gun nest. "I'm gonna raise more hell," Peter said as he elevated the barrel of the big Chink machine gun toward the hillside position of the enemy.

Peter became a madman, forgetting my presence as he sustained a constant barrage. From this location Peter neutralized the eastern segment of the Chinese entrapment, exactly what Charlie Company needed. They recognized the softened resistance in the enemy line and began a withdrawal. Peter was in his glory as he saw this corridor open up for them.

The Charlie Company withdrawal was in its early stages when Peter encountered mechanical problems with the Russian-made machine gun. It started with sporadic misfires before escalating to a total jamming.

I dragged myself up to the gun and together we manipulated parts of the unfamiliar weapon. We pulled, shoved, disengaged and reconnected all visible moving parts. It was futile.

We knew what this could mean to the withdrawal. Peter lashed out with a vicious kick at the machine gun, knocking it aside. He grabbed his rifle and braced to rush off. As he pulled away to leave, I reached out in an attempt to hold him back, pleading, "Peter. Peter …"

"I got work to do, little brother." He gave me a solid pat on the shoulder and charged away, shouting, "Take care of that leg. I got more hell to raise."

I watched Peter's departure with despair. I attempted to follow, but my wounded leg tightened. Still determined, I twisted on my side, intending to drag the disabled leg, which cramped up like a ramrod. It tied me in an agonizing knot that had me squirming and rolling from side to side in misery.

Obsessed with Peter, fearful that his bold anger was futile and that he and Charlie Company were on the road to Armageddon, my only beacon of hope was Peter's defiance. Tears filled my eyes as I exalted in his selfless courage.

Gritting my teeth, lying on my back with my rifle resting diagonally across my chest and stomach, I pushed forward with my arms. This grueling snail's pace made me sweat so much that my clothes soon became soaked and the dirt stuck on me like abrasive glue.

I pushed onward, with only a vague sense of what direction would lead me to friendly forces. Suddenly, a rifle barrel rammed into my gut. Death flashed before my eyes. "AMONOVITCH!"

I gazed up, attempting to focus, rubbing sweat from my eyes, but all I could see was a blur. That's the last I remember as I passed out.

My next conscious moment came several hours later in a UN battalion aid post. I was treated for exhaustion and shell fragments were removed from my leg. After my leg was bandaged, they tossed a crutch at me with orders to move on so they could make room for the endless line of wounded men.

Upon leaving the battalion aid post, I was directed to a causality clearing station to wait for further orders. I shuffled along with my crutch to the mess tent for coffee, where a familiar voice called out to me. "Need some help, soldier?" It was Lieutenant Grotjun. He directed me to the survivors of Charlie Company. Seeing these men brought a swell of emotion. There were nine men still alive, including the lieutenant. They had made it through the entrapment during that brief period when an escape route had been opened. They had come upon me during their withdrawal and dragged me to the battalion aid post. I told them about Peter, that he was still out there trying to reopen a withdrawal route for the remaining men of Charlie Company. "Suppose you heard about the Chinese entering the war and how they kicked the shit out of us," Lieutenant Grotjun said. "They came at us with a barrage of small arms, mortars and katysuha rockets. They destroyed damn near the whole fucking 8th Battalion."

"Some guys are still out there fighting," I said.

"They don't have a chance," said the lieutenant. "The Chinks busted through and split up our units. They're going after each segment piecemeal."

"What about Charlie Company?" I asked.

"Your brother pulled off one helleva miracle, but it won't happen again."

During this peaceful interval of recuperation the mail orderly from the 8th Battalion medical company had a letter for me. It was from Kathy Amundson, a long letter in which she told of staying up all night writing. She wrote ten pages of news from home, although she'd been living in Cambridge, Massachusetts, since September, where she was a freshman at Harvard.

"I find this war to be an abomination," she wrote. "It's beyond me why the human species cannot live in peace and love."

She told of writing to President Truman, urging negotiation for a quick end to the fighting. Aside form her news of home and her intellectual proclamation about the war, it was her feelings that touched me most.

"I wish you were here with me," she said. "I realize now that you and I have so much in common. Receiving your letter from Korea was the highlight of the fall. Maybe when the war ends, you can join me here. Peter, also. My God, do we need football players."

Kathy's letter pulled my thoughts away from the war. She reminded me that Peter and I had a life beyond Korea. I had a desire to withdraw to the south, to the safety that would lead to the beautiful life back home.

But no way could I forget about Peter. I trusted Kathy would understand. She knew what it was like between Peter and me, and admired our brotherly love and respect.

Chapter 18

If Peter was in my position and I was missing somewhere out in those hills, I know he'd come after me. People might tell him he was crazy, but he wouldn't give a shit.

It didn't take long for me to get tired of the bitching of Lieutenant Grotjun. "If that fucking MacArthur had listened to the intelligence reports, this Chinese invasion wouldn't a happened," he conjectured. There was talk among the men about how the UN leadership had let us down. In late October everyone discussed reaching the Yalu, but now all we heard were horror stories. The word was that the Chinese were coming down the peninsula like a steam roller, wounding and killing massive numbers of Americans and other UN forces.

It was hard to know what to believe. I'd seen the endless stream of wounded pouring into the aid post and I'd been wounded by a shell from the weapon of a Chinese soldier. It didn't look good. I watched for Peter as I stood by the road and saw the mangled, disoriented, and weaponless men plodding south.

The second day I cast aside my crutch. The third day I hobbled without pain. The following day a massive evacuation of the wounded would begin, leaving by air for Yokohama. That night after dark I slipped away from the tent quarters. I couldn't leave Korea without Peter.

I told the sergeant at the supply quarters that I'd been assigned to a rear guard unit. The issue of a steel helmet, carbine and cartridge belt drew no question, but when I requested a backpack filled with rations and an extra bandoleer of ammo, the sergeant in charge asked, "What the hell for?"

"Don't ask me," I responded. "Those are my orders." The sergeant issued what I requested.

At 0930 hours on November 5, I set out on the road that led to Pyongyang. The southward movement of men continued. It was a dreary sight. Many of the wounded were babbling crazy incoherent comments. Their pace was slow and feeble. There were men who couldn't keep moving, men who had fallen along the way, some now dead. There were far too many for the medics to assist. My eye was on every man that passed. Any man who resembled Peter in size drew my attention.

Anyone heading north on this road had to be considered whacko. Yet no one questioned me. Despite my limp, my gait conveyed a purpose, like my north-ward journey had an official sanction. If questioned by anyone, I had an answer ready. My duty assignment was to seek out Sergeant Peter Amonovitch and conduct his safe return.

The Chinese had pulled back after their initial successful offensive. During this reprieve, there was a UN order to withdraw and lick our wounds. The scuttlebutt was that the Chinese were rushing to amass another offensive, wanting to hit quickly while the UN forces were still disorganized and on the run.

The strategy of the Chinese November 1 offensive had been to infiltrate and penetrate deep into the UN line of defense and encircle large segments of the UN forces. But the Chinese still faced pockets of resistance. Some UN units were holding tough.

Charlie Company, along with other elements of the 3rd Battalion, 8th Cavalry, were facing total destruction. Somewhere in this scene of disaster, I was determined to locate Peter.

The hills and valleys around Ansung were familiar to me. In late October Charlie Company had moved into the area and I'd been a part of two local patrols. Most memorable was the river valley where we faced the entrapment by the Chinese, where I was headed to find Peter. I called it "the valley of death." The guns had become relatively quiet in the days following the Chinese offensive. All that could be heard was the occasional outburst of small arms fire involved in the local skirmishes and mop-up operations conducted by the Chinese.

As I approached my destination, I gazed down into the valley that skirted the Nammyon River. Clouds moved in, then light rain and cold winds. My teeth wouldn't stop chattering. Worried that the Chinese may still be in the high ground, I scampered from one point of cover to another.

As I advanced into the valley, the story of Charlie Company and the 3rd Battalion started to unfold. The mangled bodies scattered along the road had been ripped apart by extended enemy fire. The sight of arms and legs blown helter-skelter and the exposed guts of young men that had been alive only four days ago was too much to stomach.

I started to vomit. The convulsions persisted to where I was heaving up nothing but foul air and blood-tainted saliva. My energy was depleted. I crumpled to my knees, my dizzy head sagging. An enemy bullet in my direction could make it so simple. Death seemed noble at this point. To live and remember all this seemed unbearable. It was only a matter of chance that I was still breathing and the life of all these bodies had been extinguished.

The thought of Peter still out there among these bodies was enough to arouse me. I called out his name, my voice shaky and timid. It bothered me to think I was still fearful of drawing enemy fire. Boldly then, I pulled back my shoulders and shouted out his name. I had nothing to lose.

The result was alarming. There were bodies out there that still had a spark of life. It was as if my voice was a siren call—a final flicker of hope. I heard a moan of mercy a short distance to my right. The ground was piled with bodies, men who had fallen on top of their comrades. I sighted a young soldier with one eye and half his jaw blown away. "I'm Corporal Amonovitch," I said. The one eye settled on me and wouldn't let go. He tried to speak, but all that came forth was gurgling. His desperation was compelling, but I was pulled into the commitment to watch over my brother. Immobilized by indecision, I froze. The instant the young soldier sensed my reticence, he grabbed my hand and held tight.

A strange fear came over me. I jerked my hand free and pulled back. The eye was still on me. A tear glistened and trickled down his cheek. I bowed my head in painful despair. I couldn't look at him as I backed away, hearing the sound of his sobbing.

This encounter did something to me that I'd never forget. The intensity of my beckoning emotion to find Peter now heightened the acuity of my senses. My vision, hearing, and smell intensified. Had it not been for Peter's brash decision to defy orders, I'd be one of these silent bodies. Approaching the ridge ahead, it was my belief that I'd find Peter on the high ground. No way would I leave without him.

After passing over the crest of the ridge, a faint echo came that resembled my name, with an anguished eeriness that reverberated amongst the hills and valleys.

Each time after calling out for Peter, I waited and listened, concentrating, believing I was in touch with my brother.

An inner excitement had me scurrying down the far slope. It had to be Peter. I moved with abandon, obsessed, trying to zero in on the sound. In my haste I stumbled over fallen bodies. I tripped, lost balance and landed on a heap of silent young men, Americans, presumed dead. That's when I heard a groan. Someone was still alive. It frightened me. I tried to scramble free of the ground cover of fallen men, but in every direction there were bodies and body parts, lying asunder in all forms of grotesque horror.

I wanted to get up and run away. I didn't want to see what I was seeing. "Little brother. That you?"

I started to shake, thinking I'd lost my mind. I tried to figure out where I was and what I was doing. "Little brother. That you?" Was that Peter's voice? I stood in a trance. It had to be Peter, close enough for me to touch him. "Get your ass over here, little brother. I need help." I scurried forward and wrapped my arms around Peter as he lay on the ground. "I knew you'd get here," Peter whispered.

"It's a miracle," I responded.

"Bullshit. You're my brother."

I was overwhelmed by emotion and I started to sob. Peter squeezed my hand. I reciprocated. "How about helping me back for some R and R?" he asked.

"Looks like they messed you up."

"The fuckers got me in the leg, and check this out." Peter removed his helmet. His left ear flopped away from the side of his head, hanging below his jaw. "Must a been a mortar," he said. "I didn't have a chance." Peter lifted his ear and pressed it back beside his head, raising his helmet to hold it in place.

"Sure glad to find you alive," I said, trying to contain my emotion.

"Wait till I get in fightin' shape again. I'll show those fuckers," Peter threatened.

Peter clutched his head with both hands, his body trembling. He moaned a cry of distress that came from deep inside. I placed a reassuring hand on his arm, but it was like he didn't know I was there. Peter's mind had drifted out of touch. Several times I spoke to him, but he didn't answer. Moments later he surprised me. "How'd you get here?" he asked, sounding dazed and confused.

"It's a long story."

Peter took my hand. "Damn glad you're here, little brother."

"I take it you're in no shape for walking."

"You got it there, little brother. My left leg ain't worth a shit."

"Got me an idea," I said. I crawled over to several fallen comrades and removed their field jackets. After tying them together, I spread them beside Peter, and then lifted him on the jackets. I removed the sling from my carbine and secured it to the jackets. This would serve as a handle so I could pull Peter across the ground.

We set off toward the ridge. Darkness was coming quickly. I hoped we could make it to the road by nightfall.

November nights in Korea can be bitter cold. At the top of the ridge, we faced a brisk wind. Huge, slow moving clouds came out of the northwest, obliterating what little light came from the stars and moon in the early nighttime sky.

It began snowing, the first snowfall of the winter, with periods of heavy downfall that made it hard to see. When I discovered we'd crossed our own path, I knew it was time to find shelter. At those moments when the storm became intense, I became disoriented and the last thing I wanted was to mistakenly move in the direction of the enemy.

I huddled over Peter, startled by his ferocious shaking. The cold was getting to him. "God damn it!" I said while in a frenzied search to find anything to provide cover. I removed my field jacket and draped it over Peter. Soon my teeth started to chatter. When the snow lightened up, I rushed off alone, reckless and desperate, my gait now more hobbled. I fell in the snow, my knees striking small timbers that lay on the ground. Must have been a hillside farmhouse before being blown away by mortar fire. I came to an abrupt halt when I saw a large object. Shielding my eyes from the snow, I focused on the object in the darkness. It was the size of a tank, motionless and silent.

Uncertain, I inched forward, my carbine ready to fire. It was a haystack. I glanced upward in a gesture of thanks to God for this stroke of luck. Then, tracing my steps in the snow, I returned to Peter and dragged him on the jackets to the downwind side of the haystack. We nestled into the hay, huddled close together, our heads exposed enough to breathe. It didn't take long before we were cozy warm. That's when Peter started to scratch himself. The warmth set off the body lice. Soon I was also itching. We couldn't restrain ourselves, and scratched to where our skin was bleeding. Damn, it felt good.

Once we scratched our skin enough to provide fresh blood for the lice, the little bastards were satisfied and let us sleep. Judging from his painful groans, Peter couldn't have slept much. Several times I asked, "You okay?" He never answered.

By morning there were four inches of snow on the ground. Though the sun was shining and the wind had subsided, it was cold. I took a can of meat patties out of my backpack. "Hungry?" I asked Peter. There was no answer. I held a meat patty to his mouth. Nothing happened. Peter was breathing, that was it. He was out of touch, unconscious. I stuffed the meat patties in my mouth and drank water from my canteen. I washed down the greasy meat patties before raising the cup to Peter's mouth. He was still unresponsive. Worried that he should have some liquid, I dipped the strap from my backpack into the water and stuck the strap in Peter's mouth. Impulsively, he sucked on it. I repeated this until he ceased to respond.

Alarmed by Peter's condition, I felt an urgency to get him to an aid post. I squirmed out from the hay stack and was shocked by the chill of the air. Peter would need more cover to keep him warm.

I scurried off to scrounge up more fatigue jackets from the fallen men. When I lifted them to remove the jackets, their stiff bodies were hard to maneuver. With each jacket and liner I removed, I said, "Thanks, buddy."

Two jackets were laid beneath Peter to serve as a makeshift sled and two were used to cover him. As I started now to pull Peter, it was much easier than it had been pulling him over the bare ground. Again, I glanced skyward, thanking God for the snowfall.

Fatigue soon made my legs feel heavy. I lost track of time, plodding along, my eyes focused on the horizon to the south. It seemed like forever before I sighted movement on the road, far off in the distance, I checked my watch. It was 1428 hours. Moving slowly in our direction was what appeared to be a tank, accompanied by armed infantry. As it approached I recognized it as American and was amazed that I remembered its official nomenclature. It was a M4A3. I waved and shouted, "Over here!"

As it moved slowly in our direction, I could see the anti-tank crew prodding the surface for enemy mines. Perched on the turret was a man with binoculars, scanning the hillside for signs of the enemy. I knew they had sighted us when a detail of three GIs started in our direction. The sight of these men overwhelmed my pent-up emotion. I started a sobbing that I couldn't control.

By the time they reached us, my body was shaking. I was unable to speak. One of the men placed a hand on my shoulder, gently shaking me. All I could do was mumble, "My brother needs help."

Chapter 19

The unit that rescued us was George Company of the 21st Infantry. Their orders had been to facilitate the withdrawal and assist in evacuating the dead and wounded.

Peter and I were loaded in a field ambulance that had the gruesome task of gathering up the dead and wounded from the 3rd Battalion. The sight of so many fallen bodies was numbing. Many were still in their foxholes where they died. A stench from the decaying bodies polluted the air so much that it was hard to breathe.

When we reached a battalion aid post, an immediate decision was made to rush Peter to a rear lines medical unit. Peter was diagnosed as having central nervous system damage. He'd be shipped out of Korea by helicopter. Because I was his brother, they requested I accompany him.

I was happy about the medical decision on Peter's behalf, but the sudden order to leave Korea was enough to again stir my fragile emotions. My thoughts and feelings went out to the Korean people, whom I came to view as long suffering. It could be seen in the eyes of their young soldiers, most of whom came from the small hillside farms with their simple way of life. This war was not of their choosing. It was brought on by forces from outside their country. The Communist powers of Russia and China were eager to expand into Southeast Asia.

That's why we were sent here, to stop the aggression. As we prepared to leave, I felt Peter had paid a terrible price for the cause of the Korean people. What made it so sad was that there was so little to show for his effort.

I departed Korea with an emptiness inside. I wanted so much to talk with Peter, and the fact that he was in no condition to communicate made me angry and frustrated. There was no opportunity to share what we were feeling inside. We had to move on.

Our next stop was a military hospital near Yokohama, on Tokyo Bay. Peter was further diagnosed with a compound fracture of his left femur, the result of a direct hit. More serious was a head wound with damage to brain tissue, laceration of nerves, blood vessels and the brain covering.

The head wound caused Peter to fade into periods of unconsciousness. The doctor directed me to awaken him every two hours to ask him his name and location. If he didn't respond appropriately or showed signs of convulsion, I was to alert the medical staff immediately.

The military medical system faced an enormous task of caring for the influx of wounded following the November 1 Chinese offensive. They were under constant pressure with little time for rest. My presence to help Peter and others was welcome.

Day and night I remained with Peter. When it came time to check on his mental status, it was only my voice that could permeate the heavy fog that clouded his mind. When I became exhausted and had to sleep, a nurse took over. If the nurse had difficulty getting through to Peter, I was awakened. Each time I was awakened, I'd think I was still on the front line in Korea and was being awakened by a non-com. My hands would shake and I'd listen for the sound of gunfire or explosives.

A doctor or nurse would place a hand on my shoulder. "Sorry to frighten you, Corporal," they'd say, "but we need your help in getting through to your brother. He won't respond."

The fear of losing touch with Peter's mind was enough to shock me into reality. "How you doing, big guy?" I'd say to him. I'd watch for a flicker in his right eye, the uninjured one. If the doctor saw the same flicker, he'd give me a sign of approval and walk out of the room.

When alone again with Peter, I stared at the big puffy bandage that covered most of his head. His lips were skewed to one side, forming what seemed a disgruntled snarl. "Those sons a bitches," Peter muttered through clenched teeth. "I'll show those fuckers. I'll show 'em." He raised his right fist and slammed it hard on the tray beside his bed.

This brought a nurse rushing into the room, her eyes on me. I gave her a friendly wave and she departed. Then I tried to engage Peter in conversation. "Looks like the UN may get a new commander."

"I don't give a shit," Peter responded. "I just wanna get back to fightin'."

I reached over to take a firm grip on Peter's arm. "All I'm interested in is getting you healthy again."

"Right! Then you and me can go after those sons a bitches. You knock 'em down, Andrew, and I'll run over 'em. Like the old days, right, Andrew?"

"Be great if we could get back to playing football."

I felt tension in Peter's arm and he became rigid. He grimaced as he braced against the pain that kept coming back. Soon, he drifted into an unconsciousness that I couldn't penetrate. Each time it happened, I was afraid he'd never come out of it.

The medical team assigned to Peter included a neurologist, a psychiatrist and a pharmacologist. They invited me to their initial private conference. Dr. Hammer, the psychiatrist, was the spokesman. "It's likely your brother will have schizophrenic-like symptoms that will come and go," he explained.

"What do you mean?" I asked.

"There will be anger and paranoia."

"Peter was always one to get angry at times."

"I expect such incidents will become more intense and frequent in the future."

"So what do we do about it?" I asked.

"We'll try to stabilize him with medication," answered Dr. Ronald Becker, the pharmacologist.

"What do you mean … we'll try?" I asked.

"Sometimes medication works, sometimes it doesn't."

"And if it doesn't?"

"That will depend on the severity of the outbursts. If they're severe, he'll need hospitalization."

"The nut house?"

"The VA Hospitals have some of the finest mental health facilities available," Dr. Hammer explained.

Not liking what they were saying, I wanted to tell them they were wrong, that they didn't understand Peter. They remained steadfast, showing no emotion. As I got up to leave, their composure softened, but they didn't waver in their viewpoint. "One more thing," said Dr. Hammer. "We expect your brother will have a hard time living with his limitations."

"Peter's never been one to sit still for long. Anything that holds him down will be tough for him."

We stayed in Japan to give Peter's head and mind time to heal. Peter continued to have incidents where his mind drifted into unconsciousness. In the weeks that followed, these incidents of unconscious withdrawal diminished, only to be replaced by an even more disturbing symptom. Peter started having outbursts like Dr. Hammer anticipated.

The first time I saw it happen, it came on suddenly. "YOU DIRTY FUCKIN' CHINKS!" Peter shouted, over and over. His voice was so loud it would seem he wanted it heard all the way across the Sea of Japan. He became so disturbed that he pounded the wall with his fists.

"Peter!" I yelled. He ignored me. An attendant rushed in to help, but Peter knocked him to the floor. It took me and three attendants to restrain him. They shot Peter in the ass with medication. For three days he was like a zombie.

When the medication wore off, Peter had another blow up. This time he smashed a doctor in the snout. The medical team became determined to drug Peter into submission. Following this decision, the doctors were eager to ship us back to the States. They had everything ready for us to return when a special directive came from Army Intelligence.

They wanted both of us retained in Japan. They were conducting an investigation and considered it important that we remain available for questioning. It sounded like a big deal. I resented the delay but was intrigued.

The purpose of the investigation was to determine the reasons for the annihilation of the 3rd Battalion of the 8th Cavalry Regimental Combat Team. The

Department of the Army could face serious questioning and criticism in the future, and without answers, it could be an embarrassment to the military establishment.

The total casualties to the 8th Cavalry Regimental Combat Team were estimated around six hundred, more than half its authorized strength. Most of the remaining men were wounded, many seriously. The military team in charge of the inquiry wanted to question as many of the survivors as possible. Their immediate priority was to talk to men with the most serious injuries. If they were to die or be evacuated back to the States, the team would lose an important source of vital information. All men able to answer questions were to meet with the investigative team.

Before any soldier under medical care could be questioned, the investigative team had to attain permission from the doctor in charge of treatment.

Dr. Hammer was furious when he heard that the order to evacuate Peter had been postponed because of the inquiry. "It's ridiculous," Dr. Hammer told me. "Peter's in no condition to answer questions. I won't give them permission."

Peter's extraordinary acts of courage were revealed early in the investigation and became a focus of the inquiry. Peter and I became prime targets for questioning, which I resented. The war experience had been painful enough. I wanted to forget it. I wasn't in a state of mind to be subjected to further emotional trauma.

The investigating officers became frustrated. "All you give us is bare bones," they complained. "We need to know specifics."

"I don't want to talk about the war," I told them.

"Being part of the Army, it's your duty to report on what happened. You think about it, soldier. We'll be back." The following day they were back, and for the next five days they struggled to question me. Each day I became more stubborn and resistant. The questioning totally occupied my time, to the point where I was unable to make my daily visit with Peter. After the fifth day, I insisted on visiting him, but was not allowed to see him. They claimed Peter needed time alone to adjust to his new medication.

I approached Dr. Hammer. "What's happening that I can't see Peter?" I asked.

"The Army brass overruled my medical order," he responded. "They insisted on questioning Peter, claiming they had to hear his story directly from him."

"Did Peter talk with them?"

"While on medication he was totally unresponsive. They ordered the medication stopped while their questioning was taking place. It took over a week for the effect of the medication to wear off. So, yesterday, they attempted to question Peter." Dr. Hammer smiled. "We had to call in the orderlies. Peter busted ass. Couple of Army officers got popped."

"Peter went after them?"

"Hell yes. Got 'em good. Knocked one lieutenant-colonel flat on his ass."

"So, what now?"

"I warned those guys to lay off. After this they should listen."

"Can we go home now?"

"Hope so," said Dr. Hammer as he stood to shake hands. That was the last time I saw him.

Before leaving Japan I was given full instructions on the monitoring of Peter's medication. His dosage was heavy on the flight back to the States. When I escorted him on the plane, his eyes were open, but had a dull distant look brought on by the medication.

The plane ride back to the States was a tough emotional experience. It brought back memories of our flight to Japan four months ago. Back then Peter had been all eager to fight a war. He bristled with vitality. Now he sat with his jaw sagging, saliva drooling out the side of his mouth. It would have been great to talk with Peter on this momentous occasion, but attempting to do so was like talking to myself.

"We're heading home," I said. Peter gazed at me with distant, searching eyes, like he was trying to comprehend. He was unable to answer. I closed my eyes and tried to contain the deep hurt I felt inside.

We flew in an Air Force 247, outfitted with emergency medical equipment and attended by a physician and a male nurse. There were twenty-eight seriously wounded soldiers on board whose stateside medical needs were to be serviced at the Minneapolis Veterans

Hospital. Some of the men would be living at home; most would remain in the VA Hospital.

We arrived at the hospital on December 12, 1950. Dr. Henry Rogers, a psychiatrist, was Peter's doctor. Working closely with him was Anthony Stamos, a pharmacologist. I was invited to the initial treatment conference.

"We need to determine what medication and how much your brother will need to survive in the world outside the hospital," Dr. Rogers said. "Will your brother be living with you when he's discharged?"

"Yes, sir."

"Where will you be living?"

"We have a house in Northeast Minneapolis."

"I assume you'll be working."

"When we get settled, I want to go to college at the U. It would be great if Peter could get well enough to go with me."

Dr. Rogers gave me a quizzical look. "One thing at a time," he said. "First, we need to determine if your brother will be able to live in the community."

This comment bothered me. Forcefully, I said, "When Peter's leg heals, I want him home with me."

Dr. Rogers hesitated, then in a soft gentle voice responded, "We must be fully convinced that your brother's mental status is stabilized before he goes out in the community."

"My guess is that Peter will rebel if he's forced to remain in the hospital."

"We must face the facts. Our first task will be to determine what medication will be needed to guard against violent outbursts."

"I don't want Peter zonked out like a zombie."

"Our first concern must be psychotic anger. We must be sure that you and others in the community are protected before we can authorize his discharge."

"Don't worry about me. I can deal with Peter."

"We're well aware that you have a special relationship with your brother, but we need to consider the neurological and related mental health risks. We need to make a responsible decision."

"I think the best thing for Peter will be for him to be at home, so he and I can be together."

"Your concern for your brother is commendable. We'll be sure to consider that in our planning, but our first responsibility is to assure a stability that would enable your brother to live outside the hospital."

Chapter 20

While Peter was in the hospital, I made a surprise visit to Father Sikorski. "Andrew, my boy," said the ebullient priest. "You look ten years older."

"Peter and I got home two days ago. They discharged us."

"Where's Peter?"

"In the hospital."

"I read in the *Tribune* about you boys being wounded over there." Father Sikorski sized me up, looking for signs of injury. "You look great, Andrew."

"I was lucky, but Peter's in bad shape."

"He must have been some kind a soldier over there. I read stories about his exploits and his serious injuries. Must have been something awful."

A swell of emotion hit me fast, unexpected. I turned aside and covered my eyes.

"Andrew. You all right?"

I walked to the window and blinked and wiped my eyes. When my vision started to clear, I faced Father Sikorski again. "What were you talking about?" I asked.

"Forget about it. Thank God you're home."

"Came to talk with you about the house. We'll be wanting to move back."

"There's a young family renting there now."

"I don't want to force a quick move on them," I said. "Give them some time."

"Don't you worry, Andrew. We'll work something out."

"Maybe they got an extra room where I can stay for now."

"Let me talk to them. In the meantime you're welcome to stay here at the rectory."

Father Sikorski worked it out so the family would leave on the weekend of January 13. In the meantime I'd stay at the rectory.

It was uncertain when Peter would be discharged from the hospital. Dr. Rogers and the medical staff was having a hard time with him. "This brother of yours can be a handful," complained a frustrated Dr. Rogers. "Soon as we cut back on the medication, he's all over the place. Yesterday, he snuck out of the hospital."

"Sounds like Peter's getting back to normal."

Dr. Rogers gave me a contemptuous look, as if asking how I could be so stupid. "The police found him in some bar over in Northeast Minneapolis. The bartender called the police when Peter caused a disturbance."

"You know the name of the bar?"

"What difference does it make?" Dr. Rogers snapped back.

"Thought I'd go over and talk to the people. Like to hear the story of what happened."

"You don't get the point, Mr. Amonovitch. As soon as we let up on the medication, your brother can't be managed. He doesn't cooperate with anything."

"The point is, doctor, you don't understand my brother. He's been uncooperative all his life. That's Peter Amonovitch."

Dr. Rogers studied me, and then in a serious subdued voice asked, "Is that why Peter got so clobbered in Korea, because he defied orders and went off on his own?"

I wanted to back the doctor against the wall and smash him. I waited until I calmed down before responding: "What Peter did in Korea saved my life and the life of at least nine other men. Thank God he still has a life, what's left of it. Without Peter we'd all be dead, like the other six hundred men in that fucking valley."

Dr. Rogers waited to let me cool down. Then he said softly, "No doubt about it, Mr. Amonovitch, your brother did great things on the battlefield, but his soldier days are over. Now, that the battle's over, how do we control the monster inside his head."

"Peter doesn't scare me. You people are a bunch of chicken shits."

Dr. Rogers remained calm. "Your brother can be dangerous and the best way we can keep others safe is to keep him medicated."

"If that's what it takes before Peter can come home, give him medication. I know Peter would like it much better at home."

"Of course he would. He wants to do his own thing. The problem is he's an angry man who can't control himself at times. We need to be absolutely sure that you and others are safe."

We were approaching the new year and Peter was still in the hospital. "When can Peter come home?" I asked.

Dr. Rogers appeared impatient with my question, which I'd asked on many occasions. He answered, "When conditions are ready for his release."

"What conditions?"

"When we know it'll be safe." We both sat quietly, pondering what to say. "Maybe you should begin college," Dr. Rogers suggested. "You need to start thinking about your own life."

His advice annoyed me. To avoid an argument, I decided to leave. I wasn't ready for college. I wanted to wait until Peter was ready to attend with me. I prayed that he could become the Peter I'd always known. I wanted to forget that the war ever happened, but that was hard to do with all the news and talk about the war.

While living at the rectory, I isolated myself from the world, except for my daily visits with Peter at the hospital. At night it was hard to sleep. Thoughts of the war and worry about Peter's future weighed heavily on me. The church across the street from the rectory became my refuge when I couldn't sleep at night.

On the night before I was to move back home, my mind couldn't rest. Outside, the wind wailed as a winter storm charged down from the north and lashed out at the Twin Cities. It was a grim reminder that Korea was facing its most brutal winter in many years. As I walked the short distance from the rectory to the church, my shoulders were hunched and my stride was like that of a forced march. To face such a storm on the front line of Korea would be a nightmare. Just crossing the street to the church was a challenge. To be in a foxhole on a lonely Korean hillside with fear that the Chinese could sneak up from behind at any minute would test the nerves to the point of snapping.

Disturbing thoughts of the war and the uncertainty of Peter's future persisted in my mind as I trudged toward the altar in my clumsy galoshes. I kneeled at the railing and gazed up at the burning candles. Within the walls of the church, the howl of the storm seemed far away, in another world. Yet, the candles flickered, revealing that the powerful force of nature was either penetrating these walls or shaking the entire structure.

I spoke aloud, projecting my voice toward the cross that reached up toward the ceiling. "Thank you, God, for bringing Peter and me back from the war. Thanks for my arms, my legs and all my faculties. Help me to help Peter. Please, God, restore my brother to what he used to be."

The emotion of my plea for the help of God drained me, and I had to rest. Once recovered, I rose to leave, but turned back to make one last request. "Please, God, please … end the war."

On my first night home I went to bed early, expecting to sleep like I did during those innocent days of boyhood. Such magic didn't happen. I had another of my difficult nights, my mind flashing scenes of dead bodies scattered over endless hills. Every face I saw on those bodies was that of Peter, a dreary lifeless face, like when Peter was doped heavily with medication.

These horrid scenes eventually gave way to a dream of awakening in the morning to the smells of fried bacon and hot coffee. Mom was there with all her warmth, holding out her arms to greet Peter and me as we rushed into the kitchen, eager to indulge in the cuisine that only she could create. Most striking about this dream was a feeling of well-being that lifted my soul to a lofty peak.

When I awoke in the morning, there was a smile on my face. I inhaled to catch the smell of bacon, but there was no bacon. There was no Peter in the bed across the room. There was no breakfast party in the kitchen. There was no Mom—the house was empty.

Mom was gone forever. Dad and Peter were in their own little worlds, each mere ghosts of their former selves. My desire for Peter to be back home and the dream that someday he'd once again be the brother I once knew became an ever stronger force in my life. The only obstacle I saw was Dr. Rogers.

Up to now the big disagreement between us involved the use of heavy medication. I continued to see the medication as making Peter someone I didn't know. This was foremost on my mind when I went to visit Peter the following day.

On entering Peter's room I found him propped up in bed, gazing straight ahead with that disembodied glare I'd seen so many times before. "Good morning, big guy," I said. Peter didn't answer or turn his head, seeming unmindful of my presence. I touched his arm. His head turned slowly in my direction, emotionless, like his face was covered with a mask. The top button of his shirt was fastened, something I'd never seen Peter do. Someone had dressed him.

My plan for the day's visit had been to go with Peter to the recreation area for some pool and casual conversation. I could now see this was pointless in his present condition. The only thing we could do was sit in Peter's room and stare at the walls. Any conversation would be one-way, labored and unsatisfying. I sat quietly, recalling our visit with Dad before going to Korea, where he too withdrew into his own isolated world.

As we sat in silence, my eyes on Peter, his eyes on some vague aspect of the far wall, there was anger building inside me, anger so intense that I feared it would take command of me. My thoughts were on this stinking hospital, with its medical piss smell that twisted my nose every time I entered. Next on my list were Dr. Rogers and his whole damn crew. All they were interested in was making their life easy. They were afraid of Peter and cowered behind a protective shield of medication. Peter was too unpredictable to fit into the convenience of their sheltered routine. Dope him up! That was their answer. I resented everything about it.

But opposition to Dr. Rogers had gotten me nowhere. It had only made matters worse. Resistance to my ideas, even my presence, had grown daily. This intensified my anger, to the point where I considered abducting Peter from the hospital.

Fortunately, my better judgment prevailed. I realized that Peter might be transferred to a more restricted hospital and I'd face rigid restrictions on seeing him. I had to start facing facts. If Peter was ever going home, I had to begin using my head.

At my first opportunity I arranged a conference with Dr. Rogers. I was smiling and energetic as I entered the meeting. Dr. Rogers seemed surprised and unsure about how to react to my upbeat attitude. "I got a suggestion, Doc," I said.

"Let's have it," he responded, showing his typical annoyance of my presence.

"How about Peter coming home for a visit? To see how it goes."

He gave me a searching look. "So you think the circumstances are right for your brother to visit home?"

"It depends on what you think."

Dr. Rogers was quiet, appearing confused. I think he was expecting an argument from me. Finally, he responded, "Give me some time to think about it."

"Great. I'll be waiting to hear from you."

Dr. Rogers forced a smile as I departed. It was a suspicious smile that matched the skeptical look in his eyes.

Each day I visited the hospital. I had my usual time with Peter, but I also worked on cultivating a friendly approach to the hospital staff and an attitude of respect for how they managed Peter. I had to convey to these people that I appreciated what they were doing.

Every day Peter had that same emotionless expression that was hard for me to stomach. I seethed inside with anger. In the past I'd handled such feelings by seeking out Dr. Rogers and venting my disagreement with their drug-happy approach of repressing Peter.

I now controlled my emotions. When away from the hospital, I cussed and complained to myself. While in the hospital, I was diplomatic. When alone with Peter, I found satisfaction in talking privately with him. I doubted he understood, but I talked anyway.

"Just wait, big guy," I said, "our time will come." I touched his arm and gave him a big hug. He glanced at me like a puppy, unsure of what to make of my overture. When the nurse popped into the room, I gave her a smile. When she departed and was out of earshot, I said, "We got to make friends with these people."

When it came time to end my visit, my new approach was to stop at the nurse's station. I'd smile and routinely inform them that I was leaving for the day and attempted to leave them with the impression that I appreciated what they were doing for my brother. They'd glare at me, suspicious of my friendliness. It would take time for them to think I'd changed my attitude. The image of me as a bitching, complaining brother had created a barrier between us. I now realized they had no need for my friendship, but I had a need for them to see me in a favorable light.

My campaign to win favor with the hospital staff continued through the winter and early spring. Not once did I complain about the hospital's treatment approach with Peter. I held off on my request for Peter to visit home, ignoring Dr. Roger's failure to respond to my initial request. I was biding my time, covering my anger with a show of passive, congenial cooperation.

By spring the mood about the Korean War was changing. The UN forces had withstood a series of Chinese offensives, resulting in enormous enemy causalities. The latest body count was 17,000 enemy dead, 10,000 captured.

I waited for a beautiful spring day when all the world seemed uplifted by the season. I approached Dr. Rogers. "Could I have an appointment to talk with you?" I asked.

He hesitated before answering, "Check at the nurse's station. They know my schedule."

"Thank you, sir." I had the urge to salute, but held back, not wanting to go overboard.

An appointment was set for 2:00 PM that day. I arrived early. Dr. Rogers came fifteen minutes late. "Sure glad you could see me today," I said.

"It's been some time since we've talked."

"You're a busy man, Doctor. More wounded soldiers come every day."

"That's for sure."

"You were to let me know about Peter visiting home."

"Oh yes, I apologize for not getting back to you."

"I see how busy you are."

"You amaze me, Andrew. The loyalty to your brother is extraordinary."

"My brother means a lot to me and I appreciate all you've done for him."

"We've come to appreciate you too, Andrew. We know what you mean to Peter."

"Think Peter's ready for a visit home?" Dr. Roger's eyelids sagged and his forehead wrinkled, giving the impression that he was trying to see inside my head. "Some positive change has taken place in the past couple of months. We find your attitude more favorable and cooperative."

"I now have a better understanding of what you're doing for Peter."

"You're the key, Andrew. Our concern has been your attitude about the use of medication."

It surprised me that Dr. Rogers would be so frank. I smiled. "Thanks for the compliment."

"When would you want Peter to visit home?"

"How about this weekend?" I said, timidly.

"That's fine, but first we'll need to brief you on Peter's medication." Dr. Rogers reached for the phone and dialed. "That you, Hazel?" he asked, then paused and said, "Do you have time now to talk with Andrew Amonovitch about his brother's medication? We're planning a home visit for Peter this weekend." Again he listened. "Great. I'll send Andrew over."

I was tense on my way home from the hospital, worried about how my plans for Peter would work out. The talk with the nurse was still buzzing in my head: "The blue pill for paranoia comes in the evening. It will help Peter sleep. The yellow pill for anger and depression comes in the morning," she had explained. "The timing of the yellow pill is real important," she emphasized.

It seemed so simple. Friday evening Peter would leave the hospital with me. Sunday evening I'd take him back. This visit was a big event for me. I planned an elaborate agenda. I cleaned our bedroom and took pains to make sure everything was exactly as it used to be.

On Peter's first night home I brought out our high school yearbook and we sat on the edge of the bed, going through the pages. Peter gazed at pictures of high school friends and events, but showed no excitement, no emotion, as if we were paging through a dictionary. The yearbook almost fell from my numb, weakened grip.

At sundown I gave Peter the blue pill. He'd been conditioned to know that the pill meant bedtime and off to bed he went.

The next morning I was up early, planning to start the day with a famous Amonvitch breakfast. I envisioned the smell of frying bacon enticing Peter to the kitchen with a joyful smile. By 8:00 AM the bacon was sizzling, but Peter hadn't appeared. I went to our bedroom to check on him. He was sitting on the edge of the bed, his chin resting on his chest, a blank glare in his eyes as he gazed at the floor.

It was time for the yellow pill. I held it out for him. He didn't respond. I held it to his mouth. He opened wide. "Stick out your tongue," I said. I placed the pill on his tongue and handed him the glass of water. He sipped. "You get dressed," I said. "I'll go attend to our breakfast."

When Peter didn't show after twenty minutes, I went back to the bedroom. He hadn't moved or made any attempt to dress. It was obvious I had to assist in dressing him, a task I'd never imagined needing to do. This was a devastating blow to my image of Peter. Dressing him took forever. I pulled and tugged and twisted. Peter was impassive.

When finally ready, I led him to the kitchen, eager to see his reaction. I directed him to his old familiar chair and transferred my masterpiece from the stove to the table. "What you think, big guy?" I asked with enthusiasm.

There was no response. I sat down, stunned, tears squeezing out of the corners of my eyes. I wiped my cheeks and dished up our plates. I ate. Peter nibbled, eating at a pace that would take him until evening to finish the heaping portion I'd given him. I slumped down, defeated.

After giving Peter over an hour to eat, I decided it was time to clean up and do the dishes. Peter sat motionless at the table as I completed my task. I glanced at him and said, "Don't you worry, big guy. Give me some time and I'll have you home for good." Peter showed no reaction to my words. I placed a hand on his shoulder and added, "Once you're home, I'll bring you back to life."

My words were heavy with a sadness magnified by subdued anger. "Don't you worry, big guy, I'm not afraid to let you be yourself." I reached over and snatched one of his pill bottles and said, "Together, you and I will show the world you can dump these damn pills." I gritted my teeth and whipped the plastic bottle across the kitchen, slamming it against the wall.

I shouted, "RIGHT ON, BIG GUY!" Peter glared at me, the first real sign of response from him. This gave me some feeling of hope.

As soon as we returned to the hospital, Dr. Rogers requested to see me. "How was the visit?" he asked.

I forced a smile. "It was great having Peter home."

"That so? What was so great about it?"

"Just having him there."

"You're sure about that?"

"It was exactly what I expected," I lied.

"Any trouble with the medication?"

"I had to put the yellow pill in his mouth."

"After a night's sleep Peter's still sedated by the medication. In the early morning his appetite and social awareness are diminished," Dr. Rogers explained.

I hesitated, pondering his words, and then said, "When can Peter come home again?"

"Next time we'll send him home for a week. Think you're ready for that?"

I was shocked, but tried to appear calm. "Great," I said.

The meeting with Dr. Rogers made me suspicious. His eyes never left me once and his questions implied that he wasn't convinced I was giving the full story. I felt like I was on trial. Dr. Rogers smiled as he insisted I have a week of rest before they scheduled the week-long visit. I was careful not to show my appreciation for this recommendation.

We were three days into the week-long home visit when it became painfully apparent that having Peter at home over an extended period was extremely demanding. I couldn't be with him continuously. I had to take breaks to relieve my tension, which meant leaving him alone. These periods away from Peter were short, but still I felt guilty. I had to be careful not to mention any of this to Dr. Rogers.

Later, when I talked with Dr. Rogers about the week-long visit, he said, "I'm amazed with your fortitude. Next we'll schedule a month-long visit." He waited for my response. I was determined to remain calm and hold to my dream of bringing Peter back to being his old self. "Let me know when you're ready to schedule it," Dr. Rogers said after waiting out my silent contemplation.

"I'm ready any time," I forced myself to say. Dr. Rogers studied me for the longest time, then said, "I think we'll wait a couple of weeks before we set up the next visit."

I felt guilt over my reservations about Peter returning home. His quiet, dependent, non-responsiveness proved hard to tolerate day after day, but the commitment I'd made to Mom to watch after Peter held a grip on me.

Dr. Rogers must have sensed my inner turmoil when he said, "It must be incredibly difficult being alone with Peter for extended periods of time."

"Don't worry, Dr. Rogers, I can handle it."

"That's noble of you, Andrew, but my recommendation will be that the Department of Veteran's Affairs authorize funds to hire an attendant to assist you."

It sounded logical, but I was uncomfortable having another person share what I considered my responsibility. "I don't think an attendant is necessary," I responded.

"I respect your commitment to your brother, but any discharge plan will include authorization for an attendant."

His proposal made me uneasy. Secretly, I desired that Peter be freed from his medication, believing this to be the only way for him to be the brother I'd always known. I saw having an attendant as threatening the accomplishment of this secret hope.

But to fight Dr. Roger's proposal would only obstruct my secret hope. He wouldn't approve a discharge plan that didn't include an attendant. I had no choice but to concede.

I arranged another meeting with Dr. Rogers. "When can we work out the details for an attendant?" I asked him.

"So you've decided now to approve of an attendant?" he asked.

"Like you say, I have my own life to live. I can't be with Peter all the time."

"That's what I wanted to hear. I'll write up a proposal. When it's completed, you can read it. I'll need your approval and signature before sending it to the VA in Washington."

Ten days later Dr. Rogers handed me the document. "Take this home and read it," he said.
"If you agree with my recommendations, sign and return it to me."

His report began with a brief history of Peter's military career. It stated: "The Department of Army record tells of Sergeant Peter Amonovitch taking the initiative in several encounters with the enemy while on duty in Korea between September 6 and November 10, 1950. Following these encounters he was cited for exceptional bravery.

"Sergeant Peter Amonovitch was on duty with Charlie Company, 3rd Battalion of the 8th Cavalry at the time of the surprise Chinese attack on November 1, 1950.

"During this battle Peter's heroic bold action was well beyond the call of duty. Unfortunately, he was severely wounded. A bullet splintered his left femur and a mortar explosion resulted in a severe head injury. The leg injury has healed. The head injury has resulted in permanent damage, causing schizophrenic-like symptoms of impulsive anger and paranoid thinking.

"His mental condition has been stabilized with medication. We consider him ready to return home where he will live with his brother, Andrew. The demands of caring for Peter will require the assistance of an attendant. The attendant will be assigned out of this hospital and the aftercare plan determined by myself, the coordinating psychiatrist."

On June 15, 1951, Dr. Rogers notified me that the VA approved his discharge plan. A week later an attendant was assigned. His name, Harold "Skip" Hopkins, a 25-year-old redhead with freckles. He, too, had been in the military and was discharged after a year for a "nervous condition."

Dr. Rogers, Skip, and I met to discuss the details of the discharge plan. Dr. Rogers took the initiative, speaking forcefully to Skip: "It will be absolutely essential that you report at the Amonovitch home at 7:30 AM every morning except Saturday and Sunday. On weekends we have another attendant who will take over. If for some substantial reason, and I emphasize substantial, you cannot be at the Amonovitch home at the required time, you must inform the physician on duty in our mental health ward. Understand?"

"Yes, sir," was Skip's enthusiastic response.

"In the event you can't be at the Amonovitch home on time, we'll send out a nurse to administer the medication. The time for the morning medication is 8:00 AM. This is vital for Peter's stability. Understand?"

"Yes, sir," Skip again responded with a gusto to match Dr. Roger's forcefulness.

Dr. Roger's intentions were obvious. He didn't want me responsible for Peter's medication. "How about the evening medication?" I asked, struggling to restrain my anger at the mistrust implied in avoiding my involvement in Peter's aftercare.

Both Dr. Rogers and Skip showed alarm with the resentment evident in my voice. Dr. Rogers tried to placate me. "We want you to be free of the mundane tasks of caring for Peter. You have your own life to live."

What a bastard. How nice of him to plan my life. "So, what about the evening medication?" I repeated.

Doctor Rogers reached over and gave me a solicitous pat on the back and said, "We'll be counting on you for the evening medication."

"And if for some substantial reason I'm unable to perform this duty, what then?"

Dr. Rogers smiled and spoke in a voice that was calm, deliberate and respectful, "If for some reason you're unable to give Peter his evening mediation on time, the consequences won't be serious. You may see some unusual paranoia, but I trust you're capable of handling it. All you need to do is give him his medication at the first opportunity. The timing for the evening medication is not that vital."

Chapter 21

On July 16, I received a letter from the Minneapolis VA Hospital. Dr. Rogers was being transferred to the VA Hospital in Philadelphia to be replaced by Dr. Thomas Simmons, who was transferring to Minneapolis from Fargo, North Dakota. He'd now be in charge of Peter's aftercare.

I was concerned what this change might mean to Peter and me. The only information that came to me about Dr. Simmons was through Skip Hopkins, and Skip didn't have much to say about anything. Skip simply described him as "a young guy who doesn't like a lot of meetings. He likes to do business in the halls. He's more casual and relaxed."

My curiosity increased and I kept asking Skip questions. Skip became annoyed, so I backed off, but still tried to be friendly with him. Skip seemed bored with Peter, me, and the job. I sensed he preferred that I be out of the house when he was there. This was fine with me. I had plenty of time to be with Peter and there was much I could do away from home.

On a Friday morning late in July, I left the house and told Skip I'd be back shortly before noon. Soon after leaving, I discovered I'd forgotten the electricity bill on the table and it was due that day. The house was quiet when I went back to get it. The electricity bill was on the table as expected. I looked around for Skip, thinking I should explain the reason for my return. I couldn't find him. I checked on Peter. As usual for the morning, Peter sat in a chair beside his bed, gazing blankly at the opposite wall.

Curious about Skip's whereabouts, I proceeded to look for him. I went first to the bathroom, where he'd been spending quite a bit of time lately, though he never took any reading material with him. Skip wasn't in the bathroom. My immediate thought was that he'd left Peter alone temporally. This didn't shock me. After all, I'd done the same on occasion.

Assuming Skip would return shortly, I decided to wait. When Skip's absence exceeded an hour, my concern mounted. I was sitting in the front room reading the *Star Tribune* when Skip rushed in at ten to twelve. He was breathing heavy. "Had to leave for a few minutes," was his worried response.

Holding back my resentment, I said, "Peter looks to be okay." Skip remained uneasy as he busied himself with straightening up Peter's bed, a task I'd never

known him to take on before. He stayed fifteen minutes beyond his usual 4:00 PM departure time.

For the next several days I worried about Skip having left Peter unattended for so long. This could have
been a one-time happening, but I had to know for certain. I decided to keep a close watch on him. After
leaving the house each afternoon, I'd wait in hiding by
the neighbor's garage, watching for Skip. I discovered
he was leaving Peter alone every afternoon after my departure and wouldn't return until shortly before I had
agreed to be back home.

I thought about informing Dr. Simmons, but held
off, recognizing that this could present an opportunity
to achieve my secret ambition of giving Peter an opportunity to be himself, to free him from what I perceived
as the stupefying restraints of his medication. I'd take
advantage of Skip's dereliction of duty and use the leverage as a means to provide Peter the chance to be
himself again.

To solidify my leverage with Skip, I decided to
closely observe his departure, to learn more about the
motivation behind his behavior. As usual, when I was
about to leave the house for the afternoon, I informed
him of my planned return at 4:00 PM. Once again I
crossed the back alley and took my secluded position
behind Johanson's garage, where I could observe Skip
going AWOL. My curiosity about where Skip spent his
afternoons had been building, so I was eager to follow him. I discovered his destination to be a house on

Lowry Avenue, not far from the Mississippi. He had gone into the house.

I waited and watched. Shortly, Skip came out the back door accompanied by a young female. I moved closer, hiding behind the shrubbery bordering the backyard. Skip and his friend were puffing a cigarette as they strolled to a secluded corner of the backyard.

There, they sat on the lawn, obsessed with passing the cigarette back and forth, taking deep drags while smooching and fondling one another. Their intimacy intensified and soon escalated into lovemaking.

I fought off the urge to charge forward and reveal my presence. To avoid this happening, I departed in a huff, thinking of Peter at home unattended while Skip indulged his passion. After my anger cooled, it dawned on me that this illicit behavior would be excellent reinforcement to gain Skip's compliance with my bold plan.

I now became preoccupied with the plan for achieving my dream of restoring Peter to the brother I had always admired, a brother with talents that far exceeded my own, a brother with achievements that all in our family looked upon with great pride

My plan was to take Peter on a vacation to the North Shore of Lake Superior, to an isolated location where we could be alone. Back in the days before the War, when Dad was a real dad and husband, every summer he'd take Peter and me to the North Shore. Dad loved it there and we came to share this love.

Back then our visit to the North Shore was the high-light of our summer. Peter had a special fondness for these vacations because Dad was more relaxed and less demanding of him, more friendly toward Peter than at any other time. This was most evident in the evenings when we gathered around a bonfire. During the day Dad had Peter and me gather driftwood for the evening fire. I remember Peter's enthusiasm for this task as he looked forward to the festivities of the evening.

Dad always brought beer along to drink, but back then he was a light drinker. Peter liked when Dad sipped his beer, because Dad became more friendly and jovial. It was like Dad regressed to an adolescent demeanor attuned to our age.

I don't remember our exact age when Dad first invited us to taste his beer, but I'll never forget our response. When I took my first sip, the sour, unsweetened taste was so bitter my impulse was to spit it out. Dad saw my puckered up face and laughed. Embarrassed, I forced myself to swallow the putrid liquid, putting away that first mouthful. Viewing my response as less than manly, I then pretended to participate in and enjoy the drinking scene. I held the can to my mouth and faked indulging, carefully avoiding what I likened to a piss taste from entering my mouth. At the first opportunity I slyly dumped the contents of the can into the bushes. Pretending to drink beer with an empty can was much easier.

Sad in its eventual implications, Peter's response was totally different. He loved the taste and guzzled it down with gusto. This became an occasion when Dad's attention was drawn away from me and toward Peter. "A man after my own heart," quipped Dad as he gave Peter a hardy slap on the back. I still recall the proud twinkle in Peter's eyes. He'd found something besides football that brought enthusiastic acceptance from Dad.

Beer drinking became like football for Peter. Both impressed Dad and gave pleasure to Peter. Little wonder that Peter should direct such great energy to pursuits associated with beer drinking.

My hope was that a trip to the North Shore at this time would bring back the joyfulness of the past and make it a springboard for the return of Peter to the ranks of the living. I was ready to present my plan to Skip. I approached him early in the morning, shortly after his arrival. "There's something we need to discuss," I began. Skip heard me, but paid little attention as he proceeded with his usual routine. I took a position directly in front of him and repeated, "There's something we need to discuss!"

Skip glared at me with surprise. "What's on your mind?"

"Peter and I are going on a vacation to the North Shore."

Skip gave me a strange look. "Wha'd you say?" he asked.

"You heard me."

"You crazy?" he asked.

"We're leaving Monday."

"Bullshit you are. Dr. Simmons won't buy it."

"You won't be telling Dr. Simmons."

"Like hell I won't."

I smiled. "Maybe it's me who should be talking to Dr. Simmons about how you leave every day to get high and make out with your girlfriend."

Skip gasped for something to say. Finally, he responded, "What about Peter's medication? He's got to have his medication."

"Don't you worry, Skip, I'll take care of the medication."

We arrived at Two Harbors at 2:00 PM on Monday. I stopped at the Standard gas station to find out where Erik and Emily Thorgaard lived. They owned the cabin we planned to rent.

Emily Thorgaard was in the front yard weeding flowers when we arrived. "Looking for Emily and Erik Thorgaard," I said.

"I'm Emily."

"I'm Andrew Amonovitch. I called about your cabin."

"Been expecting you."

"We'd like to take a look at it," I said.

"Give me a ride in your car and I'll show you."

Emily seemed curious about Peter who sat quiet and inattentive in the passenger seat beside me. "This your brother?" she asked. I had told Emily about Peter during my initial phone call, explaining that he hadn't been well and needed some peace and quiet.

"Yes, this is my brother, Peter. He was injured in the Korean War, so I watch over him."

"Been watching over my husband Erik ten years now. He had a stroke. We had to move here to town."

"You used to live in the cabin?"

"Lived there fifty years."

"Must've been hard to leave."

"Always hoped we could move back someday." Emily gazed off to the north with wistful eyes. "Erik hasn't got better in ten years." She turned to me and said with a twinkle in her tired eyes, "I say where there's life there's hope. Right, Mr. Monovitch?"

"Right, Mrs. Thorgaard. You can't quit hoping."

"People say we should sell the cabin. Heaven knows we could use the money. Selling's like losing hope and I say hope is priceless. Life isn't worth living if you lose hope."

We had something in common. I liked Emily and I think she liked me. "You wait here, young man. I'll go check on Erik and then show you the way to the cabin."

Without Emily I doubt if we would have found the cabin. The lettering on the mailbox had faded and the long driveway had grown over with weeds and wild flowers. We emerged from the surrounding woods into a small clearing that opened to the lake front. There was an isolation that seemed provocative in its intensity. The place was uncared for, but when Emily showed us the inside of the cabin, the cover of dust couldn't hide the years of loving care.

Emily wiped a tear from her eyes. "Except for the extra bed it's all the same," she said.

"Must be hard turning your old home over to strangers."

Emily took a gulp of air to restrain her emotion. "We do what we have to do. Right, Mr. Monovitch?"

"Don't worry, we'll take good care of things," I assured her.

"Thank you."

"I like the cabin. Want me to pay you now?"

"Hundred and fifty, okay?"

I counted out one-sixty. "An extra ten for showing us the way."

I liked what Emily had to say about dreams. It was as if this old, wise woman was giving license to my bold venture.

It made me sad that Peter didn't share my immediate admiration for the surrounding beauty. Being here by the lake did something to me. In watching Peter, with his lethargy of thought and action, I was angered. I compared his current physical and mental limitations with the strength, athletic talent and energy he once possessed. For Peter to be here at the lake and not appreciate its beauty was painful to see. The longer I watched him, the more determined became my resolve to free him from what I deemed to be the shackles of his medication.

I felt intense anticipation as the time approached for Peter's evening medication. My uneasiness was overshadowed by the excitement of my bold plan. Without the blue pill, Peter wouldn't know it was bed time. Nevertheless, the first night I guided him to bed at the usual time.

The cool lakeside air had always been conducive to sound sleep. But since Korea, any deep sleep had a way of bringing forth dreadful memories. I rolled around, fighting with myself to ward off the bad thoughts. The only solution was to crawl out of bed and connect with the real world.

I pushed aside the covers and sat up. I heard sounds. Peter was pacing, his silhouette moving back and forth before the window. "Trouble sleeping?" I asked. There was no response, but Peter stopped pacing, and then slipped back into bed.

From this time on I laid awake, waiting for morning. At the first sign of dawn I got up, dressed warm and went outdoors. I was standing by the lake, engrossed in its beauty when Peter joined me. "Good morning, big brother," I said.

Peter looked at me but didn't answer. We walked along the shoreline in silence. I watched for signs of enthusiasm in Peter's stride. My attempts to engage him in conversation went unheeded.

When it came time for Peter's morning yellow pill, I held the plastic bottle in my hand, thinking how pleasant it would be to toss it far out into the lake. I raised my arm in a gesture of defiance, but stuffed the bottle back in my pocket, proud, but a bit uneasy about my decision not to give him his pill.

That day Peter and I hiked through the woods and along the rocky shore. Late in the afternoon we began collecting driftwood, preparing for the big fire. Tonight we'd celebrate like in the days of our youth when Dad was here with us.

I started the fire early, eager to renew the ritual that Dad had established. As soon as the flames started to flicker, I brought out the beer. "Catch!" I said, intending to toss a beer to Peter. He didn't comprehend, so I handed the beer to him. I then opened my beer can and took a sip, expecting Peter to do the same. He held the can, unopened, gazing out across the water. I touched his shoulder to gain his attention. When he shifted his gaze back on me, I took another sip. My performance brought the same results. Disappointed, I set my can of beer aside and later poured out its contents. My attention now went to the fire. Peter sat quiet, gazing toward the moonlight reflecting off the water, still holding the unopened can of Hamm's beer. I decided to let the fire burn down, concluding that it was unrealistic of me to expect change in Peter's behavior after one day of withdrawing his medication. I held out my hand and he gave me back the can of beer. I'd try again tomorrow evening.

Three more evenings of attempting to free Peter from the shackles of his medication brought similar results. It had me thinking of the commitment I'd made to our mother. I had to keep trying. On the fourth night of our North Shore adventure, I went through the same ritual. On this occasion I forced myself into several sips of beer. Tonight Peter was more interested in watching me than gazing blankly out over the water. To my pleasant surprise, when I gave him a beer, he snapped open the can of Hamm's and raised it to his mouth like the Peter Amonovitch of old. There'd be no dumping my beer in the bushes tonight. I wanted this to be the special occasion I'd hoped for.

I was on my third beer when the sun faded over the tree tops that lined the high bluffs along the shore. It was time to get the food started. While Peter gazed into the fire, I went back to the cabin to fetch the steaks and a bag of chips. When I returned Peter actually greeted me with a smile. "Fetch me a beer, little brother," he said while tossing his empty can at me.

This simple act had me excited. This was more like the Peter I once knew. The empty can struck me in the chest and fell to the ground. "Get you own beer," I said.

"Fuck you, little brother," Peter responded as he took off toward the cabin for more beer. I watched him move. It was hard to believe he was showing signs of being himself.

By the time Peter returned, the steaks were sizzling. Peter had come back with a beer in each hand and tossed one toward me. I moved quickly to catch it.

Peter and I then settled down by the fire, in positions where we could indulge in the warmth and the mystical dance of the flames and listen to a silence broken only by the splash of waves against the rocky shore, the crackling of the fire and the sizzle of burning fat.

"Coming here to the North Shore is the greatest decision I made in a long time," I said.

"You want another beer?" Peter asked.

I had taken only a few sips from the last can he'd tossed to me. "Go ahead, fetch yourself a beer," I said, remembering that I'd never been able to drink beer like Peter. He soon returned with another beer and guzzled it without coming up for air. As Peter sustained his indulgence, he became gradually more distant, seeming preoccupied with his own thoughts. All that moved were his eyes, from side to side, so slow it was hard to detect their motion. "What's wrong?" I asked. Peter's eyes bored down on me with unflinching intensity. "What's wrong?" I repeated. Peter remained silent while I gazed with apprehension at the suspicious glare in his eyes.

Chapter 22

There had been a long period of uncertain silence between us when I said, "S ... steaks are ready."

Peter didn't move or respond. I placed the steaks on paper plates and handed one to Peter. He drew back, his disturbed eyes darting from the steak to me, as if each were a venomous snake poised to lash out at him.

With his eyes flashing anger, Peter crouched down, his hands in a defensive posture, like a linebacker prepared to fend off a blocking lineman. Suddenly, he dashed off toward the cabin. His behavior had me dumbfounded. I considered rushing after him, but decided that may only intensify his suspicion of me. Still holding the paper plates, I carried the steaks to the cabin. Maybe Peter would settle down later and join me in eating them.

It was dark inside the cabin when I arrived. I flipped the light switch. Nothing happened.

For some reason the lights weren't working. I stood in the dark and listened, the stillness making it seem darker. Feeling edgy, I took several deep breaths, remembering the book of matches in my pocket, left over from the bonfire.

With nervous fingers I fumbled for the matches, finally finding them and lighting one after several anxious attempts. In my eagerness, I moved too quickly, causing the flame to flutter and go out. With forced deliberate moves I repeated the procedure and managed to sustain a flame long enough to light the candle in the holder on the table.

This momentarily eased my tension, which quickly elevated again when I discovered that Peter was not there. In my search of the cabin I found that the light bulb had been removed from the ceiling socket. The only other light was in the refrigerator. I opened the refrigerator door. That bulb had also been removed.

In my candle light search I also found that all the remaining beer was missing. Peter must be mighty thirsty. I glanced out the door, shivering as a cool lake breeze had commenced to blow off the lake. By morning it could be mighty cold. Squinting into the darkness, all that was visible was the silvery glistening of the moon across the lake.

My guess was that Peter was also observing from nearby. Were I to pursue him, he'd most likely elude me. The look that I'd seen earlier in his eyes was painful to witness, revealing that he now viewed me as an enemy from whom he must escape. His damaged mind was twisting the fact that I was his twin brother, desperate to fulfill my responsibility to watch over him. No way were we enemies. We were loving brothers, who had shared so much together in our young lives.

I heard a noise. My body stiffened, my eyes flickered to the sides as I glanced out the window and listened with intense concentration. All was now quiet, but I couldn't relax. Tension gripped my body. I was afraid, afraid of my own brother.

Like a sentinel guarding a lonely outpost on a Korean hillside, the constant vigilance wore on my nerves. The effects of the alcohol, the constant slush of waves pounding the shore and the mesmerizing glow of the candle on the table were hypnotic, making me sleepy. My head drooped into extended moments of semi-consciousness. I was losing the fight to keep awake.

Fear told me it was not safe to sleep, but if I couldn't stay awake, it may be wise to lock the door. In contemplating this protective measure, my conscience wouldn't allow me to lock Peter out. I had to leave the door unlocked, with the candle burning, so Peter could see if he decided to join me in the warmth of the cabin.

I devised a crude alarm system. A chair was placed beside the closed door with two empty beer cans on its edge. If Peter opened the door, it would strike the chair and knock the beer cans to the floor with a bang, a sound that surely would awaken me.

With grave trepidation, I crawled into bed. At some unconscious point the warmth of the covers erased my fear as fatigue and alcohol induced sleep.

An abrupt rattling shattered the silence. It seemed remote, like a dream. For a moment I thought I was back in Korea, curled up in a foxhole at night, afraid the Chinese had infiltrated our lines and were about to blast us with their burp guns.

I listened with an intensity that only fear can incite. I clutched the covers and peeked out, awestruck at seeing Peter hold the flickering candle to the blanket that covered my bed. It quickly swelled into a blazing flame. Peter's back was to me as he rushed to flee the cabin. After he departed and closed the door, I panicked, scrambling wildly out of bed in search of something to douse the flames.

Frustrated in my frantic search, I charged to escape out the door. I was shocked to discover that the door would open only several inches. Something solid was blocking it.

The flames expanded. I ripped the curtain off the front window and grabbed a chair to smash out the glass. That's when the glow of the flames revealed that Peter had pushed the rental car flush up against the front of the cabin, with the passenger section blocking the front window, the engine section blocking the door.

Shielding my eyes from the heat and glow of the flames, I focused on the narrow opening between the top of the car and the top of the window. It was my only chance of escape.

I ripped off a shred of the window curtain, wrapped it around my right hand and slammed my fist at the topmost glass of the window. The glass crashed to the floor, leaving jagged sharp teeth of glass protruding from the upper edge of the shattered window. The heat and smoke were suffocating. My body dripped sweat. I had to move quickly. Frantically, I grabbed the top of the window frame, braced my feet on the bottom sill and pushed myself upward, my head rising through the narrow opening. Now came the tough part, forcing my chest and torso through the same opening. Fear mobilized desperation as I squeezed upward and out-ward, cringing from lacerations inflicted by the jagged protrusions of glass at the top of the window. Blood and sweat served as lubrication as I gasped to suck life out of the smoky air. Each inhalation stabbed like a hot arrow piercing my throat and lungs; blue stars floating through my field of vision; fear of death hanging over me.

I found the strength to force movement up into the cool air of the outdoors, refreshing my lungs with life-giving oxygen, and supplying the strength to erupt through the opening. I landed with a thud on the roof of the scorched hot car, scrambling wildly from its sweltering metal surface. I plunged to the ground with a bouncing *whomp*.

I rolled about on the cool, damp grass, my arms and legs flailing out of control as I wheezed and moaned for air. Engrossed in my fight for life, the burning cabin and the lurking presence of Peter were oblivious to me.

Then came a loud blast, like an exploding mortar. I clutched my ears and scrambled off to the side for fear of another strike. It was quiet. I glanced toward the cabin and now realized that the deafening explosion was the result of the fire igniting the gas tank of the car.

This dramatic episode shocked my mind back to reality, to awareness that Peter was still out there. I had to find cover.

I sighted a clump of bushes off to the side, away from the heat of the flames. I crawled on hands and knees over to the dark shadow behind the bushes and huddled down.

The curtain remained wrapped around my right hand. As I removed it, I sighted movement near the gutted cabin. It was Peter, surveying the remnants of the disaster. He moved closer, and then pulled back from the heat. He sat on the ground, observing the diminished, still-hungry flames finish devouring their prey. Peter appeared in deep thought.

My eyes fixed on his silhouette. He sat motionless, facing the red glow of the dying timbers, his back to me. I was afraid to move. If he turned around, he'd see me and come after me. He seemed in a trance, like he'd lost touch with time and place.

I was getting cold, being dressed only in my under-wear. All I could do now was hunker down and hope

Peter couldn't hear my chattering teeth. Thank God I was alive, but what a letdown. I'd wanted so much for our lives to be what they used to be. My bold experiment had turned against me with unbelievable horror.

Somehow, I had to survive. I had to tell Peter's story. The ordeal of Korea had conditioned my mind to believe that if I could survive there, I could survive anything life would present. Believing now that if Peter discovered I was still alive, he'd come after me like a demented wild man, blinded by the distorted thinking of his damaged mind, with the same ferocious aggression that he had pursued the enemy in Korea. Now, I understood the anger that Dr. Rogers recognized, an anger that possessed Peter and presented danger.

Thanks to my humanitarian venture to free Peter from the shackles of his medication, I had contrived this whole reckless scheme, reaching for a dream that was proving a nightmare.

Fortunately, I had thus far avoided paying the terrible price of death for my ignorance. I'd learned a costly lesson. Peter's war-damaged mind had declared war on the world and I was a part of that world.

I waited for Peter to retreat into the woods, and then crawled from behind the bushes, constantly watching for him. My plan was to go to Highway 61, flag down a car and appeal to the driver to take me to the nearest town where I could inform the police.

Being dressed in my underwear was quick to draw the attention of the first long-awaited car that passed. It was moving south, driven by a young man who introduced himself as Jerome Hill. He was heading home to Two Harbors after dropping his girl friend off at her country home west of Silver Bay.

When Jerome heard my story and plan to go to the police, he turned on the speed, making me nervous because he smelled of beer and drove with wild abandon, squealing the tires around the numerous sharp curves.

At 3:10 AM we arrived in Two Harbors. All was quiet, including the police station. Both officers on duty were asleep. After they were awakened and heard my story, an immediate call was made to the Duluth Police Department, requesting reinforcements to track down what the young officer referred to as "a nut case."

An argument ensued between the two officers. "I say we go after this whacko right now!" insisted officer Wade Gustafson, who fit my image of a young, inexperienced, spit polished, gung-ho type.

"We best wait until help comes from Duluth," responded his gray-haired, laid-back partner, Henry Oswald.

"This guy tried to kill his own brother, who knows what he'll do next? I say we go after him, like now. If we wait until tomorrow, we may end up searching the whole damn shoreline," pressed young Wade.

"I say we wait for help," I said. "Peter can be tough to handle."

"What can he do against an armed officer?" Wade said, his right hand on his holstered weapon.

"Why take chances?" Henry answered. "I'm for waiting."

"Bullshit on waiting," Wade said. "If you guys won't go, I'll go myself."

"You're talking stupid," Henry answered. "You can't go after him alone."

"Who the hell says I can't," Wade responded. "I'm going after that nut."

Wade took off running. Henry turned to me and said, "Looks like my deputy's mind snapped just like your brother. Who knows what the hell might happen? I better follow along." He motioned for me to join him, saying, "Maybe you can help us find him."

Wade took off alone in their new shiny '51 Ford police car. "Guess we'll have to follow in my truck," Henry said. Henry's pickup truck was a rusted out '45 Chevy. We couldn't keep up with Wade whose driving resembled that of the half drunk Jerome Hill, as he raced down the middle of the road, ignoring the center line. When a car approached from the north, Wade flashed the red alarm light, forcing the oncoming vehicle off to the side.

When Wade reached the Thorgaard property line, he parked at the edge of the woods and rushed off in the general direction of the burned-out cabin.

I suggested we leave Henry's truck well back. Henry conceded, although we'd have some distance to run to catch up with Wade.

Wade had disappeared into the woods well ahead of us. I offered to lead the way as we entered the woods. Henry followed me.

As I expected, there was no sign of Peter. "Listen," I said to Henry, "Peter's mighty clever when it comes to fighting. We need to be super cautious." Henry heeded my plea for caution and tried to stay close behind me, but in my eagerness to sight Peter in the darkness, I moved too fast for Henry and he fell behind.

That's when I heard a commotion to my rear, followed by a gurgling sound. Panic struck me. My heart pounded as I nervously retreated in the darkness to determine what happened.

I tripped. Right away I knew it was a body. "Henry," I said. There was no answer. I kneeled, lowered to listen for sounds of life. Henry was silent—dead.

It jolted me. I leaned on one knee beside Henry, overwhelmed with emotion. A hand touched my shoulder. Instinctively, I plunged forward on the ground and rolled off to the side, where I lay silent, shaking with fear.

"Wh ... what happened?" It was the voice of young Wade, who'd backtracked after hearing the commotion and now stood near me, his voice timid and sputtering.

"Take a look," I said.

Wade glared down at his partner, leaned over him and asked, "Is he dead?"

I didn't answer. I glared at Wade, who moved beside me, standing close. I clutched his arm and whispered,

"Listen, Mr. Policeman, we're going back to the car and waiting for help from Duluth."

"Guess we better," Wade conceded.

Wade kept close to me, holding his weapon in a ready position. Suddenly, we heard a loud explosion. "What was that?" Wade asked.

"Sounds like a new police car exploding," I answered.

Wade pressed closer. We made our way to Highway 61 and huddled in the weeds beside the road. "Wish they'd hurry," Wade whispered. "Your brother'll be in Canada before they get here."

"Peter doesn't run. He fights."

Wade became more fidgety, constantly turning his head, glaring and pointing his weapon toward anything that moved or made a noise.

It sounded first like the ruffle of a grouse in the weeds. Then I saw Peter charging our direction. As he plunged at us, I rolled quickly to the side. Wade was too shocked to move, and Peter landed on top of him. "PETER! PETER!" I shouted. Peter backed off, holding what appeared to be a weapon, pointed at me. It had to be the weapon he'd snatched off of Henry. My eyes were on Peter, who stood silent and motionless. "Peter," I said softly.

"Andrew, little brother," Peter responded. He was about to step toward me when a loud blast, followed by another, from close range, shattered the silence.

I stood in shock as Peter, with a surprised and anguished look on his face, dropped the weapon he held to the ground and clutched his arms to his body.

There was silence as Peter extended his arms toward me in a gesture of affection. I stepped forward and threw my arms around him. I felt his body shudder and felt the warmth of blood. His knees buckled. I tried to hold him up, but realization of what had happened weakened me. Peter slumped to the ground.

"Little brother," he uttered.

I kneeled beside Peter and hugged him. I held him close and started to sob. Peter's body quivered. "Peter! Peter!" I pleaded. "You have to make it. You have to."

Peter muttered something I couldn't understand. I gave him a gentle squeeze. He let out a muted groan and fell limp.

I lost control and became hysterical, lying beside Peter with my arms around him. I didn't want him to go away.

After a while a hand touched my shoulder. It was Wade. In the glare of the headlights from the two approaching police cars, I saw the glistening of tears on his pain-stricken face. He started crying as he uttered, "I'm sorry. I'm sorry. I … I thought he'd shoot you."

The two cars were the Duluth police. I stood in a trance, too distraught to talk. Wade tried to explain, but he wasn't making sense. He kept repeating, "I didn't know. I didn't know."

The day Peter's body was transferred to Northeast Minneapolis, Father Sikorski came to see me. I wasn't in a mood to see anyone and he was quick to recognize my aloofness. "I know this is a hard time for you, Andrew. I want you to know I'm available to give assistance."

The look on Father Sikorski's face told me he was having a hard time as well. He waited, giving me a chance to speak. I remained silent. "If it's okay with you, Andrew," Father Sikorski said, "I can take care of the funeral arrangements."

"I don't think its right putting it on you," I said.

"Don't you worry about that, Andrew." Father Sikorski wanted so much to assure me.

"All this happened because of me," I said. "I should have been taking care of Peter."

"You did take care of him, Andrew."

"It was my idea to go to the North Shore."

"You wanted the best for Peter. You were devoted in watching over him."

"I tried to play God. It was stupid."

"You tried to give life to your brother. What more could anyone ask?"

"I tried to give him life, but I gave him death."

Father Sikorski came toward me with outstretched arms. I turned away and started for the door. "Andrew! Andrew!" he called out. I didn't look back. I hurried off, feeling like I was moving down a narrow tunnel leading to peace and quiet.

Father Sikorski tried to follow me, but I was too fast for him. The sounds of the traffic along Central Avenue echoed like a dream flashing in my mind. The screech of brakes and the blast of car horns were but nightmarish intrusions as I weaved amongst the cars, oblivious to the loud insults of angry motorists.

The sight of St. Anthony Bridge renewed my resolve. My pace quickened. From far away came the sound of a siren. My eyes were on the bridge. I charged forward, exhilarated. In a mad dash I scrambled to the top of the metal railing and stood tall, raising my arms in victorious tribute before plunging into the turbulent waters.

There was a sensation of being tossed about within an immense darkness, darkness that was vast and incomprehensible, with a faint, warm, distant glow. I saw Peter and Mom waiting for me, their arms outstretched. It was exalting.

Chapter 23

I shaded my eyes and squinted into the glaring lights. Upon hearing someone entering the room, I pulled the covers over my head, leaving a small hole from which to observe. I could make out the presence of a man sitting on a chair beside my bed. He sat quietly. What was he doing here?

There came a commotion as another man and woman entered the room, dressed in white. Dreariness came over me as I realized I was in a hospital. Hushed words were exchanged, too quiet for me to hear. The man and woman in white left the room, but the man in the chair remained.

I pulled the covers over my head and imagined hearing the turbulence of St. Anthony Falls. I peeked toward the window. A shimmer of light filtered through the shade. I scrunched further under the covers, listened and waited.

Again there was commotion as someone else entered the door. I peeked from the covers. It was a young man with a food tray. "Time for breakfast," he said.

I held my breath. The attendant moved on, leaving the tray of food. I remained under the covers. To hell with the food.

Two days later they confronted me over my refusal to eat. They gave me the choice to eat or get the tubes. I agreed to eat. With someone present in my room at all times, I had to comply. I ate, taking one bite from each item on my tray. At the end of the week they transferred me to the VA Hospital, to the same ward where Peter had been.

Daily, either the psychiatrist, social worker or nurse tried to talk with me. I refused to talk. After two weeks they gave up. Dr. Smithson, the psychiatrist, said, "Let us know when you want to talk."

To hell with these people. My time would come. Someone would make a mistake and I'd have my chance. Several times Father Sikorski requested to see me, but I refused.

My choice was to be alone and wait for the opportunity to join Mom and Peter. I lost track of time as the uneventful days merged into ongoing nothingness. The hospital staff seemed content to let me wallow in my self pity. The routine was oppressive.

Then one morning loud voices erupted outside the ward entrance. "I have a legal right to see my friend." It was the voice of Kathy Amundson.

"There are to be no unauthorized visitors!"

I rolled out of my bed and rushed to the entrance. Kathy appeared shocked at the sight of me. "ANDREW," she said, then charged forward and gave me a heartfelt hug.

Her presence was overwhelming, forcing an outburst of emotion from me that so surprised the attendants that they passively stood by as I took Kathy's hand and invited her into a visiting room to talk. I closed the door and ignored the attendants who observed through the window.

"Mom called me and told me what happened," Kathy said. "I had to see you, so I flew home yesterday."

Embarrassed by my tears and sobbing, I said, "You should be back East attending to your studies."

"This is where I belong. That's why I'm here."

"I can't believe it."

"We need to get you well so you can leave this place." Kathy glared at me with a fervent, unwavering intensity and said, "It's time you had a life of your own. You deserve a medal for your devotion to Peter. If your mother was here, she'd agree with me. So would Peter."

Her words did something to me, like a dark curtain was raised, allowing the sun to shine on me. I reached out for Kathy. She stepped forward and we embraced.

"You make me feel alive again," I said.

"The same for me," she responded. "We've been friends for a long time, and I'm so happy we're back together again."

Kathy's arrival gave me the strength to pull back from my downward spiral of self destruction and accept her reaching out to me. After a week of daily visits from Kathy, my outlook and behavior changed. No longer did I isolate myself from the hospital staff and routine.

It bothered me that Kathy was absent from her studies at Harvard. "You had better return to school," I said once again. "Don't worry about me. I'll be okay."

"I made up my mind. I'm staying until you're back to living a normal life."

"Your place is at school."

"You don't tell me what to do, Andrew Amonovitch."

"Even your mother thinks you should return."

"She doesn't tell me what to do either. Those days are over."

"You can't sacrifice your school career because of me."

"Who are you to knock sacrifice? Listen, Andrew, I learned from you that there's more to life than reading big books. When you were at Edison, I saw the sacrifice you made for your brother. That letter you sent me from Korea, don't you think I can read between the lines? Your life's been sacrifice. You cared for your brother and it was beautiful."

There was no telling Kathy what to do. Her presence and smile made living fun. I wanted to be a part of it.

Father Sikorski made another of his periodic attempts to visit me. This time he claimed to have an urgent message. "I need to talk with you about the house," he said. "The Welfare wants to sell it."

Over the phone I heard his sigh of happiness that finally I was speaking to him. "The house is important to me," I said. "I'm being discharged from the hospital on Wednesday. Could you meet with me on Thursday?"

"How about 11:00 AM at the rectory?"

"Can I bring my friend, Kathy Amundson?"

"It's your meeting, Andrew. Bring whomever you want."

Father Sikorski began the meeting by explaining that the Welfare Department wanted the house sold. "They're not into managing property and they need money to help pay for your father being at the Veterans Home. The equity from the house would be divided between you and your dad. How you use your share would be up to you."

"How much would we get for the house?" I asked.

Father Sikorski responded, "I don't know what i will sell for, but I do know your parents moved in the shortly after they were married. Your dad paid on it f thirty years."

"I'd like to use the money to go to college," I sa "but first I want to take some of it to pay to Emily Erik Thorgaard."

"What's that for?" Father Sikorski asked.

"I was responsible for destroying their dream," I said.

"I don't understand," Father Sikorski said.

"I don't want to explain. I want to pay them something to augment their meager insurance settlement for the loss of their cabin."

Seeing the strength of my resolve, Kathy and Father Sikorski chose not to challenge me.

There followed an extended silence, ending when Kathy said, "How about coming back East and attending school with me at Harvard?"

"Here that, Andrew? Sounds terrific," responded Father Sikorski

"Harvard?" I said

"Why not? You're a bright young man," said Father Sikorski.

My eyes were on Kathy, whose smile was hard to resist. "Please, Andrew, come back East with me."

"They won't take me at Harvard."

"Why not? You're bright and you're a veteran. How can they say no?" "This is like a dream. It's hard to believe."

I joined Kathy at Harvard. On June 4, 1953, we were married. Kathy's parents continued to pay her tuition. With my GI allowance and money from the house there was enough to pay my tuition and rent a small, modest apartment.

Never in my life had I been so happy.